right where you left me

WILLOW'S COVE
BOOK 1

LANA VARGAS

First Edition, Paperback. May 2025. United States

ISBN: 979-8-9901048-3-9

Editing/Proofreading by Alexa at The Fiction Fix

Formatted by Grace Elena at GraceElenaFormatting

Cover Designed by Layla Brown

❀ Created with Vellum

"The cure for anything is salt water: sweat, tears, or the sea."

- Isak Dinesen

playlist

Right Where You Left Me — Taylor Swift
Never Really Over — Katy Perry
I Love You, I'm Sorry — Gracie Abrams
About You — The 1975
Oh shit…are we in love? — Valley
Already Over — Sabrina Carpenter
When We Were Kids — Young Friend
So High School — Taylor Swift
18 - One Direction
We can't be friends — Ariana Grande
This Love — Taylor Swift
Wave of You — Surfaces
Forever and Always — Taylor Swift
What A Time — Julia Michaels (feat. Niall Horan)

To all the hopeless romantics who hide away. The world is waiting for you whenever you're ready.

content warnings

This book contains themes such as: alcohol addiction, and a brief mention of abuse.

Please only read if you're comfortable.

WELCOME TO

Willow's
Cove, Ca

POPULATION: 1,431

prologue

CAMILLA

You know the moment in a movie or book when you're shouting into the void at the main character? This was one of those moments, except I was shouting at myself.

"Do you love him?" I expected him to be angry, but he waited for me to speak with a touch of sadness in his eyes, which made the next word feel heavy. "Ye-yes." I swallowed the lump in my throat as our eyes met from across our kitchen table—the same table at which we'd shared countless meals and conversations.

After reading endless books and watching every rom-com under the sun, I always wondered how people fell in love with two people, but that summer, I discovered just how easy it was. The choice was laid out in front of me—Julian, who was part of the past I thought I'd left behind, and Greyson, a part of a future I thought I was sure of.

"Who do you love more?" he asked.

I froze. Goddamn Willow's Cove.

one

CAMILLA

IT HAD BEEN six years since I left my hometown. If you asked me then, I would have said it was my shitty luck that landed me in the town's only bookstore that day, but I didn't know it would change everything.

Willow's Cove is a small beach town you'd need a microscope to find on any map of California. It was named after the founding family whose last name is, you guessed it—Willow. It's most known for the small cove it harbors, which happens to be the most notorious hang out spot in town. With a population of one thousand four hundred, it was easy to feel small.

I was eighteen when I left, and that summer, I was nearing my twenty-fifth birthday, but it was as if time stood still in my absence. As I drove into town, I was immediately greeted by the familiar scent of salt air. It filled my nostrils and seeped into my bones like I craved it. People in their bathing suits flooded the sidewalks on the walk down to the pier, and cars passed by with surfboards strapped to the top so they could head to the cove at a moment's notice. It was practically summer all year round, but during the months of May through August, the weather was exceptionally perfect. I was happy to see the bakery owned by

3

Mr. and Mrs. Wilson still in business, and I could almost taste the freshly baked blueberry scones they'd give me every time I left the library. While it all looked familiar, after living in New York for six years, I felt out of place where I'd spent my entire life.

I was hit with a wave of nostalgia when I walked across the threshold of the bookstore. Between the pages of books is the only place I truly felt peace, so I was there almost every day, and I considered it my second home. Despite the previous owner retiring, the new owner kept up its aesthetic of earth tones and vintage posters covering the walls. The woody scent was just as comforting as it was when I was a kid, and the shelves held dust-covered books no one bothered to touch.

Out the window was a perfect view of the cove's rigid cliffs I once jumped from on a dare. I traced the scar on my right hand, remembering the version of myself who did things on a whim, but she was long gone.

"Cami." A familiar voice called after me, and I walked to the display of a blown-up photo of myself alongside the stack of my books on the table. My debut novel, *The Story of Us*, published a year earlier and shot up to the New York Times Best-Seller list shortly after. Between the book tour, interviews, and countless meetings keeping me busy, I hadn't had much time to digest how the book's success was all I'd ever dreamed of since I was a kid. I still found it hard to wrap my head around, and sometimes, I even wondered if I was worthy of it.

"I love that headshot of you." Elena's stiletto heels tapped against the wooden floor, and I looked up to see her ginger wisps of hair that framed her blue eyes. She made me feel under-dressed in her pink floral Roberto Cavalli dress, but whether it was a book event, a coffee shop date, or New York Fashion Week, it was all the same to her. She was the poster child of a fashionista—I called her a red-haired version of Carrie Bradshaw from Sex and The City when I met her in college, but underneath the designer clothes and handbags, she was a girl who shows up at your doorstep at two in the morning with a pint of ice cream and a box of tissues if you need a good cry. She'd also show up with matches and a bottle of wine if you wanted to burn someone's stuff. She's chaotic in the best ways and has the biggest heart, which sometimes ends up in the hands of the wrong people, but that's a different story.

Someone like her who majored in fashion and business, and me, who majored in English literature, weren't supposed to click, but somehow we did. I never went anywhere without her—not just because she was my newly appointed assistant, but because she was one of the only people who could keep me centered, both feet on the ground, when I felt overwhelmed by my new life.

"I'm still mad at you," I mumbled as she pulled me towards the chair designated for me. After failing to tell me she had added Willow's Cove as a stop on my book tour, I was trying to give her the silent treatment, but considering she was my only friend, it didn't last long.

"Can you be mad and sign books at the same time? We're starting soon." She brushed her almond-shaped acrylics through my hair.

"What if no one shows up?" I'd never felt unsettled before a book signing, but the thing with small towns is, it's impossible not to know everyone, especially in Willow's Cove, and I dreaded being minutes away from seeing people who hadn't seen me since I was eighteen.

She placed her hands on my shoulders. "I need you to snap out of it and remember you're Camilla Vega. How many other best-selling authors do we know?"

I rolled my eyes. "None, but—"

"Exactly." She interrupted. "They'll come. Besides, I don't exactly see anything else going on around here." I chuckled.

Nothing remotely exciting ever happened, so people jumped at any opportunity.

The store owner's long, dark hair swayed with every step as she approached us with a smile. "Ladies, I'll give you a few more minutes until we open the doors."

"Thanks Lauren,"

Elena looked at me, a gleam in her blue eyes. "I'll go take a peek at the turnout. Don't go sneaking out the back while I'm gone." I didn't tell her it crossed my mind once or twice since I'd walked in. I had done plenty of signings before without breaking a sweat, including one back in New York for over two hundred people, but Willow's Cove was different. There were reasons I stayed away all those years, and I feared one in particular was going to walk through the door. A pit in my stomach grew as I traced my fingers along the title of my book, but I couldn't dwell on it long before Elena strode back with a wide smile on her face, which faded once she approached me. "Why are you so pouty? You love signings."

"I'm not pouty." My face split into the grin I'd practiced in the mirror for hours.

"I know when you're fake smiling, but I'll take it. We have a line wrapped around the building." She nodded at the bookstore owner, who opened the doors and let people trickle in one after the other. My chest started to constrict at the sight of so many familiar faces, but I told myself the faster I got through it, the faster Willow's Cove would be behind me once again.

I should have known it wouldn't be that easy.

Very few people left my hometown, much less left and came back, so every face in the line had a string of questions for me, and with each one, the walls started to close in tighter. *How's the*

city? Is New York everything people say it is? Why didn't you ever come back to visit? How long before we see you again?

It made me appreciate how, in New York, everyone I walked past was a stranger, but in Willow's Cove, everyone either watched me grow up or grew up *with* me.

"It was good to see you, Camilla. I can't wait to make your book my class' reading assignment for the semester." I let out my first genuine smile when my English teacher from senior year appeared in line. "Thank you for coming, Mrs. Hope. There wouldn't even be a book if it wasn't for you." Without her letter of recommendation, I'm not sure I would have gotten into NYU and later got the courage to publish.

"As someone who graded your essays, I'm sure there would have." She winked before turning away, leaving me and Elena in an empty bookstore. "Holy shit. That was amazing. I think we sold out." I only half-listened as my heart leaped while reading the text waiting for me.

> Just left the meeting with my Dad. You might be looking at the new CEO sooner than we thought. Call me later to tell me how the book signing went. I love you

Greyson Carter was considered one of the most well-known heirs in New York. His dad owned a renowned advertising agency in the city, and if he had it his way, he would be next in line to take over. His status seemed to work on almost every girl at NYU when we met our freshman year, but I wasn't so easily wooed. I thought he was just a rich kid there to pass the time, but it didn't take long for me to realize how off I was. He was kind, someone who always went the extra mile to prove he deserved to be in any room because of his hard work and not his last name.

Despite him pining over me for four years, we decided to stay friends, and by we, I meant me. I thought I would never see him any other way, but one night after college graduation while we were eating takeout in my apartment, it just clicked. He'd always been there—from reading to me when I could no longer keep my eyes open to study, to walking me home from my late shifts at the school library, to helping me move furniture into my first apartment, and so many other pivotal moments of my early twenties. Not long after we started dating, my stuff was moved to his penthouse perfectly overlooking lower Manhattan. It might've been a little hasty, but one thing about Greyson was, if he wanted something, he stopped at nothing to get it.

As I typed a message to send back, I froze at the sudden change in the air when the bell above the entrance rang. I didn't have to look up to see who walked in; somehow, I just knew.

I could hear his jagged breaths, as if he just ran like his life depended on it. "Did I miss it? Are there any books left?" Some things were impossible to forget, no matter how much time passed—the sound of your dad's footsteps when he came home from work, your favorite song growing up, your best friend's laughter. For me, it was the sound of Julian Perez's deep voice.

I couldn't look up at him, so instead, my eyes stayed glued to the floor. Elena must've seen how uneasy I was because she spoke for me. "We sold out, but I think I might have one more left in the car." She was gone before I could tell her not to go through the trouble. I usually appreciated how she could always make a book sale, but I wished she would've let it go just that one time.

"Mila." The sound of my old nickname falling from his lips made me stop counting down the minutes until Elena returned. I swallowed the lump in my throat when I finally looked up at the face I tried to forget for six years. He was a man—so much different than the boy I fell in love with at sixteen, but in some ways, he was exactly the same. I never forgot the depth of his soft brown eyes, or how his dark, wavy hair complemented his tan skin. The stubble beard growing on his jaw, along with the new muscles strained against the fabric of his shirt gave him a rugged look he didn't have before.

I had forbidden myself from speaking his name before then, so I had to force it out. "Julian."

His eyes clung to mine, as if he was making sure I was real, and it brought me back to how lost they were the last time I looked into them. "It's been a long time." *No kidding.*

"Yeah. How long?" My voice hardened.

His hands slipped into the front pockets of his jeans. "I lost count." Of course, I was the pathetic one who knew exactly how long it had been. Before I could continue the awkward small talk, Elena returned with a copy of my book in her hands. "I always keep one in my travel bag, just in case." *Lucky me.* He was the last person I wanted it in the hands of.

"Do you mind signing it for me, Mila?" I flinched at the nickname and the memories it came with. I couldn't exactly say no at my own book signing, so I plastered on a fake smile. His heated stare made my hands tremble as I scribbled my signature. "You still sign your name with a heart in the I?"

I stifled a smile. "Not since my senior research paper." Our fingers grazed when I handed him the book, and his mouth curved into a devastating grin. The memories flooded back—of car rides full of our laughter, bonfires at the cove, late-night cliff dives into the ocean.

"Thanks. So, how long are you in town?" he asked.

"We fly back home tomorrow morning." An odd twinge of guilt washed over me when his face fell. "So eager to leave?"

"I didn't even want to come back in the first place." My bitterness towards the place I grew up felt heavy on my tongue.

"Can we at least catch up before you go?" I could hear the desperation in his voice, but catching up meant possibly bringing up the past, and I didn't wake up that morning ready for that conversation. I could never tell him no, not while looking into his brown eyes, so I forced myself to look away. "I can't, Julian."

He sighed. "Alright. I just thought you'd want to see what I did with the house."

My brows furrowed. "What house?"

I only pictured one in my head, and I thought there was no way it was the same one until he gazed out of the window towards the rocky cliffs with a smirk. "The only one on the hill. I think you know it."

I stuttered around to look for the words that fell out of my head. "You…you live in the old house by the cove?"

He nodded. "I bought it a year ago. It doesn't look so rough anymore, but you could see for yourself." There was a voice in my head saying to send him on his way, but I couldn't help but wonder what he had done to the very house we'd had countless conversations about. "One look, and then I leave."

His face lit up as he fought back a smile. "Great. I'll meet you there. You remember the way." He threw me a wink, and even after he left, I couldn't bring myself to move until Elena came to stand at my side. "Now that he's gone, are you going to fess up about who the hell he is?"

"What are you talking about?" I needed time to stall from her question, so I grabbed my purse and headed for the door, smiling over at the owner before walking out. "Thank you for hosting the event, Lauren."

Elena followed on my heels back to the Range Rover Greyson had arranged as our rental. "I've had my fair share of exes, Cami, so I know that kind of tension when I see it. Spill." Even if I did want to tell her, I wouldn't know where to start.

I let out a heavy breath as I started up the car. "We just know each other from school." Technically, it wasn't a lie; I just left out the part about how we dated for nearly three years in high school.

She pursed her lips. "I call bullshit. You can't lie to save your life, remember?" Unfortunately, she was right.

"Can we drop it, please?" She'd been my best friend since freshman year at NYU, so if anyone should've known about Julian, it was her, but after spending six years trying to forget Willow's Cove, I could never bring myself to tell her. I guess I thought if I never spoke about my past, eventually, it'd be like it never existed.

She sighed. "When we get back home, we're not leaving the coffee shop until I get every detail." I barely registered her words as I started to recognize the suburban neighborhood we were driving through. I knew it by heart, and could even picture it with my eyes closed. I never realized how much I took the peace and quiet for granted until then. The only sound was laughter as children raced down the pavement—no blaring horns, no echoing voices of people speaking all at once, no sounds of the busy city.

"I lived in this neighborhood growing up," I said as I stared vacantly at the houses. They all looked exactly the same—green grass, white picket fences with vibrant trees blossoming in the front yard. I pressed on the brakes as we passed the only one on the entire block that stood out. "This was my house." I spent hours trying to convince my mom to paint it any color other than yellow, but she never liked fitting in. I grew to love that about her.

"It's so cute," Elena said softly. It held so many precious memories—being pushed on the swing my dad built when I was four, tea parties I hosted my stuffed animals when I was seven, climbing out of my bedroom window in the middle of the night when I was seventeen. But it was also haunted by some of my worst moments, making the moment bittersweet.

"Do your parents still live there?" Elena pulled me back to the moment. The last I'd heard, it was sold to newcomers in town who had a newborn baby. I hoped they made better memories in it than we ever did. "No. We should get going." Unlike the last time I saw it, I didn't look in my rearview mirror when I drove away.

Willow's Cove was so small, you could drive from one end to the other in fifteen minutes. On the way to Julian's house on the edge of town, I noticed how the roads were still embedded in my mind as if I never left.

"Just one look, and then you leave, Cami," I whispered to myself as we crept up the inclined hill, which led to the old white house that stood alone at the top. To some, it might've looked like just another abandoned house; the white paint was nearly peeling off, piles of wood thrown in the yard, the giant hole in the porch still sat untouched, but I always saw its potential. I couldn't believe it was still standing, much less that it belonged to Julian.

Elena rushed out of the car and went straight to the ledge overlooking the Pacific Ocean. "You have to come see this view, Cami. It's breathtaking!" she shouted. I'd seen it a thousand times, but I still went to join her.

The view of the widespread ocean was the same. It was comforting to know that no matter how much time had passed or how different I was the last time I was there, it was the only thing constant and never changing. The breeze blew through my hair in a way I knew all too well, and I could never forget the smell of salt water and seaweed. As I listened to the waves crashing against each other, I recognized a familiar flutter in my stomach like I was being greeted by an old friend. My mom said when I was fussy as a baby, she'd come to sit in front of the ocean, rocking me to sleep. Ever since then, I felt most at home near the ocean.

"Come on, let's go feel the water." She squeezed my hand and dragged me down the hill where the grass met the warm sand. Instead of being grainy like most beaches, the sand at the cove was almost cushioned.

"You had a view like this at your disposal and left it for the city? I mean, I'm thankful you did, because then we would've never met, but wow." She let out a yelp of excitement before running down the empty beach, and I couldn't help but smile as I watched her keep her stiletto heels above her head. There were beaches in New York, but we were guilty of not appreciating them the way we should've.

As if I felt his presence, I looked back toward the top of the hill where Julian's broad silhouette stood. His olive skin glistened under the sun's rays as he waved me up. "Come on, I'll get you reacquainted with the place while your friend enjoys the view." As much as I didn't want to be alone with him, Elena had never smiled so hard, so I left her running barefoot in the sand.

"Just one look, then you leave Cami," I whispered again on the steep walk back up.

"I see you still talk to yourself." He startled me from behind when I got to the top. "I see you still sneak up on people, so I'm not the only one who hasn't changed."

He didn't seem put off by my snarky remark. "Touché, Vega." I forced myself to look away from the smile that touched his lips, and that's when I saw the house up close for the first time in six years. The once-broken windows were replaced by panels with white trim, and the walkway wasn't just a pile of rocks anymore; instead, it was pebbled and lined with flowers barely starting to bloom. The roof once covered in old tree vines was completely clear, and the patches of grass in the yard were growing back bright green. He was turning it into a home, which made me relieved it landed in his hands instead of anyone else's.

"It needs a few more tweaks before it's perfect," he said as we admired it from afar. It always was in my eyes.

"I'm glad I got to see it before I go back home."

He winced. "How is New York?" I spoke carefully to make sure we didn't fall into a conversation neither of us was ready for. "It's everything I imagined it would be." Was I was trying to convince him or myself?

He forced a tight-lipped smile and nodded. "I'm glad." I could sense the unsaid words, the unanswered questions looming between us, but neither of us acknowledged them.

"Come on, I'll show you inside." He led me up the steps and around the gaping hole in the porch. I still remembered the first time he saved me from falling through it. "I swear it's getting fixed this week." I smiled.

When we stepped across the threshold, I let out a gasp. I'd never seen it during the day since the only light coming in was from the moon the last time I saw it. I was happy to notice cobwebs no longer filled every corner, and a new floor was put in to replace the rotted wood. Despite the lack of furniture, it was everything I imagined it would be.

"When did you start renovating?" I asked, his eyes followed me as I moved through the foyer.

"Six months ago. I couldn't bring myself to touch it for a while after I bought it, but now, I work on it every day until it's dark." I traced my fingers over the design painted on the white walls. "Can I see the rest?" I should have gotten in my car and drove away, but curiosity ate at me.

A warm smile played at the corners of his lips. "I thought you'd never ask." When he opened the door to the first room on the left of the long hallway, my attention went straight to the forest-green walls and then to the queen-sized bed occupying most of the space. "This is supposed to be a guest room, but I don't get very many guests."

"Green walls? You hate green." Ironically, it was my favorite color. "Not anymore." He said softly. I could feel the heat of his stare on my neck.

The air grew thick, so I rushed into the room right across, where a telescope adjusted perfectly to look out at the ocean stood by the window. "I use it to watch the dolphins at sunset."

He said as I walked over and caught how the sun's rays glistened on the waves through the lens.

"Speaking of a sunset, we could watch one later, for old time's sake if you want." He kept his distance, but I felt the natural pull towards him.

You hadn't experienced a sunset until you'd seen one from the top of the cliffs in Willow's Cove. It was once my favorite view in the entire world, and coincidentally, the last one I saw was with the only other person in the room.

"There're more rooms, right?" He got the memo—I wanted to change the subject. He led us into the next room, which was completely empty with bare walls. "What's this one going to be?" I couldn't help but think the arch by the window would be perfect for a reading space.

"It's a secret project." He slowly shut the door, his eyes searing into mine as he towered over me. The hallway suddenly felt cramped, but his brown eyes, my own personal kryptonite, made it impossible to move. His woodsy scent filled my nose as he inched closer, and I sucked in a breath when his fingers softly brushed against mine. "This way leads to my room."

Where the hell was Elena when I needed her?

I followed him to the room at the end of the hall and immediately noticed how everything was spotless. The corners of his sheet were tucked in perfectly, the clothes hanging in his closet were sorted by color with no wrinkles in sight, and nothing seemed to be out of place. "More green walls?" I fought back a smile.

"What can I say? It grew on me." His eyes followed me as I snooped, but he didn't stop me. The photos perfectly lined up on his dresser caught my attention. I recognized the ones with his younger sister and friends from high school, but some faces weren't familiar at all. There were also some with just him, in places I'd only seen in travel magazines. His smile lit up in every one, which made me realize in our time apart, he seemed to have lived a happy and full life.

"Hey, Mila," his deep voice called out to me.

"Yeah?" We studied each other as our eyes met from across the room. I had sixteen-year-old Julian's face learned by heart, so his new look was something to get used to, but there was nothing unfamiliar about how my senses spun anytime I was near him. "Nothing. I just wanted to look at you." I turned away so he wouldn't see the flush of my cheeks. He never lost his charm, that was for sure. "It's good to see you too, Julian." His name fell from my lips with ease that time.

Loud footsteps suddenly filled the hallway, and Elena was out of breath when she found us. "Bad news, Cami. The hotel canceled our reservation because they were overbooked. I don't know how that's possible when this is practically a ghost town." She turned to Julian. "No offense."

He shrugged. "None taken."

"What do we do?" Her question made my mind race. "We could drive to the next town over, or fly back home tonig—"

Julian cut in. "How about you stay here? I have the extra rooms." My head was spinning after being in the same room as him for ten minutes; there was no way I was staying in his house. It was insane to even consider it, but of course, Elena didn't feel the same.

"Perfect. Thank you, stranger with the perfect hair. I'm Elena, by the way. If I'm staying in your house, you might as well know my name." If she wasn't my best friend, I would have considered firing her.

"I'm Julian."

She turned and winked at me, but if her goal was to be subtle, she failed. "Could you excuse us?" I pulled her away so Julian wouldn't overhear us. "What the hell, Lena? You can't just accept his invitation without talking to me first."

"What's the big deal? It beats sitting on a plane for another six hours back home. Besides, you two obviously know each other pretty well, so it's not like we're staying in a stranger's house." I once knew everything about him, but after so much time, he practically *was* a stranger.

"I really don't want to stay here, Lena." I was just there to do my book signing and get out of town. I wasn't supposed to have a run-in with Julian Perez, and especially sleep in his spare room, but I always had a talent for getting myself into deep shit.

"Who is he that he has you rattled like this?" I knew she was trying to get me to fess up, but no one in my new life knew about my old one in Willow's Cove. I wanted a fresh start when I got to the city, so I kept my past buried where it was unable to hurt me anymore.

"Forget it, it's fine. Just one night, and we fly back first thing tomorrow morning." I said sternly.

"That's the plan, babes." She didn't notice my look of distress, walking away, typing on her phone. I guess after years of fighting it, Willow's Cove found a way to suck me back in.

I walked back over to Julian with a tight expression. "I guess it's settled. We're staying."

The corner of his lips tugged up in a cocky smirk. "Looks like we'll have time to catch up after all." *Great.*

My phone's blaring ringtone cut through the air and saved me from saying anything else. I looked down to see Greyson's name across my screen. "I have to take this." I tried to calm my spiraling thoughts as I picked a room and shut the door behind me, my phone continuing to ring in my hand. "Hey, Grey." I greeted.

"Thank God. I was worried when I didn't hear from you earlier. Are you okay?" I could hear the cabs honking in the background.

"I'm sorry. Our hotel reservation got canceled, so we had to rearrange some stuff." I let my head sink into the pillows to soothe the pounding headache I felt coming on.

"My dad keeps his jet on standby. I could be there in a few hours and bring you home." I smiled from ear to ear. One of the reasons I fell in love with Greyson Carter was his selflessness despite his family teaching him to be the opposite his entire life.

"Don't go through the trouble. Elena and I will catch our flights back home tomorrow."

"Damn, I was hoping you'd say yes so I'd see you sooner." After nearly three years together, he still flirted like he pined after me, and I had the same butterflies for him as I felt in our early days of dating.

"Looks like you'll have to wait a little longer, Mr. Carter." I chuckled at his groan on the other end. He hated when I called him by the same name everyone called his dad.

"You're lucky I'm in love with you, Cami." My heart swelled when I pictured his wide smile. "So, tell me about the book signing. I heard you sold out the store."

A smile crept onto my face. "It seemed like the whole town showed up. The owner said it was the best turn-out she'd seen." I purposely left out the name of a certain person who showed up.

I knew he was home when a door shut on the other end, and I imagined being greeted with his forehead kisses. "I'm so proud of you. Did anything else exciting happen?"

I opened my mouth to speak, but was startled by a loud banging outside my window. I couldn't help but let my eyes linger on Julian as he hammered down pieces of wood to cover the hole on the porch. In the two years we'd been together, I never hid anything from Greyson, but I couldn't form the words to tell him I ran into an old boyfriend and was convinced to stay in his guest bedroom. It didn't help that Julian wasn't just any ex-boyfriend, but *the* ex-boyfriend.

"Nothing exciting ever happens in Willow's Cove."

two

JULIAN

8 YEARS EARLIER - AGE 16

I REMEMBER the exact moment I laid eyes on Camilla Vega. It was a Tuesday—the first day of kindergarten. Her dark, wavy hair was tied back with a green ribbon that matched her skirt, and she had a sparkly pink backpack. Even back then, you could just tell she was ten times smarter than everyone in the room. When she turned around and smiled at me, I felt my head explode. I didn't have a full grasp on what a crush was, but I knew I was done for. Two weeks later, I wrote her a note saying I liked her ribbon that went unanswered. The heartbreak was brutal for a five-year-old, but as with most crushes, it faded as time passed.

Our sophomore year at Willow High was when everything changed. First period English was typically when I caught up on sleep, since I managed to stay undetected in the back, but Mrs. Knowles started the class with an announcement that morning. "The name of your partner for the essay we discussed last week on Pride and Prejudice is pinned up on the wall. Come on up one by one and then gather with your partner." I stayed seated and watched Camilla's eyes roll to the back of her head when she turned around, which meant we were partnered together. Before then, we'd only had run-ins when I asked to borrow her homework and she made me pay for it with a snide remark. I could've borrowed anyone's, insult-free, but I fed off of the moments I'd see a sliver of a smile as she tried to act annoyed. Camilla stayed generally off the radar, but I'd be lying if I said she wasn't always on mine. I always found her.

I held back a grin as she walked over to my desk with a cold glare and slammed her books down. "If you think I'm doing all the work just because you're on varsity now, think again, Julian." I was secretly flattered she knew I made the varsity football team.

"I'm offended you think so little of me, Camilla Vega." Being one, if not *the* smartest person in the entire school, she had a right to ridicule me. I just scooted by enough to keep my grades up to play sports.

"Sorry, what do I know? I've only gone to school with you since we were five." She was the only person who could make me smile while being insulted, but her snarky remarks never scared me away; if anything, they drew me in.

"I'm gonna pretend you underestimating me doesn't sting a little bit." Her blue eyes met mine with a challenge, but all I could think of was how mesmerizing they were behind her long eyelashes. It was easy to get overwhelmed by Camilla's delicate beauty if you looked at her too long. The thick brown hair that fell over her shoulders in waves softened her golden tan skin, and her rosy cheeks looked permanently sun-kissed.

"I bet you haven't even read the book." Her soft-looking lips stole my attention before I met her gaze. "My sister forced me to watch the movie. That's good enough, right?" It was a hobby of mine to get her riled up.

Her eyes widened, and I could tell she was on the verge of exploding, which made me relent. "Relax, Camilla. I've got this.

Just tell me what to do." The green notebook she always wrote in was tabbed by subject, but I expected nothing less from someone who was constantly on the honor roll. Every page was filled with notes from lessons except one titled *Books*. I laid my hand on it to stop her from turning the page. "What's that?"

She hesitated to answer. "A list of books I want to read before the year ends." I chuckled with amusement. People we went to school with saw books as their kryptonite, but she had an endless list of ones to read in a matter of months. It further proved she never cared about fitting into a box because she'd made her own, and I was envious.

"I'll write the thesis and opening paragraph. I'll also cite the sources. All you have to do is write one paragraph, then the conclusion. Easy enough for your jock brain?" I hadn't heard a word she said, because I was too busy noticing the way her eyes had a speck of green in them if you looked closely enough.

I hid a smile behind my hand as an idea popped into my head. "Sure, but I think we should make this assignment interesting." It was a long shot, but after watching her for years, I wanted to know her, and I saw an opportunity. Her eyes perked with interest, but she didn't stop writing in her notebook.

"I'll read the book, and if we get at least a B on the essay, you have to come to my game next Friday."

Since she was the class president, she worked the ticket booth at every football game. I knew she left before we came on the field because she was never in the stands when I looked for her face. "How about a counteroffer? No to the game, but you get the satisfaction that you did your part and got a good grade for once in your life?"

My face spread into a smile. "Where's the fun in that, Vega?" She rolled her eyes, but I saw when her brows subtly flickered with interest. "Why would I go?"

"Maybe to have fun like a normal teenager instead of being in bed by nine?" Our playful banter was refreshing, since all anyone I hung out with talked about was girls, football, and parties—in that order.

"How do you know I'm in bed by nine?" People looked over at us when I threw my head back with laughter. "Just a guess."

Her bright blue eyes sucked me in again when she boldly met my gaze. "Let's say for argument's sake I agree to this stupid bet. We would have to get an A on the essay or no deal." I knew she only agreed because she knew I couldn't write an A-worthy essay, but that only made me want to accept the challenge more. Between football practice every day, away games on Thursdays, and home games every other Friday, I hardly had time to sleep, much less read a three-hundred-fifty-page book and write an essay, but Camilla had to be at my game—even if it meant paying someone to do the work for me and feeling like shit about it later. When I reached over to shake her hand, I could see her fighting back a smile. "Deal."

Neither of us knew it then, but I was hers from that day on.

three

JULIAN

I LIED. When Camilla asked how long it'd been since we last saw each other, I lied when I said I lost count. It had been two thousand, two hundred and fifty-seven days. After so long without someone, you start to go a little stir-crazy. I'd been hallucinating her for years, so I had to make sure she was real when I saw her in that bookstore. I never forgot the depth of her blue eyes, which reminded me of the waves we used to watch together, or how her smile could make anyone crumble. She might've changed her hair and worn a little more makeup, but she was still Mila.

She was nearly three thousand miles away for six years, yet when we were only a few doors down from each other, the unspoken words between us made it feel like she was the farthest she'd ever been. The constant reminder that I was the one to blame for our disconnect made it nearly impossible to sleep that night.

After tossing and turning for hours, I got out of bed and leaned against the window overlooking the same view I'd seen every day, but my heart lurched when I saw her silhouette glowing under the moonlight as she watched the high tides from the sand. If there was one thing you could always count on, it was that you'd always find Mila by the ocean. Without a second thought, I hurried out my front door and down the grass hill to join her. I wasn't surprised when she didn't notice my presence at first, since nothing else existed once she got lost in the sounds around her.

I didn't think it was possible, but her beauty was even more ethereal than before. Her hair was shorter and dyed a rich honey color that only enhanced the rest of her perfect features, and her smile lit up brighter than the moonlight shining down on us. I questioned how I survived so long without it, and took mental photos in case I'd never get to see her that way again.

"I didn't expect to see you out here." Her shoulders eased when I approached her. "Hey. I'm just taking advantage of the empty beach." She shoved her hands in the pockets of her oversized cardigan.

"Couldn't sleep?" I asked.

"Actually, I just woke up. I guess I'm still on New York time. You?"

"It's a rough night. I thought a walk on the beach might clear my head." I left out the part about not being able to sleep because it was driving me stir-crazy to know we were under the same roof.

She nudged further down the beach that stretched for miles. "I'll walk with you. I have some thoughts to clear up too." As I watched her bare feet seep into the sand with every step; it took me back to when we were two teenagers plunging into the cold waters after dark without a care in the world of what was ahead of us.

"I wasn't expecting you to be the same." She spoke over the sounds of water crashing on the rocks nearby.

"What do you mean?"

She smiled tenderly. "You're still you, just…grown up. It's a good thing, but I could do without that crap on your face, though."

I chuckled while running my fingers over my stubble beard in desperate need of a groom. "Cut me some slack. It took me three years to grow this." Our laughter echoed until it died off as she took in the view. I wished we could've just stayed there so I wouldn't have to wake up and watch her leave for a second time.

"Do you miss anything, Mila?" My question surprised us both, but she tried to recover. "Definitely this view."

"Anything else?" We both knew what I was implying, but neither of us said it out loud.

Her face fell before she spoke softly. "The city has everything I want. I have a great job, great friends. Everything is great." Even years later, I could still read her like a book, so I wasn't fully convinced, but I kept the thought to myself. "That's…great."

The silence loomed as we continued through the soft sand until she changed the subject. "I can't believe you did it."

My brows furrowed. "Did what?"

"The house. It's not even done yet, but it's beautiful." My heart thudded against my chest when her face split into a grin.

"I owed it to you to fix it." Her steps halted, and I watched her swallow hard before turning to face me. I knew I shouldn't have said it, but I had nothing else to lose.

"I uhh…should get inside. I have an early flight," she started back up the hill, but I craved her closeness, so I called after her in hopes she'd stay there with me. "I'm happy for you. You did what you said you always wanted to, Mila." Something in the air shifted, and it wasn't the wind. Her blue eyes lacked their normal shine when they met mine again. "Not everything." She mumbled, and then she was gone.

I stayed in the same spot until the sun rose that morning, thinking of everything I should have confessed, not knowing how different everything would have played out if I had.

four

CAMILLA

8 YEARS EARLIER - AGE 16

THE FIRST TIME I saw Julian Perez, I was five. He wore a Spiderman shirt that matched his backpack, and even then, he had confidence most kids didn't. When he flashed his smile missing a few teeth, my heart skipped a beat and a crush was born.

One day, he passed me a note that said, *I like your ribbon.* He was referring to the one I wore in my hair almost every day, and it was the first definitive memory I had of not feeling invisible. I preferred the company of books early on, but Julian was the first person to see me when no one else seemed to.

Since I knew another girl in class, Jaime Torres liked him, I never wrote anything back, and it was the last note I received from him. My crush lasted an embarrassing amount of time, but finally fizzled out sometime in middle school. To my surprise, it came back with full force during our sophomore year at Willow High.

Before we partnered on the essay in English class, he was

26

just someone I had a silly childhood crush on and always asked to borrow my homework, but after, he was *Julian*.

"Your tickets, madam president." My best friend, Taylor, skipped towards me with the roll of ticket stubs we'd be selling later that night. As class president, it was my job to set up the ticket and snack booths, which was the only part I enjoyed about high school football games. "I can't believe people pay seven dollars to come watch guys run around a field," I said.

She wiped the sweat off her fair skin from being under the sun. "It's called having fun, Cami. You should try it." She smiled. "Speaking of football, can I ask why I've seen you in the halls with Julian Perez the past week?" She was a professional prier, but being best friends since second grade, I'd learned to accept that about her.

"I got stuck with him as my partner on an essay."

"How'd that go?" I was prepared to do the entire assignment myself, but after we made the bet, I'd never seen him take school so seriously. If I hadn't seen him discreetly reading Pride and Prejudice with my own eyes, I wouldn't have believed him. He insisted on taking our essay the night before it was due to touch it up, so I hadn't had the chance to look over it before turning it into Miss Knowles. For the first time in my life, I'd hoped for a grade less than an A so I didn't have to go to the game that night.

"Good, I guess. Julian actually isn't like the other assholes he hangs out with." When we all entered high school, everyone turned into a clone of one another just to fit in, including Julian, but that week, when it was just me and him, it was as if his mask slipped off. I saw who he really was instead of the football god of Willow High.

Taylor stood with her hands on her curved hips. "I'm confused. Besides the fact you smiled when you said his name, you always said you'd swallow a jean jacket before you hung out with a jock. Now you're hanging out with one of the most notorious ones in school?"

I scoffed. "First of all, I didn't smile. Second, it's not considered hanging out since it was for an assignment, Tay."

She pursed her pink-tinted lips to hide a smile. "That probably explains why I saw you searching for him at lunch every day this week, right?" I sometimes forgot how Taylor managed to see everything, and the worst part was, she was right. I found him in every crowded room, and it freaked me out. "Can we not talk about Julian Perez anymore and get back to work?"

Her green eyes suddenly widened. "That's gonna be hard, considering he's walking towards us. You might want to fix your hair." I dropped the papers in my hand and hurried to fix myself up, but stopped when Taylor bursted out into hearty laughter. "I was kidding, Cami. I just wanted to see if you cared how you looked."

My eyes narrowed. "I hate you."

Her nose scrunched with more laughter as Julian approached us. Just like the rest of the players that day, he wore his dark blue jersey with his number twenty-one on the front and back. My eyes darted to his biceps strained against the fabric. I wasn't blind to his attractiveness—dazzling smile, staggering height, dark wavy locks, oozing confidence—but I refused to give him an ego boost, so I showed no reaction.

"What do you want, Julian?" I asked.

His face split into a wide grin. "Looks like you're watching me play tonight, Camilla Vega."

I had to strain my neck to look up at him. "What do you mean? We don't find out our grade until later today." He showed me his phone, which had a picture of our A-grade straight from Miss Knowles's desk. I still zoomed in to make sure I wasn't imagining it. "I convinced her I needed to see my grade early in order to play tonight."

I grew with suspicion. "How'd you pull this off? Pay someone to write your half, or did your coach talk to her?"

People at Willow High worshipped the football players, even teachers, so I knew he was more than capable of pulling strings.

He seemed to be amused by my defiance from the smirk that grew on his face. "You really know how to flatter me, Vega, but this was earned fair and square. A deal is a deal."

I didn't want to go to that game. I much rather would've stayed in and finished the book I was reading, so I pivoted for another excuse. "I can't go. I don't have a ride home after." I lived around the corner from school, but he didn't know that.

"It's taken care of. I'm taking you home after we hang out." He said it so confidently, as if it was already settled.

"Hang out? That wasn't part of the deal, Julian." Taylor's lips twitched with the need to smile as she watched our exchange.

"It's your turn for a challenge Camilla Vega: be a regular sixteen-year-old." He was the only person to call me by my full name.

"No." I was fully intent on standing my ground, but his soft brown eyes entranced me enough to be seconds away from breaking before Taylor spoke up. "Let's cut the shit, shall we? She'll go."

I gritted my teeth while Julian flashed a cocky smirk down at me. "Great. Wait for me outside the locker room after the game." As he walked away, I had to pry my eyes from his back muscles contracting with every step before I turned to Taylor. "Why the hell did you do that?"

"Two reasons: It's painful to watch you guys pretend you're not into each other, and because all you ever do is sit in your room and read about people who live their lives. How about you try it for once, Cami?"

I groaned. "We're not into each other, Tay. I just lost a bet. After today, Julian and I will go back to passing each other in the hallway." I didn't know why the words put a bad taste in my mouth.

"I don't get it. You read all these romance books about a girl who's so oblivious, she can't see when the guy likes her, and yet, *you* can't tell when one likes you."

I sighed. "I think you're confusing him liking me with him just being nice." My parents gave me no choice but to be smart in school, but it made me neglect every other aspect of my life, especially boys. That's where Taylor usually came in. Not many people could be both wise and headstrong at sixteen, but I always admired how she was able to do it so effortlessly.

"Maybe. Find out for yourself and prove me wrong then."

I threw my head back and groaned. "On a scale from one to ten, how insane am I for doing this?"

She put her hands on her hips while thinking it over. "A five, but we're sixteen, Cami. We're supposed to do things on a whim. Who knows; maybe you two will fall madly in love, and you'll only have me to thank." Her long, golden hair nearly whacked my face when she spun around.

She never let me live down how right she was that day.

I was ten when I realized the view from my rooftop was perfect for watching Willow High's football games, so on Friday nights, I sat alone, listening to the echoes of cheers and announcers on the microphone. If anyone ever asked why I never bothered to go to the games, I'd just say it wasn't my thing, but really, it was my fear of being seen. After going to school with the same people my entire life, I decided early on to stay off their radar, and it was working until Julian made me bend the rules.

As I sat in the stands, overwhelmed by the chaos around me, I felt like I stuck out like a sore thumb. "Let me put on record that I've been trying to drag you to a game since freshman year, yet Julian Perez is the one who convinced you." Taylor sat beside me, her eyes glued to the field while she ate popcorn.

"Let *me* put on record that I'm not here by choice." In the same breath, my eyes found number twenty-one on the field. He held his helmet in one hand while the other slicked back his wavy brown hair. Even through the sea of people, our eyes met almost immediately, as if we sensed each other. He waved and then broke out into laughter when I jokingly flipped him the middle finger.

It was almost never that a sophomore made varsity, much less became a starting tight end, but he had a family legacy on his side, considering his dad and grandpa both led their teams to state championships their senior year. Their photos lined the hallway in Willow High's Hall of Fame, and everyone knew Julian would end up there too.

"Any idea where you guys are going after this?" Taylor pulled my attention away. "Nowhere. I'm just going to ask him to take me home." Proving Taylor wrong sounded tempting at first, but the more I imagined being alone with Julian, I grew terrified. He was the first boy to make my heart race with one glance, and anytime he looked at me, it seemed like he actually saw me, meaning he was dangerous.

She shifted her entire body to face me. "Cami, you had the biggest crush on this guy when we were kids, and now he's practically begging to take you out. You're not even a little curious to see where it goes?" The only "experience" I had with relationships were those in books and my parents, and let's just say I preferred the ones I read. I grew up sheltering myself away from people to avoid disappointment, and it scared the shit out of me that I was willing to forget all of that when it came to Julian, so I had to keep my distance.

I shook my head tightly. "Nope."

"You know your cheeks turn red when you lie, right?" Taylor wasn't just my longest friend, but really, my only friend. I'd be lying if I said it didn't irk me that she knew me better than I knew myself sometimes.

I didn't have time to dwell before the crowd roared as someone flew across the field. I couldn't peel my eyes away when number twenty-one bolted farther and farther until he crossed into the end zone. I hadn't realized I was cheering along with them until I looked over and saw Taylor with a sly grin. "You sure you're not curious?"

I dropped my hands in my lap. "I hate you."

I watched Julian walk back to the bench, but instead of celebrating with his friends, he took off his helmet and offered me a wink and a bright smile. It was the smallest gesture, yet I couldn't get my heart to slow, which meant I was in deeper than I'd realized.

TAYLOR WAITED with me outside the boys' locker room after the game. My nerves only intensified with every person who walked out who wasn't him. "If we leave now, I think we can make it to the car before he comes out," I said with a shaky breath.

She grasped my shoulders and gently shook me. "Relax, Cami. I'm a phone call away if you want to bail, but give it a chance. You might enjoy yourself." I was afraid of that.

I froze when my eyes found Julian walking out in his letterman jacket and slicked back hair, freshly showered. He seemed completely oblivious that he demanded people's attention as he walked by them.

"Hey." My cheeks flushed when he greeted me and Taylor with a slanted grin. "Hi."

Neither of us said anything else until Taylor cut in. "Okay, I'll leave you two in this awkward silence. Have fun, but not too much." She winked at me before walking away, and all I could think was how much I wished I was going with her.

Julian's warmth ran down my arm when he nudged my shoulder. "I fully expected you to be gone."

"You can thank Taylor. She wouldn't let me follow through with my escape plan," I teased. As he led us to the parking lot, I let out a gasp when his touch on my back made my skin tingle enough to give me goosebumps. "Are you cold? Here."

"No, I'm fine. It's ok—" He draped his letterman jacket, which was at least two sizes too big for me, over my shoulders before I could finish. I tried not to bask in his natural scent as it wrapped around me. "Thanks."

"See, I can be a gentleman." I looked down at my feet when his face split into a grin, but I still felt my pulse quicken. "I never said you couldn't."

"Weird, because I think I remember you calling me an asshole once or twice, or was that someone else?" In my defense, I thought every jock was an asshole. When he wasn't tricking me into going on a date, he actually made me smile. Before him, I hardly did much of that.

"Julian! Are you coming with us?" A crowd of his friends huddled around their cars and looked at us in confusion when they noticed us walking close together. One outing with Julian, and all my efforts to be invisible started to unravel, but I was counting on people forgetting my face by Monday morning.

"Not tonight!" he shouted back as I got hit with an overwhelming whiff of men's cologne when I climbed into his old Mustang. Their dumbfounded expressions told me he didn't say no to them often.

"You don't have to do me any favors by taking me out instead of going with your friends. Our stupid bet is settled." It was my last attempt to get out of it before I was in too deep.

His car struggled to start, but eventually, the loud engine roared to life. "I'd much rather be here with you." I knew I was done for when just his soft gaze made my stomach tie in knots.

As we drove along the poorly lit road, I subtly snooped around his car and saw his backseat covered with sweat-stained gym shirts, enough jerseys for every day of the week, and countless empty water bottles. I wanted to know more about him, but I knew I couldn't.

"That wasn't so bad for your first football game, right?" He broke the silence. I would have never lived it down if I'd told him I actually enjoyed it. "It wasn't the worst thing in the world.""I've never scored that many touchdowns, so for the sake of the school, you'll have to come to more of my games." Thankfully, he didn't see when my cheeks turned red.

"Sorry to disappoint, but that was the first and last time." The smirk he flashed gave me the feeling that he never intended it to be a one-time thing. *Spoiler alert—it wasn't.*

"Here we are." I hesitated to get out when the car stopped on the side of an unfamiliar road near the woods. "What are we doing here?" It wasn't until I saw the *Leaving Willow's Cove* sign that I knew we were on the very edge of town.

"It's a surprise."

My brows furrowed. "Let's see, a girl on a dark road with a guy she barely knows; I think this is exactly how true crime documentaries start." I was being sarcastic, but I felt a ball of nerves settle into my stomach.

"Relax, we've known each other since we were five, Vega. Do you trust me?" I stared at his hand held out towards me, and deep down, I knew I could. I grasped his fingers for dear life as he led us through the tall grass, and his closeness filled me with an unfamiliar comfort.

He chuckled when I shuddered at every sound I heard in the pitch black. "I've been through these woods hundreds of times, and have only seen deer."

My grip tightened. "When you forced me to go on a date with you, I pictured something a lot less… sketchy."

He stopped and looked at me with a gleam in his brown eyes. "So this is a date?" Of course, that's what he was concerned about when we were at the mercy of anything out in the woods. I rolled my eyes and entwined our hands, ignoring how natural it felt to reach out for his warmth.

We finally came to a stop near the edge of the woods, but there was nothing in front of us but old tree stumps. "So, is this place imaginary?" My sarcasm made him laugh under his breath and shake his head.

"You're hard to impress, Camilla Vega." He parted a thick vine of leaves that wouldn't stick out to anyone who didn't know the most breathtaking view hid behind it. My mouth gaped at the green acres that spread for miles, with a lake that reflected the moonlight, all surrounded by hills almost as high as the cliffs at the cove. We were high enough to see everything, including the next town over, whose lights lit up the night. "What is this place?" I asked.

"Technically, it doesn't have a name, since most people don't know it's here, but I call it The Bluffs. It's my favorite place." I kept a mental picture of how he admired the view so fondly. "It's beautiful." I meant it. "How did you find it?"

He sat on the edge of the cliff so his legs dangled. "It was a happy accident. One day, I came to look at the *Leaving Willow's Cove* sign to imagine leaving it behind. My head was spinning, so I decided to walk through the woods. I like to think I found this place exactly when I needed to."

I sat next to him without any hesitation, and let my feet dangle over the cliff. "Thanks for showing it to me."

"Anytime." He scooted closer so our arms grazed each other, and I found it hard to pay more attention to the view than him.

"How many girls have you brought here? Am I number five? Ten?" I'd only ever heard of him having one girlfriend, but I was sure there was a long list.

He smirked. "I figured you'd ask that. You're actually the sixteenth."

My face instantly fell. "What?"

He threw his head back with rich laughter that quickly

became one of my favorite sounds. "I'm kidding, Vega. Not even my friends know about this place. It's sacred to me." I was confused when my stomach swarmed with butterflies. "Why'd you show me then?"

He looked out at the green acres and sighed. "I see the way you distance yourself from everyone else. Sometimes, I'm jealous I can't do the same. People around me feel like plants put there just for looks. I can't remember the last time I had a meaningful conversation with my friends. To answer your question: I'm showing you because you're the first genuine person I've been around in a long time." That was the first time I not only held sympathy for Julian Perez, but saw him in raw form, when he wasn't trying to prove himself to anyone. I liked him that way.

"I hope you know that, since I showed you my secret spot, we're officially friends whether you like it or not, Camilla Vega." The idea we could ever be friends was laughable not long before that night.

I cocked my head to the side. "Why do you always call me by my whole name?"

"Because no one else does. I'll come up with something better, don't worry." Everyone came up with their own nickname for me—Cam, Cami, Lila, and for a month when I was nine, my mom called me Lala; thankfully, that one didn't stick. Julian was the first person to ever use my whole name, but I couldn't show I liked hearing it from his lips.

"You say that like we're going to see each other more often."

He spoke gently as a boyish smile spread over his face. "I hope so."

The question that had been searing my brain since I got in his car sat on my tongue. "Why me, Julian?"

"Why not you?" He shrugged, as if the answer was obvious, and all my senses were brought to life.

"You're making it hard to stay invisible." I said while

fighting back a smile. There was a moment of utter silence where we did nothing but look at each other, as if everything around us didn't exist.

"You've never been invisible to me, Camilla Vega."

I didn't know it yet, but after he'd said those words, I was completely and utterly his.

five
CAMILLA

I COULDN'T DENY there was beauty everywhere you looked in Willow's Cove, but every part of it held memories I tried six years to forget—including Julian. Our run-in down at the beach was the only thing on my mind as I watched the sun slowly rise through the window.

I wanted to hate him. I wanted to blame him for what happened years before that landed us where we were, but as I sat and watched the waves come and go, I remembered my mom once told me there was a time for everything, and then it passes like the tides. Julian and I were in the past, which meant the mistakes we made when we were just kids had to stay there too. I reached for my phone and smiled at the text from Greyson.

> I can't wait until you're home. I couldn't sleep without you last night. Have a safe flight, Cami. I love you.

THAT MORNING WAS my first without Greyson in two years; I felt his absence deeply when I woke up and touched the empty side of the bed. He usually traveled with me for all my events, but he couldn't miss an important meeting with his dad. He'd always hated small towns anyway.

The smell of fresh coffee and bacon shot me out of bed before I could type a message back. Considering I only knew how to make toast and Greyson never learned to cook, I forgot the last time I'd had a meal that wasn't takeout.

I peeked around the corner and spied the outline of Julian's back as he flipped bacon and pancakes on the stove. I knew there had to be an old diary entry in which I imagined waking up to Julian Perez in a t-shirt that showed his rippling muscles as he made breakfast with an ocean view. As I stood by and watched, I wondered about the little things, like what his everyday routine was, and how his life turned out since the last time I saw him.

I flushed with embarrassment when he turned around and caught me lurking, but he greeted me with a dimpled smile. "Good morning. I figured you and your friend wanted breakfast before your flight." He poured fresh coffee into a mug and slid it in front of me.

"Thank you, but you did enough by letting us stay." I walked over to the sliding door with a perfect view of the rocky cliffs overlooking the cove. Julian's warmth radiated throughout my body when he joined me. "I forgot how beautiful it is," I said softly.

"I'm sure your view back in New York is better." Greyson and I could see most of lower Manhattan from our balcony, but nothing compared to the early morning rays glistening over the waters in Willow's Cove.

"Can I ask you something, Julian?" I blurted out.

He nodded without hesitation. "Are you happy?" Out of all the unanswered questions reeling through my head for six years, that was the one I thought of most often.

His brown eyes softened as he looked down at me. "Are you?" We were so close, I could feel his heart hammering, and it matched the sudden tempo of mine. I wasn't sure why I couldn't just answer the question, but thankfully, we were interrupted by the sound of a car's brakes screeching up the hill.

"Shit. Sorry about this." He mumbled.

"About wh—" Suddenly, a familiar face barged through the door with a wide smile and bounced over to wrap her arms around me. "Cami! I was hoping I'd catch you before you left."

I was surprised to see his little sister still lived in town, given that she had dreams of moving to a big city. Sofia was a year younger than us, but you'd never know it from the way she carried herself. She'd always been too wise for her own good, and she radiated kindness and warmth wherever she went. I once considered her the little sister I never had.

"Hey, Sof," I said into her dark brown hair. She was no longer the seventeen-year-old girl I knew. She was all grown up, suddenly a stranger with a familiar face, but I was to blame for that.

"We've missed you so much." I spared a glance over at Julian, who occupied himself with eating the breakfast he'd made. "I got busy at work yesterday, so I couldn't make it to your book signing, but I brought my personal copy if you'll do the honors." My eyes went straight to the huge diamond on her left finger when she slid the book across the counter. "You want to bring that up, or should I?" I raised my brows at her.

She smiled like a little kid as she looked down at her freshly pedicured hand. "Oh! I'm getting married in eight days. Can you believe it?" Sofia never shied away from the fact that she was in love with the idea of falling in love, so it was no surprise she'd done it younger than most people.

"Congratulations. Who is he? Someone I know?"

Julian scoffed. "Yeah, tell her who he is, Sof."

She hesitated before letting a smirk tip the corner of her lips. "His name is Levi…Willow."

I couldn't contain the gasp that escaped me. "As in part of

the founding family?" The only thing I knew about the founding family was their long line of members who went on to become the mayor of Willow's Cove. They were untouchable in the eyes of the townspeople, and wherever they went, a headline in the local newspaper followed.

"His dad may or may not be the mayor. Julian thinks the Willow family is full of nothing but snobs, but I promise they're not, especially Levi." Sofia had a gift of seeing through people, so I had no doubt in my mind that what she said was true.

"I wish I could be there to see you in a white dress." It was hypothetical, but her face lit up as if I'd given her the brightest idea. "Wait, why don't you? Better yet, I'm a bridesmaid short, so you can be a part of my wedding party!" She squealed with excitement while Julian and I froze. Even if I didn't have a flight back home that day, staying in Willow's Cove was a recipe for disaster. One day around Julian, and I was already rattled; eight days would be complete insanity.

"I can't. I'm flying back to New York today," I said.

"Can't you reschedule it? I mean, it feels like fate that you ended up back here. I wanted to send you an invitation, but *someone* said no." Her eyes darted to Julian, whose jaw clenched as he looked at his sister with fire in his eyes.

I stumbled for another excuse, but Elena saved me when she waltzed into the kitchen in full glam, unfazed by the strange faces. "Thank God, coffee." We all watched with amusement as she reached into the cupboard and poured some into a mug, as if she'd been in Julian's kitchen a thousand times. If there was one thing she wasn't, it was shy. I always admired that about her.

Sofia looked over at Julian with her eyes narrowed. "Since when do you bring girls home?"

Our collective chuckles echoed through the room. "That's my friend and assistant, Elena. Elena, this is Sofia." I said. If we all lived in the same place, I knew the two of them would've gotten along perfectly. A part of me gravitated towards Elena in college because she reminded me of my friends back home, but the more I got to know her, the more she stood out on her own.

She held her coffee mug in one hand and waved with the other. "Hi. Sorry, I have a habit of making myself at home."

Julian shook his head. "Any friend of Mila's is welcome to anything in my house." She subtly found my eyes and smirked, which told me she wasn't done prying. "Speaking of the house, you're so lucky you have this view. The one I have back home faces the front of a shitty restaurant."

Home. The word made me think of Greyson's smile, of getting wrapped in his natural woodsy scent every morning when we'd snooze the alarm for five more minutes of sleep.

"So can you please stay, Cami?" Sofia pleaded again.

"She's busy on her book tour." I was relieved when Julian inserted himself into the conversation, but it was immediately shot down when Elena didn't read the room. "Your schedule is clear for the next couple of weeks." I shot an irritated glance at her.

Greyson and I had never been apart longer than a day since we'd met, and the thought of being away any longer filled me with dread. "I…"

Sofia cut in as I searched for a nice way to let her down again. "Before you say it, I know it's a big ask, but you were like a sister to me. I really want you to be a part of my big day." I knew I couldn't stay in Willow's Cove. I wasn't ready to face the reasons I'd stayed away for so long, but as I looked into her soft brown eyes, they reminded me of Julian's, and I could never say no to him. Her long eyelashes batted at me, and when I looked over at Julian, his face was hard to read.

I let out a defeated sigh. "Okay, you win. I'll be a brides-maid." I figured seeing her in a wedding dress would be worth the stay.

She leaped out of her chair and hugged me so tight, I was almost breathless. "Yes! Thank you, Cami. We'll go dress shopping tomorrow and find you something perfect." She stole Julian's bacon right out of his hand before skipping out of the house.

"She hasn't changed at all," I said when the door shut behind her.

"Believe it or not, she's gotten more insufferable as she's gotten older." His sarcasm was obvious. Anyone who knew him knew he loved his little sister more than life itself, but he rarely voiced it.

I found Elena's eyes as they shifted between me and Julian, a sly expression on her face. "Do you mind—"

"Rescheduling your flight? Already ahead of you." Sometimes, it felt like we shared a brain. When she walked to her room, I tried to think of how to fill the silence when it was just me and Julian again, but I came up short. My mind reeled over the fact that I'd be in close proximity with my ex-boyfriend for the next eight days.

"You could've said no," Julian interrupted my inner turmoil. A part of me wished I had, but as much as I missed home, I knew it would have eaten at me if I'd gotten on that plane. "No, I couldn't have. She's important to me." I gulped when his eyes slowly met mine. Somehow, they were richer than they were the last time I saw them.

"Well, you might as well stay here. The hotel across town is overbooked, and Sofia will be popping in the entire week for wedding stuff anyway." The thought of being in the same town made a knot grow in my throat, much less staying under the same roof. I knew it was just a matter of time before everything we'd buried for years went off like a ticking time bomb.

"I'd hate to get in your way of renovating."

"You wouldn't. Don't be stubborn, Mila. We both know my guest room is better than anything else in town." I was quiet as I considered it. On the one hand, it saved me from staying in the shitty hotel, but on the other hand…Julian. As much as I tried to convince myself otherwise, he would never be just another face. There was a version of me who loved him with every bit of my heart, and I didn't want to find out if she was still there.

He reached over the counter and grabbed my hand as if it was still second nature. "Please stay, Mila." My body recognized his touch, making my heartbeat quicken. I suddenly couldn't push the word no from my lips.

I shot across the kitchen to put distance between us. "*If* I stay, we need to set some ground rules." When he held back a smile and ran his fingers through his wavy hair, I only saw seventeen-year-old Julian—the one I'd fallen so hard for, it felt impossible to get up.

"Okay. Set your terms." He folded his arms and listened intently.

"For one, we need distance." His chuckle echoed through the room as he took one step back. "Done." I was surprised he didn't have a rebuttal—he'd always been the type to dance around rules.

"Don't do that thing with your smile either. You know exactly what I'm talking about." He knew I'd always been a sucker for his crooked smirk. The mere sight of it had the ability to make me crumble.

He cocked his head to the side. "Anything else?"

"For the next eight days, we're friends, nothing else," I said sternly.

He looked down to hide a mischievous smile. "Okay, friends." I could hear the challenge in his tone, as if he saw the rules more like a game, which meant I was in deep shit because he'd roped me in with a similar charm in high school.

My entire body lit up in flames when his eyes slowly raked over me. "I…should go check on my friend." I practically sprinted to Elena's room to catch my breath and found her packing.

"Your flight is rescheduled for next Sunday, and your

calendar is clear from any meetings for the next eight days." I helped fold the remainder of clothes into her suitcase. "You could stay the week with me. It'll be like a vacation." I knew the answer before I even finished the words.

"You know I'd go stir-crazy, Cami." She'd grown up in a town where cows were more populous than people, which made her despise anywhere even slightly similar. "You seem to fit in here, though."

"What do you mean?" I asked.

She zipped up her suitcase and dropped it by the door. "I saw that look when you got out of the car yesterday. It's the same one I had when I first saw New York and knew that's where I was meant to be."

I shook my head. If she knew anything about Julian or the reason I never came back, I was sure her answer would have been different. "It's been years since I left. This isn't my home anymore, Lena."

She rested her hands on my shoulders, her blue eyes seared into mine. "You might have left, but did it leave you?" *I didn't have the answer at the time, but those words echoed in my head that entire week.*

Before I could speak, we were interrupted by my phone ringing with Greyson's call. "Shit. He doesn't know I'm staying yet." Usually, we ran everything by each other first, but I was forced to make a decision under Sofia's wide-eyed stare.

"Good luck, babe."

"Are you gonna be okay?" I asked.

She smirked. "I've been on my own since I was seventeen, Cami. I know how to get on a plane. I'll see you back home in a week." She threw me a wink before I rushed across the hall and shut the door behind me. "Hey." I greeted Greyson.

"How does Thai sound for dinner? I made a reservation at that restaurant you like once you land." My heart lurched at the sound of his deep voice. The thought of not being in his arms hours from then made me wince, but once I made a promise, there was no going back.

I ripped off the band-aid and let the words spill out. "Grey, I'm staying in Willow's Cove for the week." The only indication he was still on the line was the sound of office phones ringing off the hook in the background. My heart sank when I pictured the look of disappointment falling over his face, and when he finally spoke, it was in a hushed tone. "Are you okay?"

Of course, that was his first concern. "Yeah. An old friend is getting married, and I couldn't say no when she asked me to be a bridesmaid." I left out the part about the old friend being my ex-boyfriend's little sister. The more silence that fell between us, the harder my leg shook. "Are you mad?"

He didn't hesitate to answer. "Of course not. I'm disappointed I have to go an entire week without you, but as long as you're okay, that's all that matters, Cami." I smiled to myself and let out a breath of relief. "I love you. I'll call you every night, I promise."

"I love you too," he said.

I knew I should have mentioned Julian, but considering Greyson didn't know about our past, I thought it best it stay that way to keep unnecessary doubt out of his head. Besides, what was the worst that could happen?

six

JULIAN

8 YEARS EARLIER

MONDAYS AFTER FOOTBALL games always played out the same; teachers cut players slack in class, and students worshipped us more than usual. We were practically celebrities in the eyes of our classmates, and while my friends found the adoration intoxicating, I resented it. The pressure of carrying on the "family legacy" my dad and grandpa left made me eventually despise the sport I grew up loving, especially when I realized I was only valuable when I helped win games. Otherwise, I was a disappointment.

I walked down the crowded hall that morning only looking for one face, but I came up short. "Where were you on Friday, JP?" Damon asked as we headed to our first class.

"I went out." I didn't know what was more rattling—that I hadn't been able to get Camilla out of my head the entire weekend, or the thought of seeing her made me excited to get to class. Once I saw a sliver of the real her, it was too late to turn back; I wanted to know everything.

"With who?"

"You don't know her." Despite his brows raising in suspicion, I didn't want to tell him about Camilla. Not because I was embarrassed, but because telling Damon meant putting her on the entire school's radar, and weirdly, I felt the need to shield her.

When we entered Miss Knowles' class, I was disappointed when she wasn't at her desk, but I knew she would show up solely because she'd had perfect attendance since kindergarten. Instead of heading over to my seat in the back of the room, I redirected over to Johnny Miller.

His brows furrowed when I stood over him. "What's up, JP?" The last time he and I talked was in eighth grade, but he had the seat right next to Camilla, and I had to have it. "I'll give you ten bucks for your seat."

He scoffed. "You're serious? Why?"

"Would you believe me if I said I wanted to be closer to the board to take notes?" His chest rattled as he belted out with laughter. "Hell no." It was worth a shot, but I couldn't blame him for not believing me.

"You want it or not, Miller?" His smile turned mischievous when I held out a ten-dollar bill. "Make it twenty, and you have a deal." I knew I'd entered pathetic territory when I pulled out my last twenty-dollar bill, but it was the best money spent when I looked up and saw her enter right before the bell rang. The green ribbon in her hair complimented the plaid skirt emphasizing her long, tan legs. I didn't know my heart could beat so fast until then. She was way out of my league, but I wanted her anyway.

I'd pay any amount of money just to relive the look of surprise when she saw me. "Are you lost?" I caught a whiff of her flowery scent when she leaned over and whispered.

"I had Johnny switch me. It's a little hard to see from my seat back there." I lied. She looked away, but not before I saw the beginning of a warm smile that made my insides twist into knots.

I didn't realize I was watching her until Damon's voice pulled me out of my trance.

"It makes sense why you ditched us on Friday now." His lips were thin with displeasure when I turned to face him, and since he'd said it loud enough for everyone to hear, Camilla tensed from all the eyes on us.

I felt the need to defend her. "Didn't you throw two interceptions at the game? I'd worry about other things if I were you, D." He'd been one of my best friends since preschool, so I knew the only way for him to back off was to hurt his ego. Everyone used to ask why I had a friend who was notorious for being an asshole, but he wasn't always like that. We used to go down to the park every day in middle school to play football. We dreamed of playing in the pros together. He was just like any other kid, until he wasn't. I guess I was always waiting for that kid to come back.

Camilla's eyes said everything her lips didn't when she held my gaze with a softness I'd never seen before, and I spent the rest of class hoping she'd look my way again, only to be disappointed. When the bell dismissed us, she darted out so fast, I had to chase her down the hallway and ignore everyone's wide-eyed stares. "Camilla, wait!" I knew she'd heard me, but she kept her pace until I pulled her back. "Yeah?"

Just being near her made my palms sweat, so when I tried to speak, only one word came out. "Hi."

Her lips tipped into a faint smile. "Hi. Now that's out of the way, why are you chasing me down the hallway?"

I never realized how staggering our height difference was until I saw how she had to crane her neck to look up at me. "I wanted to see what you were doing later."

"It's a school night, so homework. Why?"

Spit it out. "I don't have practice today, and I sort of like hanging out with you, so I was hoping we could do it again." The words came out so fast, I wasn't sure she understood until she broke out in laughter, which wasn't great for my ego. "Julian, you can't be serious. Friday was fun, but it was just a one-time thing."

I shrugged. "What if it wasn't?"

Her arms folded across her chest. "Damon was already making comments about us in class. What do you think the rest of your friends will say?" I knew what she was trying to do, but what she didn't know yet was I never shied away once I wanted something. "Since when do you care about what other people think, Camilla Vega?" I smirked.

Her eyes widened. "I…I don't. I just think we should keep our new friendship on school grounds." She looked around at the people gawking at us. "Maybe keep our interactions to a minimum too. You attract attention wherever you go."

I leaned against the locker and looked down at her. "And if I said I don't like that idea?"

"I'd say that's too bad." Her hair nearly hit me in the face when she turned to walk away. I didn't know why, but her persistence to keep me at bay only made me want her more.

I didn't give a shit if the whole school heard me when I let my voice echo through the halls. "That sounds like another challenge, Vega!" My heart nearly leaped out of my chest when I caught the smile she threw back before disappearing around the corner.

AFTER SPENDING all of third period coming up with a plan, I realized I'd gone from borderline to full-on pathetic in one day with the lengths I was willing to go for Camilla's attention.

My hands trembled as I watched the doors to the cafeteria. She thought she stayed invisible to everyone for years, but I knew she spent the first ten minutes of lunch in the library to check out books. I just had to wait.

"Why do you keep looking at the door, Perez?" Elijah nudged my shoulder as he joined me at the end of the table.

Elijah Fisher wasn't my longest friend, but it always felt like I'd known him longer than anyone else. He was the head coach's son, so he knew pressure even more than I did, but you never saw him crumble. It's what made him the voice of reason in our friend group.

"I'm waiting for someone."

"Camilla? I just saw her leave the library." I looked around at everyone at our table, who was too busy with their own conversations to pay attention to ours. "How do you know it's her?"

"I have eyes, JP. If you guys were trying to be discreet on Friday, you were shit at it."

I chuckled. "Touché. Do you know her?"

"It's Willow's Cove. We all know each other whether we like it or not. I have her in biology, though. She's smart as hell, cute too. It's a shame she keeps to herself." The more I looked around me, the more I understood why she preferred it that way. "Are you guys a thing now, or are you just stalking her?" he asked before chugging down milk.

"It's more like I need redemption after she turned me down." He nearly choked from his abrupt laughter. "That's a first. Now I like her even more."

I grunted with frustration. "We've gone to school together our entire lives, and before, she was just the quiet girl in class who let me copy her homework—"

"Don't forget your first crush," he cut in. I wasn't surprised he remembered when it was he who told me to send the note about her ribbon in kindergarten. "Now, she's Camilla Vega, the girl I can't stop thinking about. I don't know what the fuck is happening." I buried my head in my hands.

"You like her, JP. It's not that hard to figure out." How ironic she had me wrapped around her finger after one date, and she didn't even know it.

"Well, I can't exactly do anything about it if she keeps dodging me." I'd never had to work so hard for a girl's attention; I never had to work at all. If it were anyone else, I would have given up, but with Camilla, it never crossed my mind.

"Nothing worth it comes easy, Perez."

My face twisted. "Did you just quote your dad?" Coach always said the same thing whenever we were losing a game.

He cursed under his breath. "Shit. Don't tell him, or I'll never live it down." Our laughter halted when I saw Camilla walk into the cafeteria, Taylor at her side. She tried so hard to be invisible, but was completely unaware she owned any room she entered.

Elijah patted me on my shoulder. "Go get her, Perez." I was more nervous walking up to her table than I was when I asked Summer Davis to be my girlfriend on the playground in the second grade. The closer I inched, the fuzzier the plan I'd thought so hard about got. "Fuck it," I whispered right before sitting beside her.

Her face blanched at our sudden closeness. "Are you lost again? You sit all the way over there." I was hypnotized by her flowery scent again as she pointed her green-painted fingernail to the table crowded with football players, who hadn't noticed I was gone yet.

"I came to talk about our second date." I faced Taylor, who sat across from us. "Hey, Tay." Her icy stare told me how much she didn't like being called that.

"Firstly, we didn't go on a first date; I lost a bet. Secondly, I thought we agreed our friendship would stay on school grounds?" Her rose-tinted cheeks told me I made her nervous.

I shrugged and shot her a playful smirk. "I don't remember agreeing to that."

"The answer is still no, Julian." Her firm tone screamed defiance, but her ocean-blue eyes said something different. Any time I looked at her, I was reminded of what gentle, overwhelming beauty was, and her ability to keep me on my toes only made her more captivating.

"I'll tell you what; since we're friends, I'll give you two options. You either agree to a second date, or I get on this table and ask you again in front of the entire school." I smiled when I noticed her gulp hard.

"You're bluffing." She had a bad habit of underestimating me. "Sounds like you made your choice."

I only got one foot on the table before she yanked me down. "Okay, you win. Where should I meet you?"

I glowed over my win. "It's a date, Vega. I'll pick you up."

She groaned. "Do we have to call it a date? We're just hanging out as friends, right?" It was definitely a date. I knew I only wanted Camilla Vega. I just had to wait for her to realize it.

I leaned over and ate one of her fries, as if I'd eaten lunch with her a hundred times. "Right. Friends."

seven

JULIAN

I NEVER BELIEVED in fate until it brought Camilla back to Willow's Cove. After spending six years thinking of her every single day, it felt like I'd finally gotten a break from the universe when we were put under the same roof for a week. The question I kept asking myself was, did I want to be selfish by trying to undo the past, or let her go for good? It drilled into me as I let out my pent up frustration on the wooden boards I was nailing to the porch so Mila wouldn't fall through. It was almost sunrise, but I'd been at it for nearly two hours. Four years in the Air Force left me no choice but to be an early riser.

"Good morning." I stole a glance when her soft voice came from above. I didn't know what mesmerized me more, the view of the sun greeting the day over the horizon, or the way she shined under the early morning rays. Her honey-colored hair was pulled into a messy bun, but stray strands framed her bare face. It ceased to amaze me how she got even more goddamn beautiful in our time apart. I couldn't help but feel resentful towards whoever got to watch her become the person standing in front of me.

"You're up early again," I went back to hammering the floor-boards so I wouldn't stare at her.

"You know I never miss a sunrise."

I smiled. "I'm glad the city didn't change you too much, Mila." I second-guessed if she'd heard me while she soaked up the view. Anytime she was by the ocean, nothing else existed, not even me. It was a nice reminder that part of her was still there.

Her gentle smile bathed me in warmth. "You're still the only one who ever called me that." I couldn't help but be smug that the nickname I gave her was still *mine*. I barely missed my fingers with the hammer from being too distracted by her.

"Can I help?" she asked. I was nearly finished, but I craved her closeness after going without it for so long. "Sure. Can you lay the boards down while I hammer the nails in?"

My breath hitched in my throat when her fingers grazed mine, and I was pleased to see she had the same reaction. "No more green nail polish?" I had to push out the memory of her sage green nails grazing my skin while we laid under the stars.

"Not since my freshman year of college," she said.

"What else has changed since I last saw you?" I guessed distance was good for one thing; it meant I could learn her all over again.

She sighed. "What do you want to know?" *Everything.*

"What's your new favorite book?" She sank to the floor and let a smile spread across her face. "It's still the same. You probably don't remember—"

"*Persuasion* by Jane Austen." My quickness to answer made her lips part in shock, but how could I forget after spending most of our summer before junior year watching in awe as she read pages of it to me?

She spoke in a daze. "Yeah, that's the one." She might've changed a few things about herself, but when I stared deep into her blue eyes, she was Mila. Mila, the girl I could always find by the ocean, whose face resembled sunlight, especially when she talked about books.

"What about you, Julian?" Considering I'd been in love with the same girl since high school and I still lived in my hometown, nothing had changed. "I'm still me."

Her green-flecked eyes held a glint of tenderness as they clung to me. "I can see that." I cleared my throat and distracted myself from the urge to reach out and touch her. After all, I had to follow the rules.

"Speaking of books, are you writing anything new?"

She stiffened at the question. "I'm supposed to pitch an idea when I get back to New York, but I come up blank every time I sit down to write." I was transported back to her childhood room, where I watched her with the same look of defeat when she talked about wanting to be a writer someday.

"I could help." I'm not sure what possessed me to say it, since there was no way in hell I was qualified to help write a book.Her brows flickered. "How?"

Think of something quickly. "How about a proposition? You help me with the last few touches around here, and I'll figure out how to inspire you to write." I was fully capable of finishing on my own, having nearly rebuilt the entire house with my bare hands, but for the next week, I wanted her as close as possible.

"I don't know how much help I'd be." I found it funny how she still didn't know letting me breathe the same air as her was more than enough. "Well, for starters, I need some serious help picking out furniture. I could also use an extra hand to paint the outside."

I watched her lips purse, and I realized how much I missed brushing mine against them. When she left town, people said everyone was bound to forget about their first love, but I said fuck that. Everything about Camilla Vega stayed with me like salt stays with the sea—the warmth of her touch, the serene sound of her voice, the brightness of her blue eyes, and her goddamn smile that turned me into putty in her hands.

"Okay, you got a deal." My skin tingled when it grazed hers for a handshake, and without thinking, I reached out and tucked a strand of hair behind her ear. We both froze when she cradled her face in my hand as it rested on her cheek. "Shit, that broke your rule. Sorry, I guess it's a force of habit." Her nervous laughter reminded me of our early days, when everything I did made her jumpy. "It's okay. I know the feeling."

All I wanted to do was press my lips against hers and fix everything that went wrong with us, but not everything was that easy. "Mila—" The sound of a car pulling up the dirt driveway made her turn away. *Sofia.*

"Time to shop, Cami!" I loved my little sister, but at that moment, I wished for her to trip in her four-inch heels and fall flat on her face. I noticed a familiar face following behind, but she stayed further back, as if she was nervous to approach.

"Taylor?" Mila froze when her former best friend came into view. Despite her friendship with Sofia, I'd only talked to Taylor a handful of times throughout the years, and I only ever asked about Camilla. Her answer was always the same: they hadn't spoken since she left town. "Hey, Cami," Taylor was the one to close the large gap between them and bring her in for a tight hug I could tell would last a while.

I shot Sofia a look and inched inside the house. "We'll let you guys get caught up. Julian is gonna get me a drink before we go."

"We're not kids anymore, Sof. Get your own shit," I grumbled as we entered the kitchen. She rolled her eyes and put her hands on her hips. "I don't want a drink. I just needed you alone to ask what your plan is with Cami?"

"What do you mean?" I avoided her death stare by reaching into the fridge.

"She's staying for an entire week, which should buy you

some time to win her back." I shot her a twisted expression. "I'll ask again, what the hell do you mean?"

She buried her head in her hands. "You can be so dense sometimes." She was the younger sibling, but somehow, she was always the one giving me lectures. "Julian, in the six years you've moped around for her, you didn't think of a plan in case she ever popped back up?"

My jaw tightened. "Of course I did, but she's going back to New York after your wedding, Sof. What can I do?" I knew what I *wanted* to do.

She inched closer before letting out a heavy breath. "How about you start by telling her the truth about what happened six years ago?"

I walked over to the window to watch Mila as she talked with Taylor. I'd wanted to do that since the moment she left town, and then again when I saw her in the bookstore, but after so much time, I wondered if it even mattered anymore. "Then what? Not everyone can fall in love and ride off into the goddamn sunset like you, Sofia." I'd only spoken to her that way a handful of times in our entire lives, and I always felt bad immediately after. There was so much she didn't know. Camilla occupied my every thought for six years, but the solution wasn't as simple as telling her the truth. "I'm sorry," I mumbled.

"Please, like you can hurt my feelings." My laughter paused when she moved closer and grasped my hand. "She's only here for a week, J. You can let her go back to her life in New York, or spend the rest of yours wishing you fought for her. You'll be the only person to blame if you make the same mistake twice." She whipped her hair around and walked out, leaving me with my running thoughts. The only thing I hated more than Sofia's prying was when she was right.

eight
CAMILLA

8 YEARS EARLIER

As EARLY AS FIRST GRADE, it was drilled into my head how important it was to get into a good college. I figured the only way I could avoid getting distracted was to make a pact—instead of dating in high school, all my extra time would be dedicated to studying and extracurricular activities to stack my resume for college applications. That was the plan—until Julian Perez.

Despite my resistance, he bribed me into seeing him *again*. I knew he wasn't bluffing when he said he'd ask me out in front of the entire school, proving my point that guys like him were dangerous. Everything about him was a distraction, from his charming disposition to his tempting smile.

"What the hell am I doing?" I whispered as I adjusted my oversized cardigan that hid the black mini-skirt I'd spent twenty minutes scrounging through my closet for.

"Where are you headed on a school night?" My mom crept around the corner and entered my room with a beaming smile.

"Out with a friend." I let out a grunt of frustration as I snatched the ribbon out of my hair.

"Taylor usually comes over, so I assume this friend happens to be a boy?" I sighed with relief when she walked over and helped fix my hair like she'd done since I was a little girl.

"Trust me, it's nothing. It's just a bet I lost that keeps biting me in the ass." I saw her dimpled grin in the reflection. "Who's the lucky guy?" I almost didn't answer, but I never kept anything from my mom. Before Taylor, she was my first best friend.

"Julian Perez." She froze when his name fell from my lips, but she tried to play it off. "He's a good kid. You have my approval if you want it."

"We're just friends. It's no big deal." If you asked Julian, he probably would've said the opposite, which only made my nerves grow.

"I'm just saying, I approve if you decide you're not." She winked in the mirror and took the ribbon out of my hair. "I like your hair down. It brings out your features." The features she loved about me were the same ones I grew up admiring. Her eyes reminded me of the waves down at the cove, and her dark hair cascaded down her back effortlessly. Everything I was came from her.

My cheeks flushed. "Do I look stupid? I feel like I'm over-dressed. I should cancel, right? I have homework. Force me to stay home," I rambled as my head spun with excuses.

"First, I know for a fact you already did your homework, and second, you know I hate being the strict type, Cam. You're also not overdressed. You look beautiful." My stomach churned when I heard the roar of Julian's engine outside my window. I knew it was him because no one in my neighborhood had a car that made as much noise as his.

"Shit," I said under my breath.

Mom rested her delicate hands on my cheeks. "You'll be fine. Don't worry about anything else except having fun." She practically pushed me down the stairs before I could change my mind, and my heart leaped when the doorbell rang. "He came to the door? I like him already." I thought guys only did that in movies. She opened the door and revealed Julian standing with a bouquet of green carnations. His eyes popped out of his head when he saw me, and I tried to pretend he didn't give me the same reaction.

"Hi, Mrs. Vega. This is for you." He handed my mom a stemmed flower from the bouquet, to which she showed her approval with a thumbs-up from behind the door. He won her over before even stepping into my living room, which made me wonder if there was anyone he *couldn't* charm.

"It's nice to meet you, Julian. Camilla's dad is out of town for work, but I'm sure you'll meet him soon if tonight goes well.""Mom, please." My face turned hot with embarrassment, but Julian seemed pleased as he put the bouquet of flowers in my hands. "They didn't have very much selection, so I hope you like them."

I smiled when I inhaled their fresh, faintly sweet scent. "I love them, thank you. Green is my favorite color." My pulse raced at the sight of his smirk. "I know." *I didn't tell him that.*

I broke away from the trance of his soft brown eyes. "We should get going since we have school tomorrow."

He chuckled. "Do you ever not think about school?" I inhaled a sharp breath when his warm touch rested on my back to guide me out the door.

"Don't worry, Mrs. Vega, I'll have her back by ten."

My mom failed to subtly wink at me. "Eleven." She was letting her daughter stay out late with a random boy on a school night. What could go wrong?

Despite my feet trying to stay glued to the threshold, he pulled me towards his old car. "Where are we going?" I asked with a shaky voice.

"There's always a bonfire down at the cove when there's a full moon. Before you dismiss the idea, you might have fun if you try the whole not being invisible thing for five minutes." I wanted to say no. I was in two-inch boots and a mini-skirt, so I was the least dressed for the beach, but at the same time, being invited to a bonfire at the cove was the equivalent of being invited to a celebrity party—in Willow's Cove terms, of course. Everyone wanted an invite, but apparently, you had to run with certain crowds to even be considered. I never understood that, since the cove was open to anyone in town, but it was high school, so hardly anything made sense. "Fine. Five minutes." I couldn't help but crack a smile at how he silently celebrated after shutting my door; he must have forgotten he was lit up by the street lamp.

"By the way, you look beautiful. I should have said that first, but I'm so goddamn nervous." He said when he climbed into the driver's seat. I tried masking my embarrassment with a tight-lipped smile. "Sorry. My mom can be a little much sometimes."

"I'm nervous because of you, Camilla." I was in a daze when my head snapped to him. It wasn't fair that someone I wanted to stay far away from was so ruggedly handsome. His stupidly cute smile and dazzling eyes threatened everything I'd planned.

"Why?" I didn't think people like Julian got nervous, not when he played football for crowds every Friday night and walked around school with his head high and confident.

The corner of his tempting lips tugged with a smile as he shook his head. "There's nobody like you, Camilla Vega." Thankfully, I didn't have to muster up anything to say because music blared from his speakers when he started up the car and drove away from my house. I'd lost count of how many times I snuck a peek at him while he was distracted.

The cove wasn't far, so I didn't have a lot of time to calm the doubt swirling through my head. I wasn't afraid of the people I went to school with, but I *was* afraid of leaving the bubble I'd secured for myself.

We parked on the side of the road designated for visitors, but I couldn't bring myself to move when I saw the crowd gathered at the beach. Julian set his hand on my arm and spoke softly. "Hey, the second you want to leave, just tell me. I won't leave your side. Trust me." If someone told me prior to that night I'd fully trust Julian Perez, I wouldn't have believed them, but his assurance gave me the confidence to finally climb out. The moment I heard the waves crashing against the rocks and the salty air filled my nostrils, my nerves started to unravel.

There were different sections of the beach in Willow's Cove: the pier on one end, where families tended to go; the cove, which is where the high school parties usually happened; and a third section that had been closed off to the public since I was a kid. "Watch your step." I didn't pull away when Julian grabbed my hand and guided us down the steep hill to where groups of people stood by the fires. I had the feeling he would've plunged himself in front of me if any harm came my way.

My chest tightened when I saw the beach filled with everyone I intentionally avoided at school. "You're trying to kill me, aren't you?" I said I would give it five minutes, so that's what I did.

The air was thick with the smell of smoke, and so much of it clouded the sky, I couldn't see the stars. People stayed in the small cove to swim, which you'd see often if they didn't want to go into the dark ocean at night. Despite that, there were always people who were drunk and reckless, stupid enough to accept the dare to jump off the highest point of the cliffs. You're not a local if you've never been dared to jump at least once in your life, but of course, I hadn't done it because of my rational fear of being impaled on the rigged rocks waiting at the bottom.

Julian glued me to his side as he greeted people, but I didn't want to look up and see their wary looks. I wouldn't have blamed them, since Julian and I were probably the last people they'd expect to be out together.

"Shit. Sorry for this," he leaned over and said into my ear.

"Sorry for wh—" I wasn't able to finish before being greeted by a ball of energy.

"It's so nice to meet you! I'm Sofia, Julian's little sister, who I'm sure you've heard nothing about." I knew he had a sister, but since she was a year younger than us, I never saw her in any classes. Still, I wasn't sure how I hadn't ever noticed her magnetic energy. My eyes darted to him, then back to her—their resemblance was uncanny. Their eyes were the same shade of soft brown, and they held the same sparkle. While her dark hair draped down her back, she shared the same wavy texture with her brother.

"Nice to meet you. I'm Camilla." My smile was taken as an invitation for her to hug me tightly. "I know. I had to come meet the girl my brother hasn't shut the hell up about."

"Sofia, could you not?" Julian gritted out.

"Was I not supposed to say that?" I liked her sarcasm.

"And you wonder why you're not allowed to talk to me at school unless you're in trouble. Go hang out with your friends, but if I see you with a boy, I'm dragging you home."

"Okay, Dad." She rolled her eyes but turned to offer me a bright smile before running off to her group of friends.

"I'm sorry. She can be a little…"

"She's great," I cut in. I knew immediately she was a breath of fresh air in a small town full of people who acted the same. It was hard for anyone to surprise me, but Julian and Sofia did. They had every reason to act stuck up like most people at Willow High, considering how respected their dad was in the community, but they were the opposite. I wanted to keep pushing Julian away, but all I kept finding were reasons to let him in.

I shivered when a cold breeze sent goosebumps down my spine. "Are you cold? Come on, let's warm you up." He pulled me towards a crowd hovering around a fire burning brightly, which happened to host all his football friends and cheerleaders.

I sat on a far log and hoped not to be noticed, but I quickly realized Julian attracted attention without even trying.

"Why are you so far from the fire?" he asked.

Suddenly, Damon's voice boomed over the music. "Julian! We didn't think you'd come." If the beer can occupying his hand didn't tell me he was drunk, his stumbling would've. "That's why," I said under my breath. The closer he inched, the more I started to pick at my nail beds—it was a nervous tick I developed that I never was able to kick.

"You brought your new friend, how cute is that? It's nice to see you, Camilla."

"Hi, Damon," I forced out with a disgusted tone. All the muscles in my body froze when he sat on the other side of me and I smelled the alcohol on his breath. It was comforting when Julian's grip tightened like he was ready to pounce if Damon made one wrong move, but I still hated the idea of drunk Damon so close. I didn't even like sober Damon close to me.

"Now that you guys are here, let's play a game. You in?" His sly grin told me I would regret saying yes. I hadn't trusted Damon since eighth grade, when he told the entire school he made out with Taylor, when she would never even let him breathe her air.

I wanted to throw up when everyone's eyes found me, but I couldn't give him the satisfaction of getting the best of me, so saying no wasn't an option. "Sure."

"Truth or dare."

I saw Julian's jaw tighten from the corner of my eye. "Really, Damon? Are we in middle school?"

"She said she wanted to play, so let her answer the question, JP." His mocking laughter made my blood rush. There was no way I was picking dare. "Truth."

He took another swig of beer before a sinister grin widened on his face. "Is it true Julian only went out with you because of a bet?" I wanted to crawl into a hole and never come out when I overheard everyone around us snicker. I was the least bit surprised the word got out, because nothing ever stayed a secret in Willow's Cove, no matter how hard you tried. I was sure someone in English class overheard when Julian and I made the bet, and it spread like wildfire.

"Don't be a dick." Julian's voice turned cold.

"Relax, JP. It's a yes or no question. We're all friends now, right?" He reminded me why I stayed away from that crowd of people, but I wouldn't let him see me crumble. "Yeah, it's true."

"Well, that answers a lot." His head flew back with uncontrollable laughter, which invited everyone else to join. The only people not laughing were me, Julian, and his friend Elijah, who I knew from biology class.

There were two paths to take when I entered my freshman year: the one people like Damon—people who peak in high school—chose, and the one I did. I knew what people whispered behind my back. I wasn't stupid; I just never gave a shit. None of those people knew me, and for good reason, but having them laugh in my face was a level of embarrassment I couldn't bear.

Everything began to spin when Julian shot up, fire flashed in his eyes. "Fuck you, Damon." All laughter halted when he shoved him so hard, he stumbled into the crowd behind him.

"First you ditched us, and now, you're gonna fight me over her, too?" He dusted off the sand splattering his clothes.

"I don't want to fight you, D, but I will if you say one more thing about her. So what if our first date was because of a fucking bet? If you're gonna laugh at anyone, laugh at me, because it was my idea. Go ahead. Laugh." His last words were so dark and edged, it made everyone go still, even me.

"Let's go, Camilla." He reached out to me, and I took his hand without hesitation, as if it were a lifeline.

"JP! I'm sorry." Even when Damon called after him, we walked further and further away until the crowd disappeared and his rage subsided. "I'm sorry. You didn't deserve that. I don't even know who those people are anymore." He sank into the sand in defeat while looking out at the peaceful ocean.

"It's okay. Hell will freeze over the day I let a bunch of jocks get to me." I said as I joined him.

"I'm embarrassed to call them my friends. I promise, I'm nothing like them." There was desperation in his voice, as if he was begging me to believe him, and I surprised myself at how easily I did.

"I know you're not." A light in his eyes appeared after I'd said those words. "I am curious, though: why are you still friends with someone like Damon?"

It was more personal than we'd ever gotten, but he didn't hesitate to answer. "If you really knew him growing up, you'd understand. I guess I keep waiting to see if he'll turn back into the person he was before we got to high school." Suddenly, I sympathized. I understood why he clung to his friendship when I imagined how I'd feel if one day, Taylor was unrecognizable after growing up with her practically our entire lives. I saw a softer side of him—a side that cared deeply about the people around him. "Thanks for defending me back there," I said softly. No one had ever done something like that for me, and I didn't take it lightly.

His frown disappeared. "Anytime." Seeing a vulnerable side of him had me letting him see the same from me. "Come on. I want to show you something."

"Where are we going?" he shouted as I pulled him through the heavy sand towards the closed-off area of the beach. We stopped where a grass hill as tall as some of the cliffs stood, and I ignored the *no entry past this point* sign like I always did and eagerly trailed ahead.

"What's at the top?" His shaky breath told me he was nervous, which made me chuckle to myself. "Now it's your turn to trust me, Perez." As we started up the slippery hill, I felt a hint of satisfaction when he fell behind. "Aren't you an athlete?" I shouted.

"Give me a break, Vega. I'm a football player, not a rock climber." Laughter vibrated in my chest until I reached the top, and Julian followed shortly after, out of breath. Despite being there hundreds of times, I glowed at the sight in front of us. I accidentally stumbled upon the run-down house in the middle of a dead field a couple of years before. Just by looking at it, you could tell everyone in town had forgotten it existed. The paint was worn, the wood rotten beyond repair, and it was almost completely hidden behind overgrown trees. It always had potential to me, though.

"This isn't creepy at all," Julian muttered.

"You're not the only one with a secret spot." Not even Taylor knew about it, but I figured since he'd shown me his, it was only right he knew about mine.

"An abandoned house? You're odder than I thought, Camilla Vega."

I nudged him on the shoulder. "Take a second and picture it painted sage green with white trimming, a pebbled walkway with a garden of flowers surrounding it, and one of those wraparound porches with a swing bench." I never planned on telling anyone my vision for the house, but the words just spewed out. The weird part was, I didn't want to take them back.

"Sounds like you've given it a lot of thought."

I felt the heat of him admiring *me* while I admired the house. "We all have dreams."

"Your dream is to refurbish this house and settle in Willow's Cove?"

"Is that such a bad thing?" All anyone talked about was leaving town and never coming back, but no matter how small it felt at times, I never saw leaving in the cards for me.

His gaze softened. "No, I just think there's more out there than a small town like this has to offer." Of course there was, but

I'd learned to swim in its ocean; I'd checked out nearly every book in its local library; the house I grew up in was there. Willow's Cove was home.

Without saying another word, I grabbed his hand and led him not too far from the house, where a hidden trail led down to a hollow cave. The mayor closed it off because of the sharp rocks, but I found a way to sneak in when I was fourteen. Not only was that part of the beach deserted, but it perfectly overlooked the beauty of the widespread ocean. I knew the water only reached a certain point on the sand even during high tide, so I ran freely while Julian stood back and watched. It was the only place I was truly invisible and felt the freest I'd ever felt. "I don't see anything getting better than this," I shouted as I ran barefoot through the sand without a care in the world.

"Do you just explore town and find hidden gems in your spare time, Camilla?" I looked over and memorized how perfect he looked under the moonlight as he grinned from ear to ear.

"When I'm not reading, maybe." I followed his lead when he plopped down on the cushioned sand. "I snuck down here a few years ago during the sunset, and I've watched them here since. I realized how beautiful Willow's Cove is instead of focusing on how small it feels."

"Is that when you found the house?"

I met his dreamy gaze and nodded. "What's your dream?" I asked to distract myself from the overwhelming need to close the small space between us.

"I want to travel. After that, I'm not sure. You'll be the first to know when I figure it out, though." I noticed when the sudden glint appeared in his eyes. "What?" I asked.

He gulped a lump in his throat. "Would you stop me if I tried to kiss you?" I'd never kissed anyone before Julian—shocker. The alarm going off in my head said kissing him would bury me, but every other instinct wanted him despite trying to deny it.

I got so close, our noses nearly touched. "I'm not sure. Try and find out." I shuddered from his touch on my cheek, which made it painfully obvious I was inexperienced, but his shakiness told me he was just as nervous as me.

I thought I wouldn't know what to do when it came time for my first kiss, but when Julian's soft lips brushed against mine, it was like my body was already familiar with him. The kiss was tender, like the ocean's breeze, and I was surprised at my willing response as he tangled his fingers in my hair and intensified our kiss.

I broke us apart but kept him close enough for his cologne to fill my nose. "I don't think friends are supposed to do that."His rich laughter rippled through me before he made my stomach somersault by placing a soft kiss on my forehead. "We're not going to be friends, Mila. I'm just waiting for you to catch up."

My face twisted. "What'd you call me?"

He touched a strand of my hair and grinned. "I was playing with a few nicknames in class and decided on Mila. I hope that's okay."

Mila. The name sounded perfect coming from his lips.

nine

CAMILLA

IT NEVER DAWNED on me I'd end up picking out a bridesmaid dress for Sofia Perez's wedding when I came back to Willow's Cove, but there I was, listening to her retell the story of how she and Levi met at the town's local fair as we drove into town. He was nice enough to win the big prize she'd wasted all of her money trying to get, and they'd been inseparable ever since. I think the term she used was "love at first sight". It was a relief to realize she was still the bright-eyed girl full of life I once knew.

Taylor rode in the backseat, and for the first time since we'd met in elementary school, she hardly spoke. The few times we did meet eyes, her face blanched, as if she'd seen a ghost. There was a time when she knew every aspect of my life, whether I wanted her to or not, but suddenly, we were nothing but familiar faces. The worst part of it was, I was to blame.

When we pulled into the parking lot of the only dress store in town, Sofia squealed with excitement. She and Taylor walked ahead into the store filled to the brim with dresses. "You'll love the selection they have here, Cami." I didn't have to look at the tags to know they were out of my price range. My fingers grazed the silk dresses as we walked toward the front desk, where an older woman greeted us with a smile. "Miss Perez, I was hoping you'd come to see us today. Are you ready for your last fitting?"

"Yes. Thank you, Valorie. I've also added another bridesmaid, so she'll need some styles pulled in the color we picked." The woman peered at me through her square glasses and nodded. "We'll be happy to. The fitting rooms are this way." Taylor and Sofia's giggles echoed through the store as they pranced forward with linked arms. They'd always reminded me of one another, so it wasn't surprising they grew close over the years. I knew I couldn't feel envious, but I did. Maybe if I had never left, our friendship would have turned out differently—along with so many other things.

When Sofia skipped away to try on her dress, we were left in awkward silence. "Are you leaving town right after the wedding?" she asked.

"Yeah. I was supposed to leave yesterday, but Sofia talked me into staying." Taylor always had a unique shine in her green eyes, so to see them with a hint of sadness felt like I'd just kicked a puppy. "You were going to leave town without saying goodbye again?"

I winced. "I was only supposed to be here for the book signing. It wasn't personal."

"What about last time? Was it personal when you left without as much as a phone call?" she choked out.

There were a lot of amends to be made, starting with her, but I wasn't ready to face the mess I left behind. "Whether you believe me or not, I missed you, Tay. I hope at least while I'm here, you can forgive me." It was the last thing I deserved, but what she didn't know was that while I lived in the city, I thought of her anytime I passed a store with a ridiculous colored bag, or saw long, golden hair.

She folded her arms across her chest and sighed. "Fine, but only for Sofia's sake. Everyone needs to get along until her wedding." It wasn't exactly the response I was hoping for, but I took what I could get. "Okay."

Her soft gaze found me. "How are your friends in New York? Did you make another best friend?"

I chuckled. Elena and the rest of my friends from college got me through my early twenties, but they weren't Taylor. She held a special place in my heart; she reminded me of the girl I was before I left Willow's Cove—the one who only read books and daydreamed of living in the big city one day. She failed at trying to hold back a bright smile. "Good." I knew I'd have to regain her trust before she fully forgave me, but it was a start.

Our tender moment was interrupted when Sofia swung the fitting room door open and revealed her silky lace dress. I'd never seen someone so delicate and poised. The dress perfectly hugged her curves, and the lace trim that ran along the slit emphasized her long legs. She'd always been beautiful, but she was the image of perfection in a wedding dress. "I hope this doesn't come off as cocky, but I forgot how hot I looked in this."

"Me too," Taylor gasped before joining her in front of the mirror. I wasn't expecting to choke back tears, but seeing her in a gown she and Taylor gushed over together made me finally realize just how much I'd missed. While I was gone, not only had I grown up and moved on, but so had everyone else.

"What do you think, Cami?" I sucked back the waterworks before joining them at the mirror, and it was almost eerie how much she resembled Julian when I saw her reflection. "You look beautiful. You just need one final touch." I walked over to the wall full of veils and picked one to drape seamlessly down her back. "Now you're perfect, and you're going to be the most beautiful bride Willow's Cove has ever seen." I wiped the tear that slid down her red cheek.

"Thank you, Cami. Not just for being here, but for staying. It means a lot that you did, regardless of what happened between you and Julian." I wondered how much she knew about what happened between me and her brother, but I realized none of it mattered anymore. My phone's ringtone saved me from the memories that tried to flood my mind.

"I have to take this. I'll be right back." I scurried to an empty part of the store before accepting Greyson's call.

"Miss me already?" I teased.

"I missed you the second you left, Cami, but I'm calling because I'm helpless in the grocery store right now." Greyson's family had housekeepers and handlers to do everything for them, so he never learned how to be on his own. It wasn't until we met when he decided to let me teach him the basics of adulthood—doing his own laundry, paying bills, stocking the fridge with actual food rather than just beer. He was easily flustered by it all, but his willingness to learn was one of the reasons I fell for him.

"What do you need?"

"Remind me what flavor ice cream we get?" I stifled my laughter. "Chocolate-chip cookie dough, but remember to get it last because it'll melt by the time you're finished shopping."

"Damnit, I forgot. I might need you to stay on the phone with me while I walk through the whole store." His laughter on the other end called me home. It had only been a day, and I already wanted to get on a flight back to him.

"Do you need me to send you what we usually get?" I loved any excuse to make a list.

"No. Now I get to hear your voice for a little longer." Even when we were thousands of miles apart, he still made me blush.

When I looked back at the girls, thankfully, they were too busy practicing their walks down the aisle of the store instead of looking for me. "How was your day?" I asked, the same question I did when he'd come home from work and drop his bag by the door.

"Well, this morning during a meeting, my dad was saying how great I'll do as CEO. Then later that afternoon, he stormed into my office and told me how unqualified I am because I sorted papers wrong. So, I'd say the usual."

Complicated was the friendliest way to explain his relationship with Mr. Carter. While he respected what his dad built, he hated being treated like an employee rather than a son. I saw it with my own eyes at the first Christmas I ever spent with the Carters. Greyson's younger brother, Theo, had gotten keys to a brand new truck, his mom was gifted a private beach house off the coast of Brazil, and Greyson unwrapped a sales report highlighted with all the mistakes he made the week before. He never faltered in front of his family, but I was always around when he'd shatter afterwards.

"I'm sorry, Grey," I muttered.

"It's fine. I just have to stick it out for six more months until he makes the announcement that he's stepping down." He'd been counting down the days until he took over the company. I'd lost count of how many times I woke up to him writing in his journal because an idea came to him in his sleep and he didn't want to forget it. He had big dreams—not only for the company, but for himself, which I always admired.

"I'm sorry I'm not there." I knew he needed me more than he was letting on. He always called me his tether that pulled him back when he got lost.

"Speaking of, how is it in Willow's Ocean?" I chuckled at how he never hid his disdain for small towns. "It's Willow's Cove, and it's fine. I'm shopping for a bridesmaid dress right now." I looked at the silk gowns sitting on the racks.

"When you find the one you want, just charge it to my black card."

"I have the money from my publisher, remember?" Thanks to the six-figure book deal my agent landed me, I finally didn't have a constant negative in front of my bank account balance.

"You worked hard for that, so it's yours. My money is for us." He always had a smooth way with words. "You're such a gentleman, Mr. Greyson." I couldn't see him, but I pictured his cheeks turning red and a perfect smile growing on his face. "You can't call me that when you're in another state, Cami. It's not fair."

I threw my head back with laughter loud enough to catch the attention of the front desk receptionist and looked over at Sofia in time to see her exiting the fitting room. "I gotta go. Don't forget bread. We were out when I left."

"What would I do without you? I love you."

The girls found me right as the call ended. "Where'd you run off to?" Taylor asked.

I hesitated to find an answer. "My agent called to discuss my second book." Sofia and Taylor had a talent for seeing through people's bullshit, and I saw in their eyes that neither of them believed me. Thankfully, they didn't press for more.

"Now that my fitting is done, it's your turn to find a dress, Cami. I didn't like the options they pulled for you, so that means I get to choose." Her eyes lit up before she dragged me to the racks and scoured through the dresses with a sharp eye.

"You have nice legs, so definitely something with a slit." I remembered how passionate she was about fashion. I immediately knew she had a talent when I accidentally stumbled across the sketches she kept a secret in high school.

She paused before her mouth flew open and she pulled a mermaid-style dress from the hanger. "Even if this isn't the one, I need to see you in this lace corset." It wasn't something I'd normally wear, but I trusted Sofia had a good eye. Besides, who was I to say no to the bride?

"As you wish." I let out a huff before getting dragged to the fitting room, where I squeezed into the form-fitting dress. The satin hugged my skin perfectly and emphasized curves I didn't even know I had; not to mention, the corset made my B cups look actually existent. I snapped a photo for Greyson to get his opinion, and his call came in seconds later.

"Do you like the dress?" I whispered so the girls wouldn't overhear me outside the door. I told myself I wasn't telling them about Greyson because the less they knew about my new life, the easier it'd be when I left again.

"I want you wearing that when I pick you up from the airport." My laughter echoed in the tight-fit dressing room. "I'll take that as a yes."

"Goddamn, Cami. You're so beautiful. How many days until I see you again?"

"Seven."

He groaned. "I can't make it that long." His pining reminded me of our early days. He once showed up at my dorm room at midnight just to tell me goodnight.

"How's it going in there, Cami?" Sofia startled me when she knocked on the door. "I'll be right out."

I stumbled with the price tag as I adjusted the dress and audibly gasped. "Holy shit, this dress is six hundred dollars." I was all for splurging, but spending six hundred dollars on something I only planned to wear once was unheard of for me, considering most of my wardrobe was thrifted.

"What's the problem?" I sighed at Greyson's dismissal. Between getting access to his trust fund when he turned eighteen and working for his dad's company, Greyson never saw money as an issue. Sometimes, it irked me how careless he was, but I knew old habits of coming from a wealthy family were hard to break.

"That's a lot on just a dress, don't you think?" Watching my parents count every dime just to pay the bills made me cautious about money, and even though Greyson never made me feel like I had to be, sometimes, I felt embarrassed.

"Even if it was six thousand dollars, I'd still tell you to get it. That's how amazing you look, Cami." My cheeks flushed at his compliment. I looked at my reflection in the mirror again, and I'd never felt more beautiful. I saw a confident, sophisticated version of myself I wanted to embody every day—though some days were harder than others to pull her out.

Sofia knocked on the door. "Come on out, Camilla Vega. I'll pull you out if I have to." I knew she wasn't kidding, so I scrambled. "I gotta go, Grey. I'll let you know if I end up getting the dress. I love you."

I threw my phone down and swung the door open to reveal myself to the girls, who shot out of their seats with mouths gaping. "No, you can't wear that. I can't have you looking better than me at my own wedding," Sofia said while holding her chest with a wide smile of approval.

Taylor rested her hands on my shoulders. "You look hot, Cami. This has to be the dress." *Six hundred dollars* repeated in my head, but as I ran my hands along the satin, I knew no other dress would compare. "Okay. This is it."

Before I could dodge it, they sandwiched me into a group hug. As their heads burrowed into my neck, I was overwhelmed with emotions I wasn't ready to unpack. They both had reasons to be upset at me, Taylor especially, yet they welcomed me back as if nothing happened. Though I didn't deserve their grace, I welcomed it like a familiar friend.

WHEN I CAME BACK from the dress shop, I planned to only shut my eyes for a few minutes, but it turned into two hours. Who knew spending the afternoon shopping could wear you out?

The aroma of food flooded my nostrils and woke me. I followed the smell to the kitchen, where Julian stood at the stove, managing three pans at once with headphones in his ears.

A part of me wished he'd stayed in the depths of my mind where I kept our memories, but instead, there he was, reminding me he was once the reason for my heartbeat. I watched as he plated the food and tried not to think of the nights we stayed up talking about the future—quiet dinners, walks on the beach, sunrises on the cove. We were just two teenagers with no grasp of how the world actually worked, but we didn't care.

His eyes widened with surprise when he looked up and saw me spying. "How long have you been standing there?" I walked up to the counter and grabbed the half-full wine glass. From the look of it, it was just us for dinner, so I knew I was going to need it. "Long enough," I said.

"I hope you're hungry. I made steak, potatoes, and asparagus." My mouth watered at the plate he slid in front of me. If I hadn't seen him make it, I would have thought it was takeout from a five-star restaurant.

"I'm starving. Thank you." I took the first bite and savored the layered flavors that coated my tongue. "Where'd you learn to be such a good cook?" It wasn't until then that I realized, while I knew everything about the boy I fell in love with, I knew nothing of the man in front of me.

A lazy smile ruffled his stubble mustache. "I live alone, Mila. It was either learn how to cook or live off frozen dinners." I didn't hear much after *I live alone* and tried to bury the strange sense of satisfaction that settled in my stomach.

"I still can't cook," I admitted. The restaurant around the corner from Greyson and me knew us on a first-name basis from how often we dined there. He opted for a professional chef who had been in his family for years, but I was already overwhelmed with two housekeepers, his private security, and the on-call chauffeur.

"Remember when you almost burned your house down when you forgot you left water boiling?"

The memory of him rushing to my house to clear the smoke out before my mom got home flooded my mind. "Cut me some slack. I was a kid."

"You were seventeen, Mila." Our undiluted laughter echoed

through the kitchen, slowly dying off when his gaze trickled to my lips and made heat bloom on my neck.

"I hope you hold your alcohol better than you did back then." He gestured to the almost empty glass in my hand when I took a sip.

How could I forget junior year homecoming? It was so cliché —someone spiked the punch at the dance. Unfortunately, I didn't find out until my third cup, and the room had already started to spin. The rest of the night was a blur, but I distinctly remember Julian coming to the rescue, pulling over so I could puke on the side of the road. "I still haven't had vodka since high school."

His face perked up. "Oh, speaking of high school, you're speaking at Willow High tomorrow."

Wine nearly went up my nose from the shock. "What?"

"You said you wanted inspiration, and what better way than to talk about how you started writing?" I thought he was bluffing when he said he'd help me, but I should've known he wasn't. I always had a habit of underestimating him.

My head cowered. "I'm not so good at public speaking." I nearly passed out while giving my high school valedictorian speech, and I dropped out of debate in college because I couldn't stomach standing in front of the entire class.

With the gentlest touch of his fingertips, he traced my face and tipped my chin up so I could stare into his soft brown eyes. It took everything in me not to reach out and touch where hair had grown on his cheeks. We were practically strangers again, but there was nothing unfamiliar about the way his touch felt on my skin.

"I know you can do it. Maybe there's a kid with unrealized potential waiting for someone like you to pull it out of them." He still had a talent for saying exactly what I needed to hear.

"Are you coming with me?" The question spewed out before I could stop it from leaving my lips.

He soft gaze clung to my face. "Do you want me to?"

I let out the next words as if I was in a trance. "I do." I said we needed distance, to make sure no lines got blurred, and we still did, but if I was going to speak in front of a crowd of high school kids who scrutinized just about everything, I needed all the moral support I could get.

He tried to hide a satisfied grin behind his glass. "I wouldn't miss it."

I took another bite of the perfectly cooked steak before he broke the silence again. "It'll be a little weird going back to where it all started, though."

"Where what started?" I watched the lump in his throat go down before he spoke. "Us."

The conversation of *us* was one I was actively trying to avoid, especially when I didn't even know where to begin. "That was so long ago." It had only been six years, but sometimes, it felt like it was another lifetime.

His expression turned somber. "We were just kids. We bickered a lot, but goddamn, we loved each other, didn't we, Mila?"

Don't say it was all that repeated in my head, yet the words sitting on my tongue were hard to hold back. "Yeah, we did." Quick images of a moment that changed everything flashed without warning—*my tears. His tears. Screaming and fighting. The You are Leaving Willow's Cove sign getting smaller and smaller in my rearview mirror.*

I jolted out of my seat when he reached over and dragged his fingertips along my arm, leaving my skin tingling. "Okay, new rule while I'm here: no touching."

He flashed a teasing smile. "How set in stone is that rule?" There was no denying he was the same Julian. Damn him for being so charming.

"Practically carved into it. Also, no flirting. I dated you for two years, so I know all your lines anyway."

He quirked a brow with amusement. "Anything else?"

It had been eating at me to tell him, and since we were

setting boundaries, that moment felt as good as any. "Yeah, actually. I don't want any lines to blur while I'm here, so you should know I have a boyfriend."

The air grew stiff, and guilt washed over me as I watched his smile fade into a deep frown. As much as I didn't want to hurt Julian, I couldn't keep Greyson a secret. It was a double-edged sword, and someone was bound to get wounded.

"What's his name?" he asked with a broken voice.

"Greyson." He didn't need to say a word for me to know what he was thinking. I could read him like my favorite book. "Are you happy?"

I nodded. "I am." I'd meant it with every fiber of my being, but I wished he'd never asked. I didn't want to have to watch his eyes threaten with tears.

"Then I'm happy for you, Mila. Really. I promise to follow the rules from now on." He extended his hand for me to shake but immediately brought it back to his side. "Sorry, I forgot. No touching."

I smiled and offered my hand. "We'll make an exception this one time." After only one day, he'd already begun clouding my judgment; I couldn't wrap my head around how I was going to survive another seven.

ten

CAMILLA

8 YEARS EARLIER

SOMEHOW, I'd let Julian trick me into another bet that resulted in me spending my Saturday night getting ready for homecoming. Up until then, I'd purposely avoided going, since it seemed more of a popularity contest than a dance. I fixated on the black silk dress Taylor helped pick out. She thought making a statement with a ribboned back was best, but the last thing I wanted was to attract more attention.

When my mom appeared in my door, she covered her mouth to hide what I was sure was a beaming smile. "Estás preciosa." Since Spanish was her first language, it naturally slipped out whenever she was emotional.

"I don't feel beautiful. This dress doesn't fit the way I want. Maybe it's a sign I shouldn't go." The dress fit like a glove, but I searched for any excuse to skip the dance.

She rested her hands on my shoulders. "Sounds a lot like when Julian took you out for the first time, and now look at you."

I rolled my eyes. "We're just friends, Mom." Despite Julian

and I spending almost every day together for months, and him sneaking in a kiss or two, we were still figuring out if we wanted to be more—and by we, I meant me. He was everything I wanted: kind and confident. He made me smile, and I had to admit he was a really good kisser. Still, I couldn't bring myself to let him all the way in. It was almost frustrating how his patience with me made me fall even harder for him.

"I said the same about your dad." I didn't tell her, but that was exactly what I was afraid of. "Right."

She must've sensed how high strung I was, because her voice softened. "Cami, you can't spend your teens wasting away in your room. You'll have the rest of your life to be a homebody, so go make memories while you can." It was her superpower to always say the right thing when I needed it most.

"Most moms encourage their teenage daughters to stay home," I said. She walked over to my jewelry box and returned with the emerald necklace that was once hers. "You haven't figured out by now that I'm not like those moms? Go get into trouble, just not too much where I get a knock on the door from the cops." I used to think it was weird how my parents never hovered, but they had me so young—they were teenagers not long before I was.

I smiled at the emerald dangling from my neck. "It's so pretty." It always looked better on her, but she'd handed it down to me on my thirteenth birthday. "It goes with your dress. Now, you look perfect."

I scoffed. "Isn't it a rule when you become a mom to tell your kids that?"

"Maybe, but it's easy to follow that rule when you're my kid." Our laughter halted when the doorbell rang downstairs. Julian was always right on time.

"I'll get it so you can make a grand entrance."

When she left, I took advantage of my last seconds alone and looked in the mirror one last time. The girl staring back at me was unrecognizable, and it wasn't because of the dress. One day, I was spending my Saturday nights crossing books off my long reading list, and then the next, I was on my way to homecoming with Julian Perez. I had whiplash from how fast everything had changed, and while a part of me was terrified, the other wanted to welcome it.

"Cami, get down here!" my mom shouted. My heart pounded against my chest when I heard Julian's deep voice with hers in the living room, but I started for the stairs with my head down and my hands trembling. A little voice in my head was shouting at me to run back upstairs and not come back out, but when I looked up and captured his eyes, everything ceased to exist. No one had ever made me feel beautiful without saying a word until Julian. He looked at me how I looked at the sunsets that fell over the cove each evening. He waited at the bottom of the stairs in his all-black tux that matched my dress, a bouquet of green carnations in his hands. My favorite flowers growing up were lilies, but that was just the beginning of things that changed because of him.

His mouth gaped when I finally reached him. "You look beautiful, Mila."

He looked devastatingly handsome in a fitted tux and neatly slicked back hair. "You clean up pretty well yourself." One thing I knew for certain was Julian Perez was much hotter than any fictional man I'd conjured up in my mind.

A smile touched my lips when I noticed the subtle pop of green in his pocket. "Nice touch."

"I thought you'd like it." He raked his eyes over me with a seductive look that made my insides twist. I nearly closed the distance between us, but my mom broke my daze when the flash of her camera went off. "Seriously, Mom?" I groaned.

"Just a few pictures." Since she was blocking the door, we had no choice, but I couldn't help but realize they were the first pictures Julian and I ever took together.

We couldn't have run out the door fast enough when she finished. "Have fun! Curfew is at midnight, Cami," she shouted after us as we raced to his car.

"Okay, I love you!" I yelled back.

"I thought I was meeting your dad tonight," Julian said as he opened the passenger door to his old Mustang.

I bit down on my lip to buy time. "He had to leave town last minute." It technically wasn't a lie; it just wasn't the full truth. It was better off that way, since I wasn't sure I wanted him to be a part of that night anyway.

"He must have an important job if he travels all the time." A lump grew in my throat. "If that's what you want to call it," I mumbled. The air suddenly grew thick, so I changed the subject. "I've never been to a school dance before, so cut me some slack tonight."

His irresistible grin made my heart flutter. "I just want one slow dance with you." I panicked. My only experience with dancing was when my dad put me on his toes and twirled around the living room when I was six, but it was hard to say no to him. "Deal."

THE DANCE COMMITTEE chose the "Starry Night" theme, even though I'd suggested something more original. Still, people seemed to enjoy it as they gathered under the paper mâché moon and danced until beads of sweat glistened on their foreheads. I was partly envious, but I remained a bystander who watched from my chair. Julian caught me gazing at them when he came back with drinks. "You want to dance?"

I shook my head. "No, I'm okay." I would have rather stayed in my seat the entire night than make a fool of myself.

"You might actually have some fun tonight if you stopped overthinking, Mila."

"I'm not." I said sharply.

"Prove it." All I heard were Mom's words: *Go make memories while you can.* I hated when she was right. I was seconds from leaving the comfort of my chair when Taylor approached our table, looking stunning in the navy blue dress she'd gushed over for weeks. "Thank God I found you guys. I'm leaving after they announce king and queen."

My brows narrowed. "Since when do you care who wins?" She'd always thought the entire idea was bullshit, so I was curious what the sudden change was.

A mischievous smirk grew on her face. "Since I put your name on the ballot." I froze. "You did what?"

"What's the point of being on the dance committee if I don't take advantage of the perks, Cami?"

I was horrified, but I looked over and noticed Julian glowing with pride. "I guess I'll be casting a vote for the first time." I wished she was joking, but I knew Taylor never needed an excuse to do something stupid.

I shrugged. "It's not like I'll win anyway." My only saving grace was I'd been good at staying invisible, at least before Julian, so I was confident no one would vote for me until Taylor pursed her lips. "Well…"

"Taylor Hale, I'm going to kill you," I gritted out. There were only a few instances when I used her whole name.

"Relax, Cami. I just snuck into the box and counted the votes a little early. You're tied with Jaime." Once the initial shock wore off, I looked over at Jaime Torres, who was mingling with a crowd surrounding her like vultures. She wasn't just a cheerleader, the soccer team captain, and on the varsity volleyball team as a sophomore; she also happened to be Julian's ex-girlfriend. They had a brutal public breakup, but everyone in school knew she still had feelings for Julian, even him. We had a short-lived middle school friendship, but once we started high school, she developed a new personality that clashed with mine and Taylor's.

Julian noticed goosebumps rise on my arms before I did. "Are you cold? I have an extra jacket in my car. I'll be right back." He paced out of the gym before I could tell him not to go through the trouble, and as soon as he was out of sight, Taylor turned to me. "So, are you two together yet, or are you still in the denial phase about your feelings?"

I swallowed hard. "I told you, we're just taking things slow. Honestly, I don't know if we'll ever get there."

Her face was never capable of hiding her true feelings. "We both know that's bullshit. He's already there; he's just waiting for you." When I looked around to make sure no one was near, I noticed Jaime making her way out of the gym, giggling with her group of friends.

"It's not that simple, Tay. He could break my heart into a million pieces, and I don't need that kind of distraction, especially when I'm trying to build my resume for college." I avoided relationships for a multitude of reasons, yet I found myself unable to avoid Julian.

"Everything worth it comes with risks, Cami. Do you want to stay a bystander and watch other people take them like you always have, or do you finally want to get what you want?"

Her words hit me like a truck, and I suddenly felt suffocated. "I need some air." What I really needed was to find Julian, but when I walked outside, there was no sign of him by his car in the parking lot. The crowds of people making their way in blocked my path, but I froze when I turned the corner and saw him and Jaime alone by the bleachers. I watched as he backed away the closer she got, but something in me snapped. Seeing Jaime with him wasn't what irked me; it was that it only proved what I already knew deep down: we were in two completely different worlds—his was one where everyone in school either wanted to be him, or be *with* him, and I was in the one where I wanted to stay hidden. We weren't supposed to work, so what did that mean for me if I gave him my heart?

Despite my uncomfortable heels, I bolted in the direction of my house, tears threatening my eyes, but I didn't get far before his deep voice called after me. "Mila!" I didn't stop until he caught up and blocked my path. "That wasn't what it looked like. I went to get the jacket, and she cornered me. I was trying to push her away."

"It doesn't matter, Julian. We're not together, so you can talk to your ex-girlfriend or whoever the hell you want." I tried to walk around him, but he blocked my path again.

"Why are you walking away if it doesn't matter?"

I shoved him out of my way. "I want to go home, that's why." I could have told him why I was upset, but I blamed it on being sixteen.

"Why can't you just admit it, huh?" I kept walking even after he shouted after me. "You like me, and you've been looking for any reason not to. Jaime is the excuse to push me away, am I right?" I huffed loudly enough for him to hear but kept my back turned, even though every part of me wanted to turn around and tell him he was right. I was grasping at straws to find any reason not to let him in, but all he kept giving me were reasons to do the opposite.

"I'm scared too, Mila. I've never cared about anyone like this, and that terrifies me, but you know what terrifies me more?" The desperation in his voice forced me to finally face him, tears welling in my eyes. I *was* scared. No matter how desperately I wanted to give my heart to Julian, I couldn't let go of my fear of letting someone past the walls I'd spent my entire life building. "What?" I asked with a broken voice.

He inched closer to graze my face with his fingertips, and his brown eyes pleaded as they clung to mine. "I'm terrified of missing out on you." Those were the words that won me over, but I let him continue. "I don't want to be your friend anymore,

Mila. I want the whole school to know I'm yours, but only if that's what you want too." He was too close for me to think straight. All I knew was I didn't want him to let me go.

His lips came nearly inches from mine. "The odds are against us working out, Julian."

"Fuck the odds." My train of thought halted when he crashed his soft lips to mine. The kiss was demanding, as if he was finally claiming my lips as his. It wasn't our first, but it was *different*. It felt like I'd come out of a daze, and once I was fully awake, I knew I wanted to be his just as much as he wanted to be mine.

Taylor's voice repeated in my head. *Everything worth it comes with risks.* Giving someone the power over your heart was terrifying, but so was getting on a plane, learning how to drive, or swimming into the open ocean, yet we still took the risks. If Julian was willing to make the jump, I had to let him catch me and hope we wouldn't fall.

I leaned into his hand cradling my face. "I don't want to be your friend either."

He'd never smiled so brightly. "I really want to kiss you again, Mila, but not here." I wanted to spend the rest of the night only with him, but he guided me back into the gym where the principal, Mr. M, was in the middle of announcing the king and queen. The idea of winning seemed so far-fetched, I hadn't entertained it until the moment everyone's eyes turned to the back of room, where Julian and I stood. "I can't do this," I whispered as he dragged me towards the stage to get crowned with our fingers laced together.

"All you have to do is put the crown on and walk off the stage."

I found Taylor in the crowd and threw her a narrowed-eyed gaze. "I swear, I didn't rig it!" she shouted over everyone's cheers. I didn't know if they'd voted for me as a joke or because of Julian, but either way, I couldn't get away from everyone's dissecting stares fast enough. The snarl I spotted on Jaime's face as Mr. M placed the plastic crown on my head made it a *little* satisfying, though.

"You still owe me that slow dance, Vega." When we made our way to the middle for the traditional cliché king and queen dance, I panicked from the hundreds of eyes suddenly watching our every move, and kept him at a distance. "You should know the last time I slow danced was in my living room on my dad's toes."

His lips curved into a smile before he lifted me to stand on his toes. "Any more excuses?"

"Yeah, everyone's staring." I wasn't surprised he didn't falter, because he never did. "I don't care what they think, and neither should you. Just look at me." His closeness, mixed with the sound of his voice, made all the faces around us start to blur until he was the only one who existed. I ran my fingers through his wavy hair and soaked him up as he tried to close the gap between us.

"After this, everyone will know about us," I said.

He tucked a strand of hair behind my ear and cradled my face. "It's about damn time." His last words stole my breath as he smothered my lips with his own.

At sixteen, there wasn't much I was sure of, but I knew making that bet with Julian in English class was the best risk I'd taken.

eleven

JULIAN

I WAS GREETED by the familiar sounds of birds squawking and a view of the cliffs that overlooked the ocean when I woke up. A layer of fog covered the sky, but it was to be expected at six in the morning. Mila and I didn't have to be at Willow High until nine, but I had a strict routine to to follow; it was more of a constant check list in my head to keep my days running smoothly. After getting out of the Air Force, I was dancing the line between organized and having goddamn OCD. It was 6:05 after I changed into the clothes neatly hung in my color-coded closet and headed to the kitchen to make coffee. I was right on schedule.

As I walked down the hall past Mila's room, I fought every instinct to peek in and check on her. I'd spent most of the night spiraling as I replayed her words in my head. *I have a boyfriend.* The thing about distance was, it was a gamble whether someone would miss or forget you, and hearing it from her own lips that she'd moved on was a punch to the gut I wasn't prepared for. I wondered if he knew her eyes changed color in the sun, how she'd read every book in her collection at least three times, or that her favorite color was a certain shade of green; not forest or mint, but something in between.

I busied my scattering thoughts by writing out my itinerary for the day while a pot of coffee brewed.

1. Willow High presentation w/ Mila
2. Pick up supplies from the hardware store
4. Finish patching up the patio
5. Start painting the house ??

It was light compared to most days, but between fixing up the house, Sofia's wedding, and Mila, I put everything else on hold. Honestly, I wasn't sure if I could've handled anything else.

"Good morning." I looked up at the sound of her voice and gulped at how breathtaking she looked with her messy hair and smeared mascara. In a perfect world, I'd be greeted by her face every morning before we'd share a cup of coffee and plan our day out, but instead, I had to stomach the thought of someone else doing that with her.

"I was going to let you sleep in," I said.

"I smelled coffee." I slid a mug over to her and memorized every detail as she prepared it the way she liked and took a sip with a gentle smile. "Do you always wake up this early?" she asked.

"Yeah, the military gave me no choice but to become a morning person." I grabbed at the dog tags I kept hidden under my clothes.

"You were in the military?" Her brows furrowed.

"I left for the Air Force after Sofia graduated." There wasn't enough time in the world to fill her in on everything I did to distract myself while she was gone.

"What else did you do?" It was almost poetic that the girl who once knew everything about me suddenly knew nothing.

When I looked out the open window, I saw the beach empty. Usually, I went down by myself and enjoyed the peace and quiet before it got crowded with people. "Let's take a walk."

I wrapped her in my jacket before we walked out, but she welcomed the strong winds that blew her hair wildly with a bright smile. I was in just as much awe of her at twenty-four as I was at sixteen—maybe even more, if it was possible.

As soon as my feet touched the warm sand, memories of bonfires after football games, sneaking past security guards late at night with Mila just to hear the waves, and jumping off the highest cliff on a stupid dare started to pour in, more vividly than before.

"Why didn't you tell me you went to the military?" she asked as we walked along the edge of the water. It was ice cold each time it washed up over our feet, but she didn't seem to mind.

"You didn't ask."

The corner of her lips tipped. "Touché. I'm asking now. How long did you serve?"

"Four years. I got back a little over a year ago." I picked up a rock and failed my attempt to skip it across the water.

She shook her head. "You always said you'd leave Willow's Cove behind, yet you came back." Willow's Cove was the kind of town you spent your entire life complaining about, but it wasn't until you left when you appreciated its true beauty.

"And you always said you wanted to settle here. Plans change, Mila." The dark lashes that hovered over her blue eyes shot up, and she struggled to get a word out. "So what changed your mind?"

I pondered over whether to tell her the whole truth, but after the boundaries she'd set, I opted out and only told half of it. "I thought I needed to leave to be happy, but I was still fucking miserable while traveling to different places. After my service, I could've gone anywhere, but back home was the place that felt right."

She frowned. "I know the feeling." Her head whipped around, as if she was surprised she'd said that out loud.

It's all she ever talked about—New York was her dream, which was why I was confused at her face was grim as she looked out at the waves. "Isn't New York the place that feels right for you?" I pried.

She spoke so softly, I could barely hear her. "I don't even know anymore." Before I could speak, she turned to walk towards the house. "We should get back inside."

I stayed there and watched the sun peek through the clouds while I kept all the unsaid words in my head.

THE HALLWAYS at Willow High still looked exactly like they did when Camilla and I walked down them nearly a decade before. My locker still had our initials engraved in it, and the football field still had the missing patch of grass from when our senior class painted it for our prank. The same principal even still worked there. It seemed like nothing had changed except for me and Mila.

Mr. M's salt-and-pepper mustache furrowed when we walked into the office to retrieve our visitors' badges. "Julian Perez. I was hoping I'd see you some day." Before Mila, my friends and I were frequent visitors to his office, so he knew my face all too well. "We'd love to have you come talk to the boys on the football team. They could use a pep talk after last season's losing streak." I once loved the sport, but I blamed my dad for putting a sour taste in my mouth at any mention of football.

I stuck my visitor's badge on my shirt. "I'll consider it, but today, I'm only here for Miss Vega's presentation." I took it as a sign to call her that more often when her eyes rolled to the back of her head.

"Of course. Thank you for taking the time from your book

tour to talk to the kids, Camilla. It means a lot that you remembered us."

"It's no problem, but it's Julian you should be thanking, since he set this up." I couldn't hold back my smile as I followed behind them to the cafeteria, where a full room of students waited. I could tell she was nervous from how she picked at her nails, but I wasn't sure why, since she'd done book signings for crowds bigger than the population of Willow High. It was nice to see she wasn't the superhuman she always tried to be.

"You're going to be great," I said confidently.

She leaned in close to my ear as Mr. M spoke at the microphone. "Holy shit, I wasn't expecting there to be so many of them." I fought the pull I felt towards her hand and kept it at my side instead. "I wouldn't have set this up if I didn't think you could do it. You're a bestseller, so go act like it." Her eyes brightened, as if I'd said just the right words to give her the courage to walk on stage. We always used to say we could make everyone else disappear with just a glance, and I knew I did that for her when she found my eyes in the back of the room.

Her face lit up, and I heard her shaky breaths ease over the microphone. "Hi, I'm Camilla Vega. I'm a romance author living in New York City, but I was once sitting exactly where you are. I grew up in Willow's Cove and found comfort in reading all the books in its library, dreaming of writing some of my own one day. I was invited here to answer questions on how my career came to be and everything in between, but if you take anything away from today, let it be this: whatever career path you choose, there are going to be people telling you that you can't, or shouldn't, but that's all the more reason why you should. Are there any questions to start us off?" After admiring her from a distance for years, I was in awe of finally getting to watch her be who she was always meant to be.

Almost every hand shot up, but she did exactly what I knew she would and picked on a girl hovering in the back quietly. "I really loved your book. Can I ask what the inspiration behind the story was?" Her eyes quickly darted to me, then back to the girl. "I wanted to write about how beautiful and crazy first loves can be. In a way, I sort of wrote the book for myself at your age using fictional characters." Her eyes darted to me again, but they lingered a little longer before she picked on another student. "You knew you'd be a writer someday, but did any of your friends or family know too, or was it a surprise to them?"

I was possessed with the impulse to speak. "We always knew." Everyone's heads snapped to the back of the room where I stood with my arms folded.

"You might recognize Julian Perez's face. There are photos of him in Willow High's Hall of Fame from when he was *a lot* younger." If over three hundred kids hadn't been staring at me, I would have flipped her the finger, and that was the first time in six years I felt a glimpse of our old, playful dynamic.

"How'd you know?" I wasn't expecting a follow-up question, but I didn't have to think twice. I only looked at Mila as I spoke. "She's the smartest girl I've ever met. She had this glow in English class that she didn't have in others; I knew because I would look at her a lot. Some people have something special about them, and Camilla always did."

Her breath echoed when it hitched into the microphone, and we held each other's gaze longer than we should have while being surrounded by high school students, but she found a way to recover the conversation. "That's why I'm here. You guys have potential, and I'm hoping you know it after today. It sounds cheesy, but no dream is too crazy, even if you may have to work a little harder for it."

I knew the advice was for the students, but I took the last part for myself and sank against the wall when the realization hit me. I only had one dream, and making it happen meant I had to make a borderline stupid decision, but I was willing to work a little harder for it.

Nostalgia hit me over the head on our drive back from Willow High when I looked over and saw her singing along to the radio while her hair kissed the wind. I'd relived the image of her in my head for six years, and suddenly she was real again, wrapping me in a blanket of sunshine every time she smiled.

"That was less nerve-racking than I was expecting," she said.

"I told you. The kids respected the hell out of you. Mr. M told me they decided not to send them to third period because they had so many questions." I didn't tell her I promised to talk to the football team if he did that; I didn't want her smile to disappear.

"Did you mean what you said about always knowing I'd be a writer?" I imagined her at seventeen, writing in her green journal at her desk. "I've always believed in you, Mila, even when you didn't." I had to pry myself away from her dreamy blue eyes as I turned onto the road that led downtown.

"Where are we going?" She gazed out of the window at the trees passing by. When you lived in a small town, hardly anything changed, but she took it all in as if she was experiencing it for the first time.

"I just need to grab a few things." I learned to appreciate Willow's Cove more when I grew up and realized everything I needed was in one place. You could pick up your hardware, groceries, a book, something from the bakery, and maybe even a souvenir all on one decorated block.

Mila was in a daze when I opened her door and let her see all the new shops, but what captivated her was the farmer's market that took up most of the street. At the time, it was new to everyone in town.

"Can we check it out?" It never got any easier to say no to

her. "How about we pick up some stuff from the hardware store today, and I promise we'll come back before you leave?"

Her French-tip nails grazed my arm. "I'll hold you to that, Perez." I watched as she skipped to the store, where the owner, Bill, greeted us as we walked inside.

"I wasn't expecting you until later." He adjusted his *Bill's Hardware* cap.

"You know you're my favorite old man, Billy. I can't stay away." He hated when I called him Billy, and even more when I called him an old man. Most people in town started going to the new hardware store, but I'd known Bill and his family since I was a kid, so I was more than happy to give him my business instead. He never had to say it; I knew he appreciated when I came in.

He nudged toward Mila scoping the place out. "Who's the new face?"

"An old friend visiting from New York. She's staying with me for Sofia's wedding." My gaze never strayed away from her. He clicked his tongue and smacked me on the back of my neck. "I know that look, and it'll get you into trouble."

I acted oblivious. "What look?"

"I'm old, Julian, not an idiot. A man only has that look for one woman in his lifetime." He'd been married to the same woman for over forty years, so if I was going to listen to anyone, it was him.

Before I could muster up anything to say, Mila approached us. "What are we here for?" I had a plan for the house before she arrived, but when she said she'd stay, I decided I wanted her to be a part of it. "Paint. You're helping me pick the color of the house." There was only one color I intended on painting my house. I'd kept it stored in my mind since the moment she mentioned it on our first date, but I had to act like I didn't so she'd feel included. I also didn't want her to think I was pathetic enough to remember the color she talked about years before.

"You should pick it. It's your house."

I smiled. It might've been mine, but anytime I looked at it, all I saw was her. "You always had better taste than me."

"Can't argue with you there." She headed to where hundreds of paint samples were spread out on the wall and did exactly what I knew she would—go straight for the selection of greens.

"What about this one?" I grabbed a color I knew she wouldn't like, and she made her disgust obvious before picking the only sage green shade Bill carried in the store. "This one is perfect." What she didn't know was that weeks before, I'd decided on the same color. "That one it is."

"Are you sure? You're the one who has to look at the house every day, so it should be a color you like." It was on the tip of my tongue to admit it had been my favorite color for nearly a decade because it reminded me of her. "I'm sure, Mila."

We headed to the counter, where Bill started to make the paint in the shade she'd chosen. "I'll finish up here. I'm sure Mrs. Wilson will be happy to see you stop by the bakery."

"Don't mind if I do. I've been thinking about her blueberry scones for years." I watched her hurry out and walk across the street to where Mr. And Mrs. Wilson made the best fresh baked goods money could buy. I never got enough of the sight of her.

"There's that look again. What was she? First love?" Bill asked.

"More like *the* love." Mila was *everything*.

"I see. What happened between you two? Is she the one that got away, as they say?" The last thing I wanted to do was relive the biggest mistake of my life. "Let's just say I'm paying for a decision I made at eighteen, tenfold."

A smile grew under his grey mustache. "I made a few mistakes with my wife too. Being stupid sort of comes with the territory of being that young, but take my advice, kid: before you do anything hasty, make sure you're both on the same page. I'd hate for you to be moping around my store."

I peeked with interest. "If it was your wife, would you do anything to get her back, even if it meant it could blow up in your face?" When he immediately nodded, it only solidified my thoughts from earlier. "Without question." I offered him a smile and handed him a fifty-dollar bill to cover the twenty dollar total. "Always a pleasure, old man. Keep the change."

"Thanks, Julian. By the way, my truck's making that sound again. You mind taking a look at it?" Most of the townspeople considered me their unofficial maintenance guy. I took a mechanics class in high school, but what really honed my skills was being a crew chief in the Air Force. I was good with my hands, and working on cars was a nice side gig to help finance the house rebuild.

I winked. "I'll be there after my sister's wedding chaos." As I walked out, his words flooded my ears. *A man only has that look for one woman in his lifetime.* If he'd noticed the way I looked at Mila after five minutes, I wondered if she had too.

twelve

JULIAN

8 YEARS EARLIER

EVERY WEEK, I looked forward to Friday nights. For one hour, I was able to focus on nothing but playing the sport I loved with guys I'd grown up with. Football was drilled into my life as early as I could walk. You couldn't really escape it when you came from a line of legendary quarterbacks. I never wanted to be the team leader, but as a starting tight end, I was the right-hand man. I tried to forget the pressure to be great like my dad and grandpa, but it followed me every time I stepped onto the field.

"Perez! We're down by a touchdown with a minute to go. I told Damon to get the ball to you. Do what you do best." Everyone was high-strung, since we were playing our renowned rival for the championship, but it felt like just another game. It was impossible to feel fazed by the other team with the energy that surged from the crowd and the constant adrenaline, but what really kept me grounded was knowing Mila was somewhere in the stands. We'd been officially dating for two months, and not only had she not missed a game, we hadn't lost one. The first thing I did before any game was look for her in the crowd so I'd know where to find her after I made a play.

I ran over and huddled in the circle as Damon went over the final play. Between his good arm, my speed, and the fact that we'd been playing ball together since we were kids, we gained a reputation for being a "dynamic duo". We could practically read each other's minds at that point, so we somehow got the team wins when it seemed highly unlikely.

Despite our friendship being rocky before I started dating Mila, all of that went out the window when it was a tight game. As soon as the ball snapped, I ran full sprint down the field, juking through players twice my size as fast as my legs could carry me. With Damon being swarmed, the play he'd called changed, and instead, he launched a hail Mary. By some miracle, I caught the ball with one hand and landed on my back. It wasn't until the crowd erupted in loud cheers and my teammates swarmed me that I knew I'd made it into the end zone. Winning a game was a high I was addicted to feeling, but it was nothing compared to seeing Mila through the crowd flooding the field to celebrate. I didn't care for the trophy—I just wanted her. When she leaped off the ground into my arms and crushed her soft lips against mine, that was the real win.

"I'm so proud of you." I never told her, but she was the first person to ever tell me that. I didn't know how much I needed to hear it until it came from her perfect lips.

"I made that last touchdown for you." I placed a kiss on her forehead and planted her feet back on the ground.

She smiled. "That's why I wore your jersey with pride." It was my selfish idea for her to wear my jersey on game days; I wanted everyone to be reminded she was mine—as if they'd forget from how much I talked about her.

On the walk back to the locker room, I looked at the players posing for pictures with their family and friends with a level of envy. My dad went to all my games, but contrary to what people thought, it was never for me. The only thing he loved more than himself was sitting in the stands, reliving his glory days with the his old football friends while he scrutinized every play I made.

"I'll be quick." I pecked Mila's lips before going into the locker room, where the guys were amped up on adrenaline from the win. "I can't believe we're goddamn champions! We have to celebrate. You're coming to my house tonight, right, JP?" Elijah shouted from across the room.

"I don't think so. I'm gonna hang out with Camilla." I ignored the teasing because I knew they were just jokes. Damon was nearby, completely silent; he'd learned not to make any comments about her.

Elijah shouted back. "Bring her. I invited her friend." I was surprised he and Taylor even knew each other.

"I promise, I'll be nice. You won us the game, JP; the least you can do is celebrate with us," Damon chimed in.

I quickly stuffed my gym bag with my sweaty clothes. "I'll call you guys later if I can make it, how about that?" They knew I wasn't going, but I didn't have the heart to tell them. It wasn't that I didn't want to go, or that I'd become the asshole who ditched his friends, but there was something I'd planned on doing if we won, and getting drunk with our entire school wasn't it.

"I never pegged you for the type to ditch us once you got a girlfriend," another one of my teammates nearby teased. A few months before, all I ever did was party with them until we passed out on someone's lawn, and then we'd do it all over again the next weekend. Mila made me want something different. "You would do the same if you had a girl like Camilla Vega."

I PARKED two houses down from her house so Mrs. Vega wouldn't see my car and I could stay with her for a little while longer."Thank you for coming tonight. I play better knowing you're in the stands." Our fingers grazed as they met on the middle console. She was the only person who went with no ulterior motive, for just me, and I never took that lightly. Even in the dark car, I could see her blue eyes searing into mine. "I wouldn't have missed it."

I gently took her face in my hands and kissed her deeply. I never got tired of the way her lips felt like velvet, or how they tasted like the green apple lip balm she always wore. I was only sixteen, but I knew I never wanted to kiss anyone else.

I broke us apart and gained the courage to say the words that had been sitting on my tongue for days. "I love you." It didn't surprise me when I fell so hard for her, or how fast I did. I hated myself for not having the courage to make a move sooner.

"What?" I felt when she went stiff under my fingertips.

"I love you, Mila," I repeated with the same confidence. The feeling crept up slowly, and then hit me all at once when I watched her admire a sunset from her favorite spot. I never knew home could be found in a person, but she was it. There wasn't a shred of doubt I loved her.

"I'm sorry." She reached for the handle of the passenger door and climbed out, leaving me with a feeling like I'd been punched in the gut. She neared her house, but I knew I had to go after her. "Mila! What do you mean, I'm sorry?"

She slowed down but kept a steady pace forward as I chased after her. It was déjà vu of homecoming. "I mean I can't do this right now."

She had tears rolling down her cheeks when I caught up and pulled her back to face me. "You can't just say I'm sorry after I said I love you. At least tell me you don't love me back, but don't just walk away," I pleaded.

She freed herself from my grasp. "I just need some time to think, Julian. That's all."

Something in me snapped when she gave me her back again.

"I finally get it. That's your thing, huh? When things get real, you bail?"

The anger in my voice triggered hers to crack. "If you really think that, you don't know me as well as you think."

I inched so close, I could feel how fast her heart was beating. "Who's fault is that? You don't let me all the way in. You won't even let me meet your dad!" I nearly threw up seeing her flinch when my voice rose. For a split second, I was exactly who I had feared becoming my entire life.

"You want to talk about not letting people in? You can't even look at me any time I bring up meeting your parents." She didn't know I was doing her a favor by protecting her from those people.

My voice softened as I searched her blue eyes. "Where does this leave us, Mila?"

"Just go home, Julian." I felt my heart break into pieces. I wanted nothing more than to take back what I said, but it was too late. The damage was done. The least I could do was listen to what she'd asked, even though the last place I wanted to be was somewhere she wasn't.

When I peeled away in my car and looked into the rearview mirror, the sight of her standing alone on the sidewalk triggered my eyes to fill with tears. I wasn't sure if it was just a fight or a breakup, but I refused to accept the latter.

thirteen

CAMILLA

I MISTOOK my phone's blaring ringtone for the alarm until I pried my eyes open and saw Greyson's name across the screen. Despite the sun burning my eyes, I startled awake and hurried to answer. "Good morning," I greeted him with a groggy voice.

"Did I wake you?" My eyes were still shut as I spoke, but I was willing to sacrifice sleep just to hear his voice. "No, I've been up for a while."

"I'm sorry I didn't call yesterday. My dad had me sit in on a big meeting, so I didn't get home until late."

"How'd that go?" When I finally shot up from under the covers, I was immediately disappointed by the lack of fresh coffee scent.

"I don't think any of them took me seriously, Cami." His somber tone reminded me of when we'd lie in bed after a hard day at work, and I'd run my hands through his hair until he fell asleep.

"All that matters is that your dad takes you seriously. The rest of them will fall in line when you take over. You didn't think you'd win me over, but you did." I beamed a smile he couldn't see.

"Four years of flirting and pining won't work in this instance, Cami." My laughter echoed through the room. He was known for being a bit of a player in college, so I'd admit, I made him work for my attention.

"It'll just take time, Grey. They'll see you're different than your dad." Those were some of his favorite words to hear.

"How do you always do that?"

"Do what?" I asked. "I was in a shitty mood when I picked up the phone, and now I'm not." I walked over to the window to watch the birds fly over the calm ocean. With the days I had left in town, I wanted to soak up the view as much as I could.

"What can I say? It's a talent," I joked.

"How'd your day go yesterday?" His voice carried over the sounds of chaos coming from the coffee shop in the background.

I recalled the events from the day before and only thought of Julian. "Great. I went to my old high school with Julian to talk to the kids. They asked so many questions, Grey. It inspired me to finally start writing another book and—"

"Who's Julian?" he interrupted curtly. That was the first time I ever mentioned Julian's name since I'd met him. "An old friend from high school who offered me his guest room until his sister's wedding." My hand holding the phone trembled as his silence grew on the other end. He had every right to be upset, so I waited for his anger, but of course, it never came. "Why didn't you mention him before?" Greyson wasn't the jealous type—territorial, but never jealous.

I chose my next words carefully. "I didn't think it was important. He's just a friend who had a spare room. I'll be out of his hair after the wedding. I'm sorry I didn't tell you." A pit grew in my stomach for not telling him the whole truth, but telling him Julian and I dated nearly a decade before seemed unimportant. He was my past, and Greyson was my present. That's what mattered.

He broke his silence that felt like an eternity. "It's fine, Cami.

I trust you. As long as you're okay." I was fully aware I didn't deserve someone as selfless as him.

"I am. I promise."

"Okay. I'm heading into the office, but I'll call you later. I love you." I took a breath of relief when he said the words I needed to hear. "I love you too."

The line went dead, but I didn't have a chance to sink back into my pillows before Julian's voice echoed on the other side of the door. "Mila, are you up?"

I scurried around and immediately froze when I realized I was fixing my hair in the mirror. "What the hell are you doing, Cami?" I whispered to myself. "Come in."

As he stood in the doorway, I had to peel my eyes away from how broad his shoulders and arms looked in his white tank top.

"What's up?" I asked.

"You get any writing done last night?" I smiled. "I did. It just started flowing." I ignored how my stomach swirled at the sight of his warm smile.

"Well, remember when you said you'd help with the house if I helped you?" He tossed clothes onto my lap and winked. "I'm cashing in that offer. Change into those and meet me in the kitchen."

I waited until he was out of the room to push myself out from under the covers, but he barged back in seconds later. "Julian! Get out!" I never slept in pajama bottoms, so I pulled my oversized shirt down as far as I could to cover my lace underwear.

He put his hand over his eyes so quickly, his forehead rammed into the door frame. "Shit, I'm sorry. Uhm, I was just gonna say there's coffee in the kitchen when you're finished getting dressed." I could see a sliver of a smile he fought back.

"Seriously, get out, Julian!" He managed to dodge the pillow I threw at the door as it shut, and I heard his laughter erupt in the hall seconds later. Goddamn him.

Once the embarrassment subsided and I no longer wanted to crawl into a hole, I failed at holding back laughter of my own.

AFTER STEALING glances at each other over a cup of coffee, we met outside, where a plastic cover and cans of paint were laid out on the grass. "Is this what I think it is?" I asked.

I couldn't contain my excitement when he put a paintbrush in my hand with a smirk. When our fingers grazed, I didn't know whether the shivers that ran through my body were from the cold ocean breeze or his touch. I went with the latter.

"Time to give the house some color." I'd waited over a decade to see the house the color I'd always imagined instead of the old rustic white. I adjusted the straps on the overalls he'd let me borrow that were a few sizes too big. "Show me what to do." He seemed to snap out of a daze. "There's an easier way to do this, but since I can't afford a spray painter, we'll have to do it by hand." He poured paint into the trays spread out on the plastic.

"I don't mind. I think it'll give it some character." I felt his burning glare as I admired the house and thought back to the first time I stumbled on it. I once pictured myself living in it, spending my days writing books on the porch overlooking the ocean, but life had other plans. Instead, I had to help Julian settle into it.

He pulled me back from the haunting thoughts. "I'll let you do the honors of the first paint stroke." I had no idea what I was doing, but I eagerly swiped the brush across the fresh wood with the green paint of my dreams, and reveled in how much consideration Julian had put into the house. Replenishing the rotten wood, cutting down the vines covering the roof, redoing the patio that was seconds away from caving in—it must've taken him months, but he seemed to glow with pride over how it was turning out.

"Slow, Mila. You don't want streaks." My breath hitched when his firm touch hovered over my hand to stop me. Our closeness was breaking my rule, but I let him stay at my back and guide my hands. "I always imagined this place this color," I said my inner thoughts out loud.

His jagged breaths grazed my ear. "I remember."

I was glad he couldn't tell how hot my cheeks turned. "You do?" I thought it was purely a coincidence when he agreed to the shade, despite once hating green, but I never considered he remembered from when I mentioned it years before.

"I remember everything, Mila." He couldn't say things like that. It wasn't fair I'd spent the past six years trying to forget what happened, and he was undoing everything in a matter of days. I suddenly felt suffocated, so I backed away in hopes of getting space to breathe air that wasn't the same as his.

"You okay?" I flinched when his fingertips rested on my back.

"I'm fine," I lied. What the hell was going on with me? He was just Julian, my *friend;* but last time I checked, a friend's touch shouldn't make you feel like you've been lit on fire. I tried to go back to painting, but I couldn't concentrate with a question clawing at me. "Would you do it differently if you could go back, Julian?" I let the words slip.

"Do what?"

"Everything…Us." Once again, we were dancing on the line of boundaries I'd set, but if I didn't ask, I feared I never would.

His face grew tight as he ran his fingers over his facial hair. "You and I ended up where we are because of the choices we made. It doesn't matter if I would change anything or not, Mila." It was the answer I thought I wanted from him, but I was met with an odd twinge of disappointment. He must've noticed the shift in my mood, because he approached me with a smile peeking through the corner of his lips.

"You've got paint on your face."

"No, I don't, what—" I gasped when I felt the wet paint drag across my cheek with his fingers. "You're gonna pay for that." I scooped green paint into my hands with the plan to retaliate, but once he bolted through the tall grass, I knew I'd never catch him.

"Julian!" I thought he would've lost his athletic speed as he aged, but he was just as fast as he was in high school, if not faster. When he disappeared from sight, I accepted my fate, because I knew what was coming next. It was his oldest trick, yet he still surprised me by picking me up off the ground and spinning in circles. "You still let your guard down." His deep voice ringing so close to my ear made chills rise on my arms.

I got on my tiptoes and leaned in so close, our lips nearly touched, then watched his disbelief when I slapped wet paint across his cheek. "You've got a little something on your face."

He threw his head back with rich laughter. "Okay, truce. We have to save some for the house." He wiped it off with a towel then used the same one to clean my face with trembling fingers. "Thanks." I couldn't look away from his soft eyes as they roamed over my face. No one ever looked at me with the same depth as Julian. It was as if he was looking into my soul and letting me get a peek into his.

When he tucked a strand of hair behind my ear, I saw the faded scar across his palm that matched mine. *You jump, I jump,* he told me the day Elijah Fisher dared us all to jump off the highest cliff point. It was perfect weather that day; the air felt different since we were one week away from graduating. Julian, Taylor, Sofia, Elijah, and I all packed our cars and headed to the cove in hopes of perfecting our tans and swimming in the open ocean, but of course, it didn't play out that way. You know the saying, "If your friends jumped off a cliff, would you?" I guess my answer was yes, since we all took the fifty-foot plunge together. Julian never let go of my hand the entire time, which resulted in our matching cuts from the sharp rocks at the bottom. We had no idea a week later, our lives would turn upside down.

"Does your boyfriend know how you got this?" He traced over my deep scar, leaving his warmth to travel through my arm. I shook my head, only thinking of how easy it'd be to close the distance between us and how much that made me a shitty person.

I let out a sigh of relief when a car's blaring horn echoed up the hill to the house. "Every time," I heard him faintly whisper when Sofia popped her head out from the passenger window.

An unfamiliar face helped her out of the brand new Ford Bronco before they walked over to us, holding hands. My first impression of them was they looked like luxury together. "Sorry for the surprise visit, but we were just passing by, and I wanted Levi to meet Cami."

Her fiancé pulled his sunglasses above his head to greet me with his dark green eyes. "Cami, this is Levi Willow. Levi, this is the girl I've been telling you about." At first glance, I knew he was a perfect match for Sofia. She always went for clean-cut guys like him. The strong and confident aura he had reflected in his smooth, granite-like features.

"Nice to finally meet you, Cami. Sofia hasn't stopped squealing since you agreed to be a bridesmaid." He combed his fingers through his dark, curly locks framing his ivory skin.

I smiled. "Thank you for inviting me. I'm sure it'll be beautiful."

"Wait." Sofia looked between me and Julian with furrowed brows. "Why do you guys have paint on your faces?" I looked over at him, embarrassed that I'd met a stranger with lingering green paint on my cheek.

"We were painting the house and had a little mishap." Julian looked down to hide a smile from everyone.She didn't seem to buy it, but she looked more pleased than anything else. "Anyway, since we're here, do you guys want to have lunch in town? Or do you want to get back to your *painting*?" She threw a playful smirk in Julian's direction.

I looked at our paint-covered clothes, then back at the house that wasn't even close to being finished. "Lunch sounds great." I didn't necessarily want to sit at lunch with my ex-boyfriend, his sister, and her fiancé, but I needed a break to gather my reeling thoughts, like what would have happened if Sofia hadn't shown up, or what would Greyson think about me having paint fights with my ex-boyfriend?

AFTER SOFIA and Levi treated us to lunch, Julian and I spent the rest of the evening painting what we could of the house. It was coming along perfectly, and he even made sure there was white trimming like I'd mentioned just once. If he recalled a small detail like that from years ago, did he really remember everything? Why did I care so much if he did or not?

"Mila?" I scurried to shove the journal I was writing in under my pillow as Julian let himself in. "Hey."

"You get any writing done?"

I sighed with disappointment. "I haven't even attempted yet." I was so wiped out from the day, opening my computer seemed like a huge chore.

"Show me what you have so far." My cheeks flushed when he walked over and sat at the foot of my bed.

"Absolutely not." No one had ever seen a first draft of my work before. Even my editor waited until I went over with edits before she had it in her hands.

"I'm not leaving this room until I see it, Mila. I have all night." He was stubborn as much as he was persistent, so I knew he wasn't bluffing. I rolled my eyes and grabbed my computer off my desk. "Don't judge too hard. It's only a first draft. It's supposed to be shitty." I chewed on my nails while he read the first chapter.

"It's good." His voice wasn't as confident as I'd hoped.

"But?"

He sighed. "I'm no expert on writing a book, but maybe there should be an intro chapter that grabs the a reader's attention."

My eyes narrowed. "So, a prologue that serves as a hook?"

"Exactly." The idea was different than my first book, which was exactly what my publisher wanted, so I jotted it down in my notes to visit at a later time. He laid on his back and stared up at the ceiling. "What's it even about?"

I shrugged. "I'm still playing around with ideas, which is probably why I gave up after writing the first chapter." It was getting both frustrating and discouraging that I didn't have one solid book idea yet. Even after being pumped with inspiration from the presentation at Willow High, I quickly lost momentum. I hoped one would just come to me when least expected, but I didn't exactly have the time to wait around.

His eyes never strayed from the ceiling as he asked me something that vacuum sucked all the air from the room. "Going back to what you asked me earlier. It's my turn to ask; would you do anything differently if you could go back?"

I partly expected it, but I still got the air knocked out of me. I could name a few moments I'd do differently if I suddenly had a do over, but none I was willing to admit. "I think you were right when you said we both ended up where we are because of the choices we made, but I definitely could have reacted better in some situations."

He perked up with interest. "Like?"

I knew the words only going to fuel the fire before I said them. "When you told me you loved me for the first time." His breaths halted, and the only sound was the soft crash of waves outside.

"I think about how I reacted that night a lot too, but then I see the students at Willow High and how young they are. We were just kids figuring how to handle being in love, Mila."

I cringed at the memory of storming off after he'd told me

the words I'd been waiting so desperately to hear. "I guess you're right."

After all those years, he still didn't know the whole story.

fourteen

CAMILLA

8 YEARS EARLIER

I LOVE YOU. Tears streamed down my face as Julian's voice echoed all the way up the stairs, where I heard commotion from my parents' room. I wasn't expecting my dad for another week, but it wasn't a surprise hand my mom were already fighting. I slowed my pace up the steps so I could stay undetected while listening through the cracked door.

"If you're already packing for another business trip, at least have some goddamn decency to spend time with your daughter before you go."

"What do you want me to do, Liv? You never wanted to worry about money, and this is how I do that."

"Just come out and say it already, Jeremy. We both know you're not really leaving for work." You could suddenly hear a pin drop.

"You're fucking crazy," he gritted out. I didn't stick around because I'd heard it all before. Every time he left town, they called each other every name in the book, and he'd still end up leaving. My parents knew I was aware of their problems, but they didn't know I knew *everything*. When I was ten, I accidentally eavesdropped on a conversation my dad had with his mistress about baby names. It shattered my entire world and everything I thought I knew. Every time my dad kissed me on the forehead to leave out of town for *work*, I knew where he was really going. Despite her suspicions, I didn't know if Mom knew, so I lived with the secret he'd been juggling two families for years.

For a long time, I thought that was all love stories ended up with—secrecy, silent dinners, screaming matches, no laughter. It made the idea of falling in love a terrifying concept. I found comfort in reading fictional love stories because I could live vicariously and never run the risk of ending up like my parents. They were good to me but fucking terrible for each other. Sometimes, I wished they had never crossed paths and lived happy lives, even if it meant I never existed.

I shut my door and escaped their noise by climbing out of my window onto the rooftop. When I couldn't make it down to the cove, the view from up there sufficed.

I only had Julian on my mind when I looked out at the cliffs just out of reach when I needed them the most. Tears fell down my cheeks as I replayed our fight, how I ruined what should have been a perfect moment. He was right when he said I bailed. Mom always told me she and Dad fell in love young, and I saw how they despised each other, constantly throwing digs about the life they could have had if they'd never met.

I refused to be like them, and the only way I prevented that was to stay away from relationships altogether, but I couldn't stay away from Julian. I might've been able to at one point, but he'd snuck his way into my heart and found a way to unlock my soul. For the first time in my life, I knew what love was supposed to be like.

I felt like my life started the day we were forced to be partners on that writing assignment, whether I wanted to admit it then or not. He made me feel seen, even when I didn't want to be. He brought out a version of me I didn't even know existed and taught me to love it. He made me feel at peace in a place of chaos.

When things got real, I ran, but not because I didn't love him. I ran because I did.

"CAMILLA, YOU'RE UP NEXT." I froze when Miss Knowles turned to me. I'd been so busy rotting in bed all weekend, I'd forgotten about the homework for English class. We'd been learning about Edgar Allan Poe, so the assignment was to write our own poem. I had to write mine ten minutes before the final bell rang that morning, so I wasn't confident it was any good, but in true poetic fashion, it was my raw emotions of everything I'd felt over the weekend.

I took a deep breath and walked to the front of the class, my hands shaking as I grasped the wrinkled piece of paper. I found Julian's lost eyes and almost broke into tears, but I refused to be remembered as the girl who cried in first period English.

I swallowed the lump in my throat and read with a shaky breath. "She finds it hard to trust, the same way the ocean struggles to hug the shore no longer than a few seconds, before she begins pulling herself back. When she feels safe enough to be still, she's pulled by the gravity of his words, tainted by the love she's always known. He's somehow stronger than the waves crashing onto the shore, and she finds herself willingly swimming into his arms. Why? Who are you to even do such a thing?" I looked up and found only his brown eyes to try and tell him everything I couldn't say days before. I always found it easier to put my feelings onto pages rather than speak them out loud, and I'd meant every word. I just hoped it wasn't too late.

My spot was the only place I wanted to be after school that day. I sat inside the hollow cave, rubbing sand between my fingers as I looked out at the ocean and remembered when I'd shared the peaceful place with Julian. The question lingered whether I'd lost him, and I couldn't stomach how, if I did, I only had myself to blame.

"I figured you'd be here." I sighed with relief when his deep voice rang from behind me. "Lucky guess."

He sank into the sand next to me, and we stayed quiet for what felt like hours, looking at the surfers in the distance. I was the one who screwed up, so I decided to bite the bullet first. "You were right about me. I got scared and ran, but not for the reason you think." I knew without a doubt I loved him. He had me, so there was no going back. "I didn't grow up with the best example of how love is supposed to look, Julian, and i've spent my entire life trying not to be like my parents. When you said those words, it felt real, which meant we could turn out the same way. It scared me." I let out a heavy breath once the weight was off my chest.

He turned to me and took my face in his warm hands. "Mila, you don't have to explain yourself. It was selfish to tell you that. You can say I love you tomorrow, a year from now, five years from now. I don't care. I still love you. You had me the second I saw you with the green ribbon in your hair in kindergarten. I knew it was you. It's always going to be you." With his thumb, he wiped the single tear that slid down my cheek. He was so gentle, and his eyes were filled with passion and tenderness that made the next words easy to say. "I love you, Julian. You have my heart, so don't break it."

He rested his forehead against mine. "You can do whatever

you want to mine." I ran my fingers through his wavy hair and kissed him deeply enough to tie our souls together.

"I liked your poem." He smiled against my lips.

"I thought I lost you."

His laughter vibrated in my chest before he pressed a kiss to my forehead. "You can't get rid of me that easy, Vega."

And that was it—I was a girl in love.

fifteen

JULIAN

"Sofia, where the hell are you?" I paced my kitchen and peeked out the window. My sister had been hounding me to get a tux and then had the audacity to be thirty minutes late to help me pick one out. "My meeting with my wedding planner ran late. Go without me!"

I sneered. "Goddammit, Sof. Don't complain when I show up to your wedding in an orange tux."

"Julian, I swear to—" I ended the call before she got another word out. If there was one thing I hated, it was not sticking to a schedule. I grabbed my keys and rushed out the door, but my schedule was suddenly the last thing on my mind when I saw Mila reading in the middle of the field surrounded by dead flowers. I walked over and sat next to her on the cold, wet grass. "What are you doing out here?"

"Reading."

"Tell me about it."

Her smile wrapped me in more warmth than the sun. "It's the same story just in a different font. Boy likes girl, girl likes boy, but they can never quite figure it out."

"Until they do," I cut in.

"We'll have to wait until the end to find out. It's a series, so their story is still being written." I hoped our story was still being written too, but I kept the thought to myself.

She nudged to the keys in my hand. "Where are you going?"

"I need a tux. Sofia was supposed to help me pick one out, but she bailed." She looked at me, then back at her book before closing it. "I'll come. Knowing you, you'll pick out some weird color like orange as her punishment."

I smiled to myself at how much she still knew me.

THERE WAS ONLY one place to get tuxedos in Willow's Cove, and that wasn't saying much by its small selection. Even if I wanted to get revenge on Sofia by getting a wild color, the only choices to choose from were black, white, grey, and navy blue.

Mila approached me with a black one and held it against my body with narrowed eyes. "You can never go wrong with black, and you can put a teal blue pocket to go with the theme."

I shrugged. "I'll show up in whatever you pick." She hid a smirk as she turned towards the wall of ties. "Wait here."

I couldn't look away from her as she roamed freely around the store. Doing things with her that were so domestic, like running errands, painting the house, picking out a tux, felt second-nature. It felt like we'd been doing it all this time, which made it hard to forget she was leaving in a matter of days.

Her face lit up when she came back with a teal blue pocket. "Go try this on."

I smiled down at her. "Yes, ma'am."

Only seconds went by before she barged in without knocking. "I found a tie to match your—" I watched as her eyes nearly bulged out of her head at seeing me shirtless. Unlike when I'd accidentally barged in on her, I didn't tell her to get out. "Oh my God, I'm sorry. I didn't think you'd undress so fast. Uhh…here."

The tie dropped to the ground from how fast she darted out, and I finally let my laughter ring.

"I hear you, Julian," she shouted from outside the dressing room. "Did you enjoy the show at least?" I teased.

"Just shut up and get dressed." I didn't have to see her to know her cheeks were flushed red.

Not only did the tux look perfect, but I wouldn't have to hear Sofia complain, since it went with her theme. Mila's blue eyes shined when I walked out and waited for her approval. "You still clean up nice, Perez." I tensed when she ran her hands along the seams of the fabric.

Her words brought me back to when she'd said something similar. "The last time you saw me in a tux was senior prom."

"Black tux with a green pocket." She lowered her head and murmured softly, as if she was hoping I wouldn't hear her.

"You remember that?" I asked. We were inches away when she looked up at me. "You're not the only one who remembers everything." Being close to her was a drug, and I chased the way she made my pulse pound like it was an addiction.

Her hypnotizing gaze made me slip out the question that had been lingering in my mind since she agreed to go to the wedding. "So, since we're both going to the wedding, do you just want to go together?" I spoke quickly before I could psyche myself out.

"You mean carpool?" For being so smart, she always failed to see when someone was making a move.

I looked down at my feet. "No. We'd be each other's dates." I waited with a knot the size of fucking Texas in my stomach, just like I did in high school when I'd asked her out for the first time. It wasn't every day I asked my ex-girlfriend of six years to be my date to my little sister's wedding.

I could sense the doubt swirling in her head. "Do you not remember I have a boyfriend?" How could I forget when the thought made my jaw tighten? "If it makes you feel better, we don't have to label it as a date. We'll just be saving each other from having to dance with anyone else for the night." I tried to hide my excitement when she showed a glimmer of interest.

"Okay. It's not a date, though. Just two friends going to the same wedding. Deal?" I'd take any fraction of her I was given.

"Fine. As long as I get one slow dance."

Her brows raised. "Now you're making requests?" I got so close, I could almost taste her cherry lipgloss. "It's not a request."

I felt her heart start to beat erratically and found pleasure in how she proved not to be as immune to me as I thought.

THE TUX SHOP happened to be on the same street as the farmer's market Mila was entranced by.

"You promised we'd check it out." I still had to grocery shop and cross the last things off my to-do list, but I couldn't resist her. "Please." She was like a siren capable of compelling me to do anything she asked with one look. *Fuck the list.*

"Fine, let's go." She intertwined our fingers and dragged us towards the vendors awaiting customers. I shopped there occasionally, so I knew just about everyone, but I saw Mrs. Wyatt's booth first. She happened to be my neighbor when I lived at home, so I always stopped by to see what she was selling. "Hey, Julian. You haven't been here in a while."

I felt Mila's grip loosen. "I've been busy with the new house, but you know I can't stay away from your lemon squares for too long. Do you have any left?" She baked me and Sofia a batch of them every birthday until we moved out.

"I have two, just for you."

"We'll take them."

She seemed offended when I offered her a ten dollar bill. "When was the last time I charged you, kid?" She looked at me through her round glasses.

"It never hurts to try." While she had her back turned, I slipped the money into her tip jar. Willow's Cove was mostly full of people who were just trying to make a living like me, so I never accepted the hand-outs that were offered.

Mila was nowhere to be seen when I turned around, but I knew her well enough to know she was wherever the books were. Right I was when I saw her head stuck in a copy of *Persuasion* by Jane Austen. "Of course, I found you here. Are you always so predictable, Camilla Vega?"

"Are you always pointing out the obvious, Julian Perez?"

I chuckled before scanning all the books on the table and spotting the stack of hers on display. She was too distracted reading to notice when I slipped the booth owner money for every single one of them.

"Can you do me the honor and sign these?"

Her eyes widened when she realized what was in my hands. "You're serious?" Her cheeks turned three shades darker than her natural pink as she grabbed the pen and signed every copy.

My heart swelled with pride the same way it did when we laid on her bed and she told me she wanted to be a writer for the first time.

"Why'd you buy all six?" she laughed under her breath.

I was tempted to selfishly keep them all for myself just because they had her signature, but I decided against it and put them back in their original spot. "Whoever wants a signed copy, tell them it's paid for, Lauren." Anyone who spent time at the bookstore knew the owner. I was a frequent face, so she and I became acquainted, despite the two weeks of awkward tension after she asked me out to dinner and I said no.

"Thanks, Julian." She swept her jet-black locks back and batted her long lashes. She never hid her attraction, and while I was flattered, I only ever had space in my heart for one girl, and she was standing next to me, completely oblivious. When I looked over at Mila, she'd gone from bright and bubbly to sour. "I'll see you around, Lauren," I said.

"You bet. Nice seeing you again, Camilla." She shouted as we turned to walk away. "You too, Laurel."

"It's Lauren."

"That's what I said." She forgot I knew what she looked like when she was jealous, but she changed the subject before I could question it. "Paying for all those books was really nice of you."

"It was nothing." I tried to do things like that all the time, but unfortunately, buying the house and renovating it cost most of the money I saved up while in the military, leaving me with hardly anything.

"Trust me, it wasn't. I've been around people who wouldn't give water to someone on fire. It's a nice reminder people still do nice things just because." She stared ahead at the other booths, but I only looked at her, wondering what kind of life she lived in New York to be around people like that. "Tell me about this boyfriend of yours, Mila."

Her mouth gaped. The less I knew about him, the better, for my own sanity, but I was curious if he knew just how lucky he was.

"He's, uh…a Carter, which is a big deal in New York. I met him my freshman year at NYU, but we didn't start dating until after we graduated. He's not like the other snobs on the Upper East Side, trust me. I think you'd like him." He had the girl I was in love with, so I couldn't like him that much.

"Why'd it take you so long to start dating?" Her face fell when the question slipped out. "I don't know. I guess I was waiting for it to feel like the right time." I never believed in "right person wrong time" until Mila and I became victims of it.

"What about you? Any girlfriends after me?" If she knew just how much she occupied my every thought, she'd know it was impossible for me to even look at another girl in our time apart. "It's still just you."

Her face twisted. "You're serious?" I found it funny how she didn't know she seeped herself into me to the point where I'd rather be alone for the rest of my life than live one without her.

Before I could open my mouth to speak, her face lit up as we passed familiar faces at a booth. "Is that Mrs. Asher?" The smell of citrus from the fresh produce filled my nostrils before we approached them. Everyone in town knew every fruit and vegetable Mr. and Mrs. Asher sold was hand-picked from the property they'd owned for over fifty years. They were known as everyone's grandma and grandpa. If you lived in Willow's Cove, you were family, even if you were a complete stranger. They let Mila and I pick oranges from their tree in high school, and they were better than any store-bought ones you could get.

Mrs. Asher rubbed her eyes in disbelief. "Is this who I think it is?"

"It's me, Mandy." She was suffocated by her tight hug, but didn't pull away. "It's good to see you, sweet girl. We've missed you here." I saw the shimmer in Mila's eyes as she squeezed Mrs. Asher tighter. The thing about this town was, every part of it embedded itself in your soul—the locals, the cove, the memories you made as a kid. You could talk down about how small it was, and you might even be able to leave, but I know from experience it was easy to remember how it would always be home. Whether she said it out loud or not, I saw glimmers of Mila that wanted to acknowledge it.

"How are your parents, dear?" I looked over and saw her face wash of color. "My mom moved to the city to be closer to me." We all waited for her to mention her dad, but instead, she changed the subject. "I saw your booth and had to get some fruit before I left town."

Mandy didn't think twice about the dodging of the question and pulled her salt-and-pepper hair back into a bun. "In that case, have a sample." She handed both of us a bright red strawberry, and my knees nearly buckled at how delicious it was when it coated my tongue. For being nearly eighty years old, both she and her husband still had magic hands when it came to growing fruit. I saw the red juice dripping from the corner of Mila's lips, tempting me to press mine against them and never stop. I couldn't resist sliding my finger against her warm skin to wipe it away.

She stayed frozen until my touch was gone. "Thank you."

"We'll take two baskets of strawberries, some blueberries, and might as well throw some oranges in there too." I winked at Mila, who found that amusing.

We bought more than we could carry, but hearing her laughter as we struggled to carry it all to the car was worth every penny. "I think you have enough fruit to last you all summer." "I'll just have to make us strawberry pancakes for breakfast tomorrow," I said before my attention was pulled away to a booth I'd missed on the way in. "Could you stay here, Mila? I'll be quick."

She spoke warily. "Sure."

The table was filled with jewelry, but I only had my eyes on one necklace. It wasn't made of real diamonds, and I was sure she had more extravagant jewelry back home, but I knew the sentimental value she'd see behind it. "How much?" I asked the booth owner, whose face was unfamiliar.

"Twenty-five." I gave him the last thirty dollars in my wallet and immediately took the chain out of the box.

"Who's that for?" She eyed it with suspicion.

"You. To replace your old one." My fingers trembled as I held the silver-studded *C* necklace out in front of her.

She tried to push my hand away. "Julian, I can't take that."

I held her wide-eyed gaze while I clasped it on. "Relax, Mila. It's not real diamonds. Think of it as something to remember me by when you leave." Just the thought of it made the air grow thick.

I cowered with embarrassment. "I'm sure you have real diamonds back home, but—"

"It's perfect. Thank you." Tears rimmed her eyes as she held the chain and melted into my arms. For the first time in six years, I felt true peace, and I didn't want to let her go. I memorized her sweet vanilla scent and the rhythm of our aligned heartbeats while inviting a familiar memory into my mind.

sixteen

JULIAN

7 YEARS EARLIER - AGE 17

I WATCHED from the ground as she carefully scaled her roof. It was a little after one in the morning, and her mom would have killed us if we were caught, but it was officially our one year anniversary, and I couldn't wait another second to see her.

As soon as her feet touched the ground, I backed her up against the tree and kissed her deep enough for her to lose her breath. "I missed you." It had only been a day since I'd seen her, but I genuinely missed her.

"You had me scale my roof to tell me that?" She chuckled between our kisses.

"Not exactly." I pulled away to show the box hidden in my pocket. "I figured you wanted your anniversary gift, but I guess I'll just go home." I walked off with a cocky smirk, but she pulled my arm back. "Hold it. Let me see it!" she squealed.

My breath staggered as I revealed a silver-studded *J* necklace. Everyone knew Mila always had a *C* necklace dangling from her neck since we were kids, and she was devastated when it broke. I decided to replace it, but selfishly, I wanted her to have my initial around her neck instead.

"Julian, it's beautiful." She gawked at the jewelry. "I can't take this. It must've cost you all your savings."

I looked down at my feet. "They're not real diamonds, Mila. I can save up to get you something better and—-"

She dragged her finger against my lips to get me to stop. "It's perfect. You're perfect."

Any doubts I had disappeared when she held it out in front of me. "Can you put it on for me?"

I kept her blue-eyed gaze as I clamped it around her neck. "One day, I'll buy you real diamonds, I promise." I bent down and kissed her collarbone to seal the promise I had every intention of keeping.

"You know I don't care about that stuff, right?"

I touched a strand of long brown hair that framed her delicate face. "I love you."

She got on her tiptoes and wrapped her arms around my neck. "I love you too." God, I never got tired of hearing those words. People said your first love was "puppy love"—short-lived and forgettable—but they didn't know Mila. She'd engraved her name on my heart, and I knew that, if by some unfortunate event, we parted ways, there would never be anyone else.

Her ocean eyes softened as if she'd made a decision I wasn't in on yet, but I didn't hesitate to follow when she grabbed my hand and pulled me towards the tree she used to climb down from her roof.

"What are we doing?" I whispered.

"You want to come up with me?" I couldn't do anything but nod; the knot in my throat made it impossible to speak. That was the first time she'd invited me up to her room, so I ran the risk of her mom chasing me out as I followed her up the thick branches and onto the rooftop. Thankfully, Mrs. Vega was a heavy sleeper, so our heavy footsteps didn't wake her when we passed her bedroom window.

I started to memorize every detail about her room when I climbed over the windowsill and my feet touched her floor—the smell of her sandalwood candle burning, the names of the CDs scattered across her desk, titles of books with worn-out spines that told me those were her favorites. Posters of her favorite artists plastered on her white walls, along with a board full of printed pictures of her and Taylor as kids. I almost felt left out until I picked up the framed picture of us on her desk from our date at the town fair. Seeing her room was like getting a peek at the last unknown piece of Camilla Vega, and I finally had all of her.

The last thing I noticed was behind the door, a pinboard labeled *dream board* with only three things listed:

1. Go to college in the city
2. Buy the house by the cove
3. Become a writer

I wasn't sure how, but she still found ways to amaze me. Her dreams weren't extravagant; all she wanted was a simple yet meaningful life, and I wanted to give her that.

When I finally met her eyes, she admired me with a dreamy glaze I'd never seen before. "What?" She didn't say another word before slowly stalking over and pulling me into her with an eagerness unfamiliar to both of us. Her hands explored until they found the edges of my shirt, but I stopped her when she tried to lift it about my head.

"Mila, are you sure? You said you wanted to wait." As eager as I was, the last thing I wanted was for her to wake up the next morning and regret her decision.

Her eyes fell to my lips. "I want it to be you, Julian." That's all I needed to hear to recapture her lips and match the urgency of her movements. Contrary to what people thought, I never slept with anyone before Mila, so while I seemed confident on the outside, my stomach was tied in knots the entire time. The way she took command and eased us onto her bed was a side of her I hadn't seen before. I wanted to see more; I just had to get my shit together.

I slid my ice-cold fingers along the length of her back, then moved to undo the buttons on her shirt, but they kept getting stuck. "Shit, sorry. This is a mood kill." She stifled her laughter so we wouldn't wake her mom next door and started leaving trails of kisses down my arms. "It's just me," she whispered.

I traced the lines of her perfect face, basking in how I got so lucky before letting everything but her disappear from my mind.

WHEN THE SUN greeted us through Mila's curtains, I had yet to get any sleep. How could I? I was too busy watching her, memorizing the tune of her heart, while imagining a life where I woke up every morning with her sleeping in the hollow of my neck. She had every part of me, and I didn't want it back.

The soft caress of my hand on her cheek woke her, and I was greeted with her blue eyes. "I thought you'd be gone."

"And miss seeing your early morning look? Yikes." I couldn't help but admire how the sun shone on her bare face, the way her messy brown hair fell across her pillows. Goddamn, she was beautiful. I was fucked. "Can I ask you something?"

She sank more into her mattress and nodded. "It's about number three on your dream board. You've never talked about how you wanted to be a writer."

There was a distant look on her face as she trailed her fingernails over my bare chest. "I've never told anyone, not even Taylor. It's just a silly dream. The chances of becoming a writer are discouragingly low." No matter what she said, no one put something on a dream board if they thought it was silly.

"The poem you wrote in English class begs to differ. You even had Damon paying attention, and he hates that class." If there was one person who could make their dream come true, it was her. She had the drive and passion people craved.

"You really think I could?" I saw her potential, even when she didn't. I cradled her face in my hand before answering with the whole truth. "I do, and I'll tell you every day until you think so too." She crushed her lips against mine before we disappeared under the sheets.

seventeen

CAMILLA

I DELETED all ten pages of the chapter I'd spent an hour writing before going into the kitchen to get a third refill on my coffee. My frustration started early that day when I woke up to an email from my agent, Lucy, with the deadline to submit the first few chapters of the new book. Three hours and many grunts of frustration later, I still had nothing to show for it.

Writing my first book came with ease, almost like it poured out of me, and suddenly, I'd stumbled on a brick wall that blocked any creativity. I started to wonder if maybe I only had one book in me. People back home gave Greyson most of the credit for my success, since he'd helped with the marketing, and what if they were right? What if I was just someone who got lucky and wasn't meant to be a writer after all?

I opened the window and let the sounds of birds squawking and the laughter of people down at the beach fill the room. With only a few more days until I had to leave, I wanted to take in all the peace and quiet before my days were filled with loud traffic and crowded sidewalks again. I thought I would have been homesick after almost a week away, but other than Greyson, I'd hardly given anything from the city a second thought. Was it possible to have a mid-life crisis at twenty-four? New York was once everything I wanted, but when I wasn't sure anymore, I didn't know where that left me.

My numbing thoughts were interrupted when Julian entered the kitchen, startled at the sight of me. "What are you doing?"

"Failing at getting any writing done. I made coffee." I gestured to the coffee pot I helped myself to earlier that morning.

"You're a lifesaver." I darted my eyes away from the grin he flashed while pouring himself a cup. "Do you plan on writing all day?"

"I probably should because of my deadline, but everything I'm writing is crap." I buried my head in my hands.

He sat in the stool next to me. "I highly doubt that, Mila." That was one thing that never changed about Julian—he always believed in my writing. "Maybe we can figure it out together. I'm all ears."

I was going stir-crazy, so I figured I might as well tell someone my doubts. "The story doesn't feel right. It feels like it's being written by someone else. I'm not sure I know what kind of writer I am anymore." I bit back tears of frustration as I picked at my nails.

"How did you feel while writing your first?"

"Not like this." My first book felt freeing to tell, almost like a journal told from someone else's point of view.

His gaze softened. "Maybe because with your first, there were no expectations. Dig deep and find a story you want to tell, and even if that takes some time, the book you put in front of your publisher will be so good, they won't even care about a deadline."

I chuckled at how oblivious he was about the industry, but he said it so confidently, it was almost convincing. "Everything is so simple for you, isn't it?"

His gentle eyes searched my face long enough for time to

stand still. "Not everything." Despite the window letting in fresh air, I felt suffocated by his closeness.

"What do you have planned for the day?"

I looked up to find a smirk threatening his lips. "How about you take a break and find out?" I shot him a look of confusion when he tossed a set of keys into my hand. "You drive."

The cold metal on my skin brought back memories of all the driving lessons he gave me in his Mustang. It was an unwritten rule he was the only one who could drive it, but he made an exception for me.

I glanced over at the mess of a manuscript on my computer, then back to the set of keys. I knew I had the deadline, but something screamed at me to get in that car with Julian, so that's what I did.

I WAS afraid I wouldn't remember how to drive a stick shift after so long, but as soon as I felt the familiar leather under my fingertips, it was like greeting an old friend, and everything rushed back.

I took for granted how freeing it felt to have an open road to myself, letting the wind blow my hair in every direction. "I haven't driven since I left town." I admitted.

Julian shot me a look of concern from the passenger seat. "That's comforting to hear while you're behind the wheel of my car."

I grinned. "You have full-coverage insurance, right?" "Since the day you almost plowed down that fence senior year." Our familiar laughter fluttered through the car. "I swear, it came out of nowhere." I still stood by the same excuse I used that day.

"I thought you'd be different when you came back, but you're still the same, Mila."

"Is that bad?" He shook his head and glowed with a smile that nearly distracted me from the road. "Not at all." In that moment, I was hit over the head with feelings I thought were dead.

I knew a part of me would always care about Julian. First loves were supposed to own a piece of your heart forever, but that was all they were—the first. I'd love Julian the same way I loved my first apartment in the city, or the first book I ever picked up, but our story was finished. *Wasn't it?*

"Are you gonna get that?" My attention pulled back in time to see my phone ringing in the middle console, Greyson's name across the screen. "Is that the boyfriend?" Julian asked with a tight jaw.

I stared at the call coming in and pondered whether to answer it. I wanted to hear his voice, but I didn't think he'd take it well that I was on a spontaneous errand with another guy, so I let it go unanswered, though not without a guilty conscience. "He's just getting off work and wanted to talk. I'll call him back." Even though we were navigating being just friends, I couldn't ignore the underlying feeling I was betraying Greyson by just being around Julian.

"What does he do?"

I looked at him with narrowed eyes. "You really want to talk about this?" Telling my old boyfriend about my new one wasn't an ideal conversation to have, but I knew he would've just kept on prying. "He works for his dad's advertising company. It won't be long until he becomes CEO."

He scoffed. "So he's a spoiled rich kid who works for his dad?" His dismissive tone made my face twist. "You don't know him. He worked hard to get where he is."

"With some advantages, of course." Greyson was the opposite of what people thought of him, and I made it a point for them to know how hardworking and dedicated he was.

"If you're gonna be an asshole when we talk about Greyson,

then we shouldn't talk at all." The car grew silent as my anger rose.

"Shit, I'm sorry, Mila. You're right. I shouldn't have said that." I wanted to stay angry, but it was hard when I sensed his regret. "New rule. You can ask about him, but don't be a dick about it."

I could see in his eyes—he was being sincere. "Deal." I had to start writing down the rules to remember them all.

"You can pull into the parking lot here." I hesitated to stop in front of the abandoned building. "Don't take this the wrong way, but I need you to tell me where we are before I go inside."

He chuckled. "I need help picking out furniture. It might look like a dump on the outside, but I promise, the stuff in there is way better than anything we'll find downtown; they'll just need a little care." It took seeing him talk about old furniture to remember how passionate he was, even about the little things.

"What are we still doing in the car then?" He grinned and led us inside, where furniture and art pieces you only came across on your luckiest day filled every inch of the store. It was more like a graveyard for impeccable pieces people either forgot about or threw away. Everything had a personality and a unique style you couldn't find anywhere else.

"What's the color scheme you're going for?" I stopped and appreciated the detail on each piece we passed.

"I was hoping you would choose." My boots squeaked against the laminate floor when I stopped abruptly. "Julian, it's one thing to choose the color of your house, but the entire interior design?"

"I have something to contribute that won't come until the end. Please, Mila? If I ask Sofia, she'll turn my house into a goddamn museum filled with expensive art I can't even breathe around." It was crazy, and even though I shouldn't have agreed, I still couldn't say no to him. "Fine, but you owe me dinner on your new table."

A smile lit up against his tan skin. "Anything you want."

As PROMISED, we ate dinner on Julian's new farm-style table I chose. We were so tired after spending three hours rearranging all the furniture, he made us grilled cheeses, but he could never do the bare minimum, so he added five types of cheese. It was the best I'd ever had.

"You should look into interior design. The place looks great." I looked around at the fully furnished living room and swelled with pride. We'd stumbled on this white velvet couch I couldn't leave behind, and by luck, we found the matching ottoman. I had to inhale a mountain of dust for a wooden coffee table, but it was worth how perfectly it balanced the modern farmhouse style. I always loved the concept but never could execute it in the penthouse back home, since Greyson's family had an interior designer who decorated all their houses.

"Is this how you pictured it on your dream board?"

My shoulders straightened. "You remember that?" He was the only one who'd ever seen that board. Funny enough, I did just about everything, yet I wasn't sure if seventeen-year-old me would be happy with how her life turned out six years later.

His lazy smile greeted me. "I thought we already established I remember everything, Mila."

I couldn't ignore the anguish that gnawed at me. "It's exactly how I pictured it." Sitting in the fully furnished house made it even harder to face that, while I was off chasing my new dream, my old one had slipped through my fingers.

I changed the subject. "Is the house how you pictured it'd be when you bought it?"

He hesitated to answer. "Yes and no."

I sensed I needed a refill of wine before I asked for clarification. "What do you mean?"

His face dropped as if he'd been hit. "Did you ever want to come back once you left, Mila?" I chugged my glass and refilled it again. I'd been trying to avoid that conversation all week, but he gave me no choice. "A couple of times, when the city got hectic and I wanted some peace and quiet."

"That's the only reason?" I nodded; I wasn't ready to let him in on the whole truth yet. A long pause grew between us as he ran his fingers over his facial hair, but when he finally spoke, it was in a fragile tone. "Sometimes, I would stupidly let myself imagine what life would have been like if you did come back."

I could have let the conversation die—I *should* have—but curiosity hammered at me. "What did you imagine?"

His expression grew so tight, I thought he wasn't going to answer. "Everything we promised each other." My shoulders sank when I remembered a glimpse of the memory he was referring to.

"We were teenagers, Julian, and promises are easy to make when you're that age." It seemed as if everything was easier then, though it didn't feel like it at the time.

"It doesn't make what we said any less real, at least for me. What about you?" There wasn't enough wine in the house that could unravel the ball of nerves in my stomach. Telling him the truth would've been betraying Greyson on some level, but not telling him felt like betraying a part of myself that once loved him with every piece of my heart. "It doesn't matter anymore." I felt a stab in my chest when he shriveled.

"I didn't tell you the truth when you asked what brought me back to town after I was done with the military." So many questions ran through my head: Did I want to know? Would it change anything? Would it make it harder to leave Willow's Cove once again?

As I opened my mouth to speak, my phone blared in my pocket, cutting through the thick air.

His voice turned cold. "You should answer that. Don't want

Greyson to get suspicious, do we?" I watched with a blank stare as he shot up and stormed to his room while my phone continued to echo with the call. I finally snapped out of it before another one of his check-ins went to voicemail. "Hey, Grey."

"Hey, I was worried about you. Are you okay?" A few minutes before, I would've said yes, but I was suddenly a confused wreck who had her face buried in her hands.

"I'm sorry. It's been a little hectic here with the wedding in a few days." The only chaos seemed to be in my head.

"I get it. As long as you're okay."

"I am, I promise." I listened to him vent about his day, but my mind kept wandering to Julian. There was a time I wished more than anything to know why everything played out the way it did all those years before. Maybe even get closure, but things were different. *I* was different. As much as past Camilla loved Julian, the present version of myself loved Greyson, and I had to keep that in the forefront of my mind before the lines I was afraid of blurring disappeared altogether.

eighteen

CAMILLA

7 YEARS EARLIER

I was in the middle of writing in my journal, just as I did every night before I went to bed, when the tapping on my window startled me. It was past midnight, and I knew my mom was already asleep in the next room, so my heart pounded against my chest as I approached the curtain and yanked it back to peek outside. "Julian! Holy shit, what are you doing?" I rushed to let him crawl through.

"A guy can't sneak through his girlfriend's window to see her?" I rested my hand over my heart to slow its rapid beating. "I thought you were a goddamn serial killer trying to break in."

He grabbed both sides of my face and kissed me. "You watch too many murder documentaries, Mila." He was probably right. That was the first time he'd snuck in on his own, but when his visits became more frequent, I always left my window unlocked —probably risking an actual serial killer coming through.

"So you drove ten minutes and scaled my roof in the middle of the night just because?" I sat on my bed and watched him snoop around like he always did.

"I had nothing else going on." He ran his finger along the scattered books on my desk and stopped at the one with *Cami* written on the front. I nearly tripped over my feet to shut it before he could see what was inside. "Wait, what was in there?"

"Uh, homework assignments I need to catch up on." It wasn't my best lie, but it was all that came to mind.

His brows scrunched together. "You're a shitty liar, Camilla Vega. You do your homework the same day it's assigned." Sometimes, I hated being so predictable.

"Okay, you got me. You still can't read what's in here." The thought of anyone reading my journal was too embarrassing to stomach.

"Why? Did you scribble my name on every page or something? Because I'm completely okay with that." I covered my mouth to quiet my laughter. "You wish."

He pried the green journal I'd had since I was thirteen out of my hands and held it with a firm grip. "Then what could be so bad that I can't see it?"

I chewed on my lip and contemplated whether to let him be the first person to see the part of me I hid away from everyone, even Mom. "I've been thinking about what you said about being a writer. I still think it's a silly dream, but I had this idea for a story and I started writing it. It's crap, though, so I don't want you to read it."

I knew once he gave me a boyish grin and his brown eyes lit up, I wasn't going to say no if he asked again. "Well, now I have to read it. What about the first couple of pages? I could be like your editor." Since I helped him with all his English homework, that idea was laughable, but he was the reason I started that first story, so the least I could do was let him read it. "Fine."

I went back to sit on my bed and waited anxiously. It didn't have a name, or a solid plot, and I wasn't even sure it was going to leave the pages of my journal, but I'd never forget seeing the smile grow on Julian's face when he finished reading.

"This is great, Mila, seriously. I think you should finish it and get it published."

I scoffed at the idea of actually be a published author. "Yeah, right. I don't think I'll make anything of it, but I'm glad someone sees the potential." No one ever saw me the way Julian Perez did, not even myself.

He wedged himself on the bed and held my face in his hands. "You wouldn't be doing the world any good if you let this sit in that journal, Mila, and who knows? Maybe one day, you'll write the story of us." He leaned in and kissed my forehead. "Maybe I will."

nineteen

JULIAN

"It doesn't matter anymore." Mila's words were the first thing I heard when I opened my eyes the next morning, and they echoed until my body went numb. I'd hoped it was just a bad dream, but of course, I wasn't so lucky. It wasn't what she said that was so hard to stomach; it was the vacancy in her ocean eyes that once held so much love for me. I didn't want to accept I'd lost her, but she had a flight back home right after the wedding, and despite what I thought, it was clear she wanted nothing to do with Willow's Cove, which included me.

I wanted to spend the entire day in bed, but I knew Sofia would come to drag me out if I even thought of missing her and Levi's co-ed bachelor and bachelorette parties later that day. The last place I wanted to be was a room full of people celebrating love and the happy-ever-after bullshit, but that weekend wasn't about my inability to get Mila out of my head; it was about my little sister, so I put my sourness away.

"Julian? Are you awake?" Mila's timid voice on the other side of the door pulled me out of my haziness.

When I swung it open and stood in the doorway, she looked

fine, but why wouldn't she? She wasn't the one who got her heart stomped on. "Hi," she greeted softly.

I avoided her eyes so she wouldn't see the restlessness in mine. "Morning." There wasn't anything *good* about that morning.

"Sofia insisted on taking me to find an outfit for the party later, but can we talk first?" My heart couldn't take any more hits, but her eyes pleaded, so I let her pass me to come into my room.

"What's up?" I folded my arms across my chest and finally met her eyes. Even after she'd shattered my heart, I relished in how beautiful she looked when she first woke up. It was pathetic how much of a grip she still had on me.

"I wanted to talk about what I said last night. I—"

"You don't have to say anything. You're right. After you go back to New York, it won't matter anymore what happened in the past."

She cowered her head. "I still shouldn't have said it. I'm sorry." I kept my face stern so she wouldn't see the pain clawing at my heart. They said grief comes in stages: denial, anger, bargaining, depression, and finally, acceptance, but there are no guidelines on how to grieve someone still alive. There she was, standing in front of me, but the girl who loved me with all her heart was gone. "Apology accepted, Mila." I forced a smile to ease her guilt.

Suddenly, a high-pitched voice echoed through my living room. "Cami! Time to shop." If I had a dollar for every moment my sister interrupted, I'd be able to retire at twenty-four.

I followed behind Mila towards the kitchen, where Sofia greeted us with a look of suspicion. "You guys both just came out of Julian's room? Shit, did I interrupt something?" If she was trying to be subtle about her excitement, she was horrible at it.

"No," we said in unison.

"I just had to talk to Julian about something before we left, but he was still in bed."

She was never good at hiding her facial expressions. "Whatever you say. I'll be raiding Julian's fridge while you get dressed."

As soon as Mila's door shut, Sofia wasted no time breaking the silence as she ate from the bowl of fresh strawberries we'd bought from Mrs. Asher. "Okay, spill."

"I don't know what you're talking about." I snatched away the berry in her hand and shoved it in my mouth.

"Oh, got it. You're still in denial. I thought you'd be over that by now and more onto trying to get her back." I was already having a bad enough morning without her smart remarks. "Don't you have other things to worry about? Like your wedding in two days? Get off my case."

She smiled and flipped me the middle finger. "Fine, but don't come complaining to me when you're moping around after she leaves."

I pushed away her hand that ruffled my hair. "Are you always going to be a pain in my ass, Sof?" I knew the answer before she spoke.

"Someone has to call you out when you're being an idiot, and who else but me?" She walked towards Mila's room but turned back. "By the way, don't forget to write your best man speech. I expect to cry until my mascara smears."

Suddenly, staying in my bed sounded like the plan I should've gone with.

I WAS FINISHING up painting the trim on the house when I heard a car pulling up the gravel driveway. I knew the girls would be out for hours shopping, so I was on high alert until I saw a familiar face get out of the car and walk towards me.

"Elijah Fisher?"

"Ouch, JP, has it really been that long?" The last time I saw him was our high school graduation, which happened to also be the last time anyone had called me by that nickname.

After getting a full ride to UC Davis on an academic scholarship, he never returned to town. At first, our check-ins were frequent, but as the years passed, they stopped altogether.

I wasn't much of a hugger, but I brought him in for a tight embrace, and suddenly, we were just little kids throwing around a football to each other again. "What are you doing here?" I led him up to the house.

"Your sister's wedding, of course. I almost didn't come, but she sort of threatened me." I laughed at how she'd always had the guys in town wrapped around her finger.

"Have you heard from Damon?"

I shook my head. Just like with Elijah, we checked in on each other often after high school, but eventually, the calls stopped. When I came back to Willow's Cove, I went by his childhood home where his mom still lived, and she told me he'd taken a job in upstate New York a few months prior. "No, but I imagine he got the same call from Sofia, so he'll be showing his face soon."

He gawked at the house. "I never even knew this was here." No one did except for Mila. "She needed a little TLC, but she's getting there."

He patted me on the back with a wide smile. "You're all grown up, JP. You served in the Air Force, and now look at you, a beautiful house with a nice view. Seems like everything worked out." It was funny how it seemed that way on the outside, but really, I was a fucking mess.

"Not exactly, Fisher."

He sighed and nudged inside the house. "You have beer in there?" If you could count on anything, it was that Elijah was always there when you needed him, and funny enough, he'd shown up the day when I felt like hope had been lost with Mila.

He helped himself to my fridge and cracked open a beer I only kept for company. "What's on your mind, Perez?" I couldn't talk to Sofia about Mila, and I definitely couldn't talk to Mila about Mila, so I had no choice but to sort through my reeling thoughts. "Camilla Vega."

He froze with his beer hovered over his mouth. "*The* Camilla Vega? The girl you enlisted in the military to get over?" I nodded.

"Time really stands still in this goddamn town. So, what about her has you looking like a lost puppy?" I replayed the days from the moment Camilla arrived in town, up until she stomped on my heart. "Pathetic, right? Here I am, twenty-four years old, still moping around for the same girl from high school."

He didn't hold a speck of judgment. "Camilla was never just any girl to you, JP, so of course seeing her again would have you spiraling. It could happen to anyone. When she goes back to New York, everything will go back to normal." The thing was, I didn't want to go back to normal, because that meant a life without Mila. A life where I walked around a house that reminded me of her, in a town where we'd made all our memories.

"I want her back, Fisher." It felt free to finally say the words out loud to someone other than myself.

"What's stopping you?"

"She has a boyfriend." He chuckled under his breath. "You always gotta do things the hard way, huh? I think the first thing to do is ask yourself if you're still in love with her."

"I love her more than anything," I said with no hesitation.

"Yeah, but are you *in* love with her? There's a difference. You can love someone for the rest of your life but not be in love with them." Mila was the reason I believed in love in the first place. Every good memory of mine had her in it, and her name would always be tattooed across my heart, no matter what happened when she left Willow's Cove. "I'll be in love with her for the rest of my life, whether she feels the same or not."

His brows shot up as he finished off his beer. "It's worse than I thought. If you really feel that way, then you have no choice but to fight for her, Perez. Maybe she'll see she belongs here instead of New York."

"I've tried that," All I focused on that entire week was showing her everything she'd been missing out on, but it didn't seem to work.

"Have you said the words *I want you to stay* out loud to her?" He took my silence as the answer. "I figured. You haven't tried hard enough then."

Another thing about Elijah—he was always right.

I IMAGINED a bachelor party a lot differently—beer, poker, and other guys. Instead, I had to watch my little sister dance with her fiancé at the local bar. Despite the urge to throw up, I'd also never seen her smile as much as she did that night. She was happy, and after everything we went through growing up, she deserved it.

"What's with the long face, Julian?" The bar owner, Vance, approached me and slid over another Jack and Coke. I hardly drank, but I made an exception that night to get my mind off Mila, who was making it difficult by demanding my attention even from the other side of the room.

"I'm just celebrating my life going to shit." I held my glass up to him before taking a sip. I was usually optimistic, but even after talking with Elijah, I couldn't seem to get a grip. "You're a kid, Perez. Your life will go to shit eventually, but not today." He was referred to as the drunk uncle by everyone in town—he was good for a laugh but horrible at giving advice.

"Thanks, Vance. You always know what to say." He lived up to his reputation when he was oblivious to my sarcasm.

"Another round of whatever he's having." Levi took a seat on the barstool next to me and laid a twenty-dollar bill on the counter.

Despite my opinion about the Willow family, I tried not to hold it against him, because my sister happened to be head over heels for him. We'd only spoken a couple of times, on account of my distrust in the founding family. It always rubbed me the wrong way how they seemed to care more about their reputations than the hard working people in town. I knew Sofia was a good judge of character, but I still kept a watchful eye to protect her; that was never going to go away.

"Thanks, but you don't have to do that."

"Consider it my payment to find out if your shitty mood has anything to do with the girl over there with my fiancée." I glanced back at the dance floor where Mila was laughing with Sofia and Taylor over the loud music. I couldn't help but notice how she looked in her element with them around.

I'd already had enough pouring of my heart out for one day, so I dodged the question by finishing off my drink. "I don't know what you're talking about."

He snickered. "Sofia told me you'd say that."

Curiosity clawed at me on what else my little sister blabbed about. "What else did she tell you?"

"That you're in love with Camilla but too stubborn to tell her. Those are her words, not mine." She never could keep a secret, so at least she was consistent.

"Well, as much as she doesn't like to hear it, she's wrong," I deflected. There was no way my so-called "love life" was up for discussion.

He sighed and waved Vance back over. "On second thought, another Jameson on the rocks. I'm gonna need it."

"Deny all you want, but we hardly know each other, and

even I can see how you look at her." I hated how easily I was baited into talking about Mila. "How do I look at her?"

A crooked smirk grew on his face. "How I looked at Sofia when I knew she was the one."

My face fell into a frown. "The difference between yours and Sofia's story is that you guys get the happy ending. Not all of us do." When I snuck a glance back at Mila again, her smile lighting up the entire room made my chest tighten.

"Maybe you're right, but if I were in your position and it was Sofia we were talking about, I'd do whatever it took not to lose her. It beats wishing you did something about it while you still could." God, he even sounded like Sofia. If anyone told me someone with the last name Willow would be the one to finally knock the sense back into me, I would've told them they were full of shit.

"You're alright for a Willow," I joked.

He shrugged as if he took the joke with a grain of salt. "We're not all assholes."

Suddenly, we were joined by a familiar face. "I was wondering when I'd see you somewhere other than the bookstore." Lauren's long black hair came into view when she sat in the stool on the other side of me.

"I have to get back before your sister gets alcohol poisoning." I'd never admit it to his face, but I was comfortable trusting him with Sofia, and considering how we grew up, that was rare.

"What brings you here on a Thursday night?" I asked.

"Same as you. I need to drown my sorrows. A shot of the usual, Vance. Thanks."

"What makes you think I have sorrows to drown?" I scooted away when she inched close enough for her intense perfume to flood my nose.

"The fact that you're here alone was dead giveaway number one, and the fact that you look like an injured puppy." If one more person commented on how sad I looked, I was going to lose it.

"You're not the first person to tell me that today. Actually, you're not even the second person to tell me that." When I couldn't hold back my laughter, guilt settled in my stomach. Laughing with someone who wasn't Mila felt wrong and unnatural.

"I hope this doesn't come off too forward, but can I ask why you never agreed to dinner?" She swallowed down her shot in one gulp. Lauren was smart, witty, beautiful, but she wasn't my Mila. Her smile didn't feel like sunshine, she didn't light up whenever she was by the ocean, and she didn't make my heart ram against my chest by just existing.

"If I'm being honest, I've been in love with the same girl since I was sixteen."

She slammed back another shot. "Damnit, I always go for the ones who aren't over their exes."

I figured it was okay to laugh when she did. "Sorry," I said.

"It's okay. Maybe one day, I'll be the girl some guy agonizes over at the bar." She was surprisingly nice to talk to when she wasn't hitting on me. "Out of curiosity, does the girl you're in love with happen to be the brunette on the dance floor who keeps staring at us?"

I subtly turned and was met with Mila's hardened blue eyes. Her dissatisfaction was obvious, which gave me an idea to use it to my advantage. I guess I still had some fight in me after all.

twenty

JULIAN

6 YEARS EARLIER - AGE 18

BY THE TIME I was five, my life had already been planned out for me. It was how every story went—when a dad can't live out his dreams, he passed them on to his son. My dad played for UCLA his freshman year of college on a football scholarship but had to quit his sophomore year, so naturally, it was engraved in my mind I'd follow in his footsteps from the moment I got a Bruin sweatshirt on my fifth birthday.

Not once did anyone ask me what I wanted, but it wasn't until I fell in love with Mila that I really knew. She made me want something different—something more—so, when she applied to colleges in New York, so did I. Since NYU didn't have a football program, I applied to a school not far from her.

I thought it was a long shot, until I sat frozen on my bed with Columbia's acceptance letter in one hand, UCLA's in the other. Two completely different paths, and I was going to disappoint my dad or myself with whatever one I chose.

"Julian, can I borrow your—" Sofia barged into my room and

halted when she saw what I was holding. "You got into Columbia?" She and I pulled an all-nighter to fill out the application months before, so she was just as anxious as I was to hear from them. She was also the only other person who knew the consequences if I chose the path I actually wanted to take.

Despite what I'd heard about following your high school sweetheart after you graduated being a recipe for disaster and it'd be wiser to go separate ways, I knew my way always included Mila. We were going to be the exception, so the choice was obvious. The only issue was breaking the news to my dad.

Sofia joined me at the foot of the bed. "I'd say congratulations, but your face says otherwise. I'm guessing you're spiraling over what to tell Dad."

I ran my fingers through my wavy locks to settle the nerves. "What would you do if you were me?" She was younger by a year, but a lot wiser. I'd deny it if she ever asked, but most of the time, I was the one who looked up to her.

"Isn't it obvious? I'd go with whatever was going to make me happier in the long run."

"You know it's not that simple, Sof." My voice was calm, but I felt the opposite. Sofia must've noticed, because she held my shaking hand while she spoke. "You shouldn't have to live in his shadow, J. You'll turn out just like him if you choose the path you know will make you miserable. Be different than him."

The thought of turning out even the slightest bit like my dad made my stomach churn. He was nothing but a rotten drunk who lived off the ego boost he got from his glory days twenty years prior. If everyone in town knew what he was really like, they would've never looked his way again.

"You don't think going to New York with Mila is crazy?"

She placed the acceptance letter back in my hand. "I think you'd be a dumbass if you let her slip through your fingers, so there's only one option."

Another realization hit me. "What about you?" I mumbled. No one talked about the guilt of being the oldest child. Part of you wanted to pack your things and move as far away as possible, but another part wanted to stay just so your sibling wouldn't have to face what you endured together all alone.

She smiled blandly. "Don't worry about me. I'll be out of here next year. You deserve to be happy, Julian, so go be happy." Leaving her behind filled me with dread, but if I didn't get out then, I was afraid I never would.

I kissed her on top of her head. "Thanks, Sof.""You want me to go down there with you to tell him?" The edge in her voice told me she wanted me to say no. It was something I had to do on my own anyway.

"No, but lock your door, okay? You know how unpredictable he is." There was no doubt he wasn't going to take it well, and I didn't want her to face his inevitable wrath because of me.

"Good luck." Her voice carried down the hall as I built up the courage to go downstairs, where my dad flipped through sports channels with a case of beer close to him. I stopped being afraid of my dad when I was fifteen, but it was a known fact he had a short fuse, and I knew the slightest mishap could set him off. I approached him with the acceptance letter glued to my hand. "Can we talk?"

He already looked annoyed by the fact I made him lower the TV. "I'm missing the basketball game, so make it quick." His hazel eyes had a glaze as he looked at me with disgust. Between us never having a close relationship and him seeing me as nothing but a pawn to live vicariously through, it was a relief to say the next words. "I'm not going to UCLA."

His anger flashed almost immediately, but since I was expecting it, I was unfazed. "What do you mean?" I knew he was giving me a chance to change my mind, but I was firm on my decision to leave and never come back, so I stood up straighter and spoke with defiance.

"I got accepted into Columbia. I'll still play football, just not on a scholarship. I'll figure out the rest as I go. My plan won't have anything to do with you, though."

My jaw ticked when his dark laughter filled the room. "It's because of that girl, isn't it? You're following her like a goddamn fool to New York?" His audacity to even mention Mila's name made me seethe with anger.

"By *that girl,* you mean my girlfriend of two years you've never bothered to meet?" I would have never let him breathe the same air as her, but in two years, he never asked about her once.

"What's your new plan then? You follow her to the city and then what? Get married and live happily ever after? I bought into that bullshit and look where that got me, Julian. I could've played professionally, but instead, my whole life is fucked. I thought I raised you to be better than this." He chugged down the rest of his beer and opened another can.

He never stopped reminding me I was the reason he never played in the pros. My mom got pregnant in the middle of their sophomore year at UCLA, and the load of parenthood made them both drop out not long after I was born. He blamed me so much that, after a while, I started to believe it was all my fault their life went to shit. I was done holding that burden.

"You didn't raise me at all, but I feel sorry for you, Dad. Deep down, you know after I leave, you'll have no one to live through, and you'll realize all you are is a piece of shit who punished his kids for his own failures."

He shot up from the couch and yanked the collar of my shirt so hard, I almost stumbled over. "Are you gonna hit me? Do it. It won't go as smoothly as it used to." He hadn't laid a hand on me since I was sixteen and finally stood up to him, but that never stopped him from trying.

"I won't watch you throw away your future," he gritted out. I stood emotionless in the face of his familiar rage. For as long as I could remember, all I wanted was for him to accept me for who I was and not who I could be. I wanted him to love me because I was his son and not Julian, a future pro football player. That day, I realized even if I did exactly what he wanted, it wouldn't matter. After killing myself trying to be the best at everything, he still hated me, but how could he like me when he didn't even like himself?

I shoved him hard enough for him to lose his grip. "It's a good thing you won't be there to watch then." I bolted out the door and sprinted for my car like my life depended on it. I figured, why delay the inevitable crash and burn of our relationship?

"Once you back out of that driveway, don't ever come back!" His words slurred as he shouted after me, but the only thing I paid attention to was Sofia looking down at us from her window on the second floor with a deep frown.

I'd come back for her too, but at eighteen, I was helpless. With tears threatening my eyes, I waved before I got in my car and raced in the direction of the only place I wanted to be.

DESPITE IT BEING BROAD DAYLIGHT, I still chose to scale Mila's roof and sneak through her window to avoid an awkward run-in with Mrs. Vega with puffy eyes.

I leaned on the glass and soaked in the sight of her on the bed reading. My dad thought my future wasn't bright, but if all it amounted to was getting far away from him and coming home at the end of the day to see Mila reading, I'd consider myself lucky.

My day did a complete one-eighty when she greeted me with her blue eyes and lifted up her window. "I have a front door, you know?"

I smiled at her sarcasm as I climbed through. "It's more fun to risk my life by scaling your roof."

"Why are you here in the middle of the day?" I heard her

breath hitch when she saw the evidence of tears on my face. "What happened?"

I held her fingers that gently traced my face. "Nothing I can't handle." Everything that just happened with my dad escaped my mind when I held her in my arms.

"I know you can, but whatever it is, you don't have to do it alone." As I looked down at her perfect, delicate face, I knew I was looking at my future, and I might as well start planning it.

I guided her to the bed and entwined our hands. "How do you see your future, Mila?"

She didn't hesitate. "Go to college in New York, hopefully become a writer and travel, then settle back in Willow's Cove. Why?"

I spoke with a shaky breath. "When you picture that life, am I there?"

Color crept into her cheeks as she blushed. "We haven't really talked about the future, but yeah, of course you are." I didn't think there was room to love her any more than I did until she said those words.

I left a soft kiss on her forehead. "I'm glad, because I applied to colleges in New York, and I got accepted into Columbia."

She went still. "What?"

"When I picture my future, it's you, Mila. Wherever you go, I go."

She stumbled around for the words. "What about football? Your scholarship? UCLA was your future, Julian. I can't let you throw it away for me."

Of course her immediate thought was what was best for me. "I'll play football at Columbia, and whatever grants don't cover, I'll pay off by working a job on campus. It's done, Mila. After we graduate, we can start living the kind of life you always gush about."

I caught the single tear that fell down her cheek with my thumb. "Are you sure?" she asked.

I had never been more sure of anything. I made my decision, and there was no doubt in my mind it was the right one.

I placed my hand over her heart—the same heart I'd memorized the natural rhythm of. "It's you and me."

"You and me," she repeated.

twenty-one

CAMILLA

IT WASN'T until Taylor nudged me on the shoulder that I noticed I was staring at Julian and Lauren laughing together at the bar. What could she be saying that was so funny?

"Lauren flirts with everyone in town, but she's innocent, don't worry," she said before sipping on her cocktail.

"What makes you think I'm worried? He can flirt with who he wants."

Her grin had mischief written all over it. "Did you forget we've known each other our entire lives? I know when something is bothering you, Cami." The first couple of days trying to earn back Taylor's friendship were bumpy, but we'd finally gotten to a place where it felt like the old us.

Still, I couldn't tell her why I was spiraling. I didn't want to admit seeing Julian and Lauren together brought up uncertainty I thought I was past. It took me four years to make peace with the fact that Julian had probably moved on after I left town. When I came back and found out he hadn't, I grieved for the version of myself that agonized over wanting to pick up the phone, and constantly went through scenarios of what could've been.

"The only thing bothering me is the lack of shots at our

table." I waved down the waitress taking orders. "Can you keep the tequila shots coming? Thank you."

I hardly drank. The most I'd ever had was a few glasses of wine and whatever was spiked in the punch at a school dance, but that night was an exception, and it wasn't only because we were there to celebrate.

"It's okay to still have feelings for him, you know? Your first love is the hardest to forget, or so I'm told."

Julian was the first person I gave my heart to. He taught me that love could be scary but also beautiful. Greyson loved me when I was afraid of letting anyone in, and he mended a heart he didn't break. My mind racked over which love was stronger.

"Julian and I are practically strangers. The person he knows doesn't exist anymore, Tay." I nearly choked on the last words.

"Strangers don't look at each other the way you guys do." I threw back another shot to drown her words out. The last thing I wanted when I came to Willow's Cove was to dig up the past, and it seemed as if it was happening all on its own. If I was going to endure the night, I had to make sure I didn't remember it in the morning.

BEING with Sofia and Taylor under the lights of the dance floor reminded me of senior prom when the three of us danced the night away before going off on our own paths. In a way, it was the same circumstance because in a matter of days, I'd go back to my life in New York, and they'd continue theirs in Willow's Cove; but for that moment, we were together.

When the waitress came back with another round of tequila shots, I shot it back despite the room beginning to slow. It was like I was possessed with the inability to stop. The more I looked over at Julian and Lauren, who had been sitting together for almost an hour, the worse I felt.

"You don't look so good, Cami. Let's go sit down," Sofia shouted over the blaring music as she and Taylor dragged me back to the table. "I'm fine."

"You can barely keep your eyes open. Don't move while we get you some water." They left me alone at the table as I fought not to look over at the bar while the room spun.

"Shit." I realized how overboard I'd gone, and if I didn't sober up, I'd have to be carried out of the bar. What the hell was wrong with me? I'd moved on with Greyson, who I was going back home to in a couple of days, so why did I care so much if Julian moved on too?

"Camilla Vega?" I looked over my shoulder to find where the deep voice came from, but I didn't recognize their face. "Do I know you?"

"Alex Young. We had math together freshman and sophomore year." I wasn't sure if it was my bad memory or the alcohol, but the name didn't ring a bell. "I would always ask to copy your tests."

It wasn't until he brushed his blonde, wavy hair back and flashed a charming smile that I faintly remembered he played the trumpet in the school's marching band. He'd asked me out a few times and I said no. "Now I remember. You asked to copy off my final and I said no."

His laughter carried over the loud voices around us. "Yeah, that's me. It's so funny running into you. Didn't you move to New York or something?"

"I still live there. I'm just visiting for a wedding." I tried to keep a straight face when I felt bile travel up my throat.

"The Willow wedding, right? Don't you know Sofia from when you dated her brother?"

I groaned. Even talking to a stranger couldn't distract me from Julian. "Yeah, but that was a long time ago."

His lips tipped up into a crooked smirk. "I had the biggest crush on you back in high school, but Julian got to you first." I faked a smile and looked around for anyone who could pull me out of the conversation. *Where the hell were Sofia and Taylor?*

"Do you wanna dance?" He grabbed my wrist and tried to pull me out of my chair before I could answer.

"I'm okay. I'm just waiting for my friends to come back." I tried to stay alert while the room faded in and out, but my body started to go limp.

"Come on, just one dance."

"REALLY, I'M OKAY." Trying to free myself from his iron grip made me remember his unsettling persistence in high school. Some people didn't change.

"Do we have a problem?" I took a breath of relief when Taylor's voice came from behind me and she stood in the middle of me and Alex.

"Not at all, I was just asking her to dance." He said.

"You were gonna take her to dance when she can't even stand on her own?" Sofia's voice was curt when she chimed in. I chugged down the water they put on the table, but I could still feel the alcohol taking over, making my vision blur.

"How about you two just go back to whatever you were doing?"

"How about you fuck off? That sounds like a better idea." Taylor yanked his grip away from my wrist, while Sofia stood in front of me as a shield.

"Is everything okay over here?" I could hardly see at that point, but I immediately knew the voice was Julian from his warm touch on my back. "Great, I'm assuming you're here to save the day? This doesn't concern you, Julian." Alex tried to meet his gaze with a challenge, but Julian towered over him, making him look intimidating.

"It does now."

I knew I was seconds away from fainting when everything

around me started to sound muffled, but I managed to get out one word. "Julian." My feet were no longer on the ground when he swooped me into his arms and effortlessly carried me towards the exit.

"Don't worry, we got it from here." I heard another voice I assumed was Levi.

"I got you, Mila. Let's go home." His woodsy scent wrapped around me as I sank more into his arms.

"Home," I whispered before everything went black.

It FELT like I'd only been asleep for a few minutes before I startled awake as Julian lowered me into bed. The graze of his hand on my arm when he draped a blanket made my skin ignite, but it was quickly overshadowed by the wave of nausea that rushed through me. "I'm never drinking again," I mumbled.

The room was dark, but the moonlight coming in from the window illuminated his tender smile."You never could hold your alcohol, Mila." He held a strand of my hair in between his fingers before he caressed my cheek. "Shit, sorry. I keep breaking the rules."

I sighed. "You're not the only one." Even as my head rested on the pillow, the room spun violently. "I'm sorry for ruining your night with Lauren."

He shook his head but kept the smile on his face. "You didn't. We're just friends."

"You looked like a little more than friends at the bar." I blamed my boldness on the alcohol still in my system.

He moved to the spot next to me and laid on his side to burn his brown eyes into mine. He looked at me the same way he did when we were just two kids blindly in love. "Why do you care so much?"

"I don't," I said defensively. My heart jolted when he inched so close, I could feel his natural heat radiating off him. "If I'm being honest, we were talking about you."

I was spooked with curiosity. "What about me?"

He gulped. "Do you ever think about what your life would be like if we worked out, Mila?"

I'd always felt like our story was unfinished, but after four years, I faced reality he wasn't coming to find me. "I try not to. If we had, there wouldn't have been Greyson."

I memorized Julian's features, wondering if I had truly let him go, or if I just pushed him deep into the depths of my mind, where I couldn't acknowledge the invisible string that pulled me to him.

A frown set into his face as he traced the outlines of my cheek. "If I did the right thing when it came to you, we'd have that life we talked about." My breath hitched.

When he said things like that, it was easy to fall under an illusion, but reality was, in a matter of days, I was going back to New York to live the life he gave me no choice to build without him. So many questions sat on my tongue, but my eyes felt heavy as I fought exhaustion.

"Get some sleep, Mila. We'll talk more tomorrow." He draped another blanket over me before trying to slip out of my room.

"Can you stay with me?"

He settled in to the pillow next to me. "For as long as you want me to." His faint whisper was the last thing I heard before my eyes slowly shut.

twenty-two

CAMILLA

6 YEARS EARLIER

WITH ALL THE seniors graduating in a matter of weeks, the air on prom night felt different—electric. Everyone smiled as they danced into the late hours of the night, even me. Taylor's date bailed at the last minute, so she tagged along with me and Julian, but I didn't see much of her after Julian's best friend, Elijah, pulled her away. Even Sofia found us on the dance floor at some point—it was no surprise she was one of the only juniors to be asked by a senior.

That night was the first time I looked around and appreciated the simplicity of high school. In that moment, we were all just teenagers living in a bubble. While you were in it, all you wanted was to get out, until you look back and realize how easy it was when your only concerns were passing the SAT and filling out college applications.

I must've looked over at Julian at least a dozen times and wondered what we'd be like together in the real world. Everyone said never take your high school sweetheart with you to college, but while living in New York sounded grand, the idea of being there without Julian made it sound the opposite. I wanted the breakfast-in-bed dates, study sessions at the kitchen table we picked out together, watching him cook in our kitchen since I burned everything I touched. I wanted a love story opposite of what I watched growing up, and I couldn't wait to start writing it.

"Do you want to go somewhere?" Julian whispered in my ear as we swayed on the crowded dance floor. Prom was coming close to an end, but we fit in one last slow dance—no need for any trickery or bets that night.

"Where?"

A smile greeted his lips. "Do you even have to ask?"

I HAD to tread lightly so I wouldn't trip over my dress that dragged behind on the wet grass. The air was typically hot in late May, but as we overlooked the ocean from the top of the hill, its cold breeze sent shivers down my arms. I tried not to make it obvious, since I'd left my jacket in the car and told Julian I wouldn't need it, but it was a bad time to have a strapless dress on.

His eyes darted to the goosebumps on my arms. "Are you cold?"

I shook my head. "Nope." I would've rather froze than admit I was wrong.

"You're so stubborn, Vega." Thankfully, he ignored my defiance and draped his tux jacket over my shoulders, engulfing me with his scent of amber and spice.

I held back a smile as he entwined our hands to walk over and stand in front of the abandoned house, like we had so many times before. Nothing about the house changed over time, especially my vision for it, but I still never tired of looking at it, picturing my future.

"You've never been inside?" he asked.

"Never." I was always tempted, but a small part of me wanted my first time walking inside to be when I bought it some-day. "I think it's time we rectify that."

I pulled him back. "Shouldn't we wait? What if it's bad luck to see it before?"

Laughter vibrated in his chest. "It's gonna be yours one day anyway, Mila. Might as well get a good look at the work it needs."

My heart pounded against my chest as he led us up the porch steps, where I made a note that the first step of remodeling had to be patching up the huge hole in the rotted wood floor. The old door wouldn't budge, but with enough force, Julian was able to push it open and reveal the inside no one had occupied for years. The walls were completely stripped of paint, the laminate floors ripped out, all the furniture left behind was covered in layers of dirt, but when the moon lit up the room, all I saw was everything it could be. I'd built it up in my head for years, but somehow, it exceeded everything I imagined.

Julian and I walked carefully across the floors that creaked with every step we took. The only indication a kitchen was near the living room was the rusted stove ripped from the wall, but I smiled when I noticed the island barely standing. It was always my dream to have a marble island to host parties.

"Watch your step," Julian warned before we walked down the dark hallway to check out the vacant rooms next. My favorite was the biggest room because it overlooked the cove perfectly from the window. How could you have a bad day when all your mornings started with a view so beautiful?

"What will you do to this place when it's yours, Mila?" I smiled.

"It'd be easier to give you a visual." I pulled him to the first room we entered and moved around to different sections. "For starters, this house calls for new floors. We'll paint the walls off-white but with a design I haven't chosen yet. The couches would go here, next to our coffee table." I moved to the farthest wall next to the window. "We'll also knock some of this wall out to build a fireplace for the cold winters. That's just the living room. Don't get me started on the kitchen or the bedrooms."

He stood still and watched me with a soft smile trembling over his full lips. "What?" I asked.

"It's just…while you were talking about it, you said we. It's just nice you see me living here too." His voice caught in his throat.

We'd spent all our time talking about life after high school, but we hadn't talked about what it would look like after college. "I know you said you never wanted to settle in Willow's Cove." My dream always was to leave town for college and see the world, then come back when I was ready to settle down perma-nently. Julian saw leaving town as an escape from a prison sentence. At the time, I didn't understand why.

"What if I said I changed my mind?" The room went silent enough for him to hear the sharp intake of my breath. "What do you mean?"

The anticipation of him slowly walking over killed me. He held my gaze as he caressed my face. "It's you and me, remem-ber? I go wherever you go."

I gulped down as tears threatened my eyes. "You promise?"

"After you become a famous author and you're ready to come back, I'll rebuild this house exactly how you want. I promise."

"What about traveling? You said you wanted that." He wanted to make sure I got everything I dreamed of, and I wanted the same for him.

"We'll do it together. All I want now is to be part of the life you want, Mila."

A hot tear rolled down my cheek and ruined the makeup my mom had spent hours doing. "You are." He pulled me in and pressed my lips to his, as if sealing the promises we just made to.

The thing about promises was, they were easy to make when you didn't know what was ahead.

twenty-three

JULIAN

I MUST'VE lain awake for hours after Mila fell asleep, just watching her calm breathing I waited six years to hear again. I replayed our conversation before she passed out and agonized over everything I didn't say—like how she belonged in Willow's Cove with me instead of in New York, or I was stupid for letting her go all those years ago, that I've mourned the life we could've had every day since.

While she stayed sleeping, I slipped out of her room to start a pot of coffee I knew she'd need to cure her inevitable hangover. I started writing out my itinerary for the day and grunted at Sofia's handwritten note plastered on my fridge.

> ### WEDDING REHEARSAL @ 7. DON'T YOU DARE BE LATE.

In any other circumstance, I would've been happy my little sister was getting married in a day, but it meant Mila was closer to leaving, and there was still so much I hadn't said.

I smiled to myself when I heard footsteps dragging slowly

down the hallway to the kitchen. "Good morning, Sunshine." I prepared her coffee the way I memorized it and slid her mug across the counter. "I figured you'd need this."

She sighed with contentment. "Oh my God, thank you. I feel like shit."

"Do you remember last night?" I asked.

Her brows rose as she took a sip from her mug. "Honestly, everything is a little blurry after I passed out at the bar. How bad was it?"

I was sort of relieved she didn't remember rejecting me. "You woke up looking for a trash can and asked me to stay with you for the night."

I chuckled when her face blanched. "So you slept…" She stopped mid-sentence as if she didn't dare to finish.

"Right next to you."

She groaned and buried her face in her hands. "I'm sorry. It won't happen again, I swear. I'm not touching a drop of alcohol the rest of the time I'm here."

"I didn't mind." It was on the tip of my tongue to tell her if she asked me to stay with her again, I wouldn't hesitate. Her eyes went wide when she saw Sofia's note on the fridge. "Shit, I forgot about the rehearsal."

"That's not the worst of it. Sofia will barge through the door any minute to drag us to help set up." I knew my sister, so I knew she'd milk the excuse of being the bride to get me to do her dirty work as much as she could.

"I can't believe she's getting married tomorrow. It seems like yesterday we were all just hanging out at the cove together."

"Tell me about it. She was just a kid who had just finished high school when I left for the Air Force, and when I came back, she was dating the mayor's son. It's still hard to wrap my head around." It was just like Sofia to do the most unpredictable thing while I was away.

"I've never been a part of a wedding party before. I'm kind of nervous," she said.

"You just have to stand there and look beautiful, which won't be hard." I knew I couldn't say things like that, but it was like word vomit.

Speaking of the devil, Sofia barged in with a wide split grin. "I'm getting married tomorrow!" I tried to push her off when she rushed up and hugged me tightly. "Can you believe it, Julian?"

"I can't believe he's still going through with it after your bridezilla phase these past few months." There was no doubt Levi loved her after seeing her spiral over the smallest details during their wedding planning.

When she tried to shove my shoulder, it only made her angrier when I didn't budge. "Screw you. I just like things done a certain way. You would too if you were getting married." Suddenly, I was back in turmoil, and Mila seemed to have the same reaction when my eyes darted over to her. One thing I knew for sure was, I had to pull it the hell together if I was going to survive the day.

"Where is the infamous Levi?" I would never tell her I didn't hate talking with him at the bar. Underneath his wealth and family scandals, he seemed...normal.

"Waiting at the venue. Breakfast is on us for anyone willing to help set up before the florists get there, so chop-chop." She pulled her luxury sunglasses over her eyes.

"If I make my own breakfast here, can I opt out of going?" Even through her dark lenses, I saw her eyes narrow with anger. "No. You have five minutes to get dressed and be in my car before I pull you out myself." She turned and walked out.

"See what I mean? Bridezilla," I said. Somehow, she'd gotten even scarier under the pressure of a wedding.

Mila laughed under her breath. "You ready?"

"Absolutely not."

I EXPECTED nothing less from a wedding thrown by the founding family than to have it in the town's most renowned building. The white carpet that led a path inside was lined with flowers, and every tree was wrapped with lights, but inside, it seemed as if it were a royal wedding. Crystal chandeliers hung from the high ceilings, creating the illusion we'd stepped into a cathedral church, and there were flowers in every corner that made my nose scrunch.

The staff of people setting up chairs nearly knocked me over as they filled the room to the point where there was hardly anywhere to stand. "Did they invite the whole goddamn town?" I whispered to myself.

"Just about." The voice came from Levi, who had been standing next to me longer than I'd noticed. "Let me guess: my sister?" I watched people dressed in uniforms roam chaotically around the room.

"Actually, Sofia and I wanted something more intimate, but unfortunately, when you're a Willow, you have to keep up appearances." His grim expression changed the instant an elderly woman walked up and greeted him as if he were a celebrity.

"I should've asked this a long time ago, but how does my sister fit into all of this once she marries you?" I knew Sofia could handle herself, but it was second nature to look after her.

He adjusted his tie before he spoke. "She knew before we got engaged my family expects a certain image. The whole damn town does." He forced a smile as people walked by. I could barely handle being put under a microscope by my dad when I was younger, I couldn't imagine having a whole town of people watching my every move.

"That's a lot of pressure to put on people," I said.

He scoffed with no trace of humor. "You have no idea." I'd

be honest—I'd spent most of their engagement judging him for his last name and over analyzing anything he did. I never made an effort to actually get to know the guy Sofia was marrying.

"By the way, as Sofia's big brother, I'm obligated to threaten you not to break her heart, but I kind of like you, so I'll just ask you nicely."

He erupted into laughter. "I appreciate that. She was the first person who made me feel normal despite who my family was, so I promise I'll take care of her."

Sofia and I used to always say it was us against the world. I protected her and she protected me for our entire lives, so while it was hard to let go and let someone else take over, it was then I knew she was in good hands. "I'll hold you to that."

"Julian! Levi!" I flinched when a high-pitched voice echoed from across the room. "What are you guys doing just standing here? We're rehearsing our walks down the aisle."

"I was giving him relationship advice. Don't worry, Sof, he's good to go." I placed a quick peck on her forehead, but she wasn't amused.

"Please, you're the last person who should be giving advice. You couldn't even ask Cami to be your date to the wedding. A dance partner, Julian? Really?"

I shrugged. "She was put off by the idea of it being a date, so I pivoted."

"I love you, but you're an idiot." She pulled both me and Levi to the group already waiting by the altar still being built. I tried not to look at Mila, but she was like a magnet pulling my attention to her.

"Okay, since we're all here, Taylor and Elijah will walk together first, then Jasmine and Trevor, Chloe and Josh, and finally, Cami and Julian." Our eyes shot up at the same time with a hint of panic.

"I thought I was walking with Taylor?" I tried to mask the shakiness in my voice.

Sofia's smile wasn't friendly in the slightest. "I changed it. Do you want to ask any more questions less than twenty-four hours before my wedding?"

I shuddered from her shrill voice. "Nope."

"Good choice."

I was trembling when I joined Mila behind the other pairs. I always imagined the first time I walked down an aisle with her would be under different circumstances, like her in a white dress, me in a tux, and after we'd just said our vows. Staring at the altar was just another reminder of how much I'd fucked everything up. "Are you okay? Your hands are shaking," she whispered.

I couldn't speak once the music started up, and each couple walked down together one by one. When it was finally our turn, she gripped my hand. "Usually, it's the groom who gets cold feet, Perez."

Only shallow breaths escaped me as we walked further down, with everyone at the altar staring at us with watchful eyes. "I'm just nervous about all of the eyes that'll be on us," I lied.

"It's just a quick walk to the end, then everyone will be looking at Sofia. We'll do it together." When I looked over at her, her beautiful blue eyes had a familiar sparkle in them. She was my Mila, who could make everything else disappear.

AFTER FOUR RUN-THROUGHS of walking down the aisle, practicing Sofia and Levi's vow exchanges, speeches, and finally, the rehearsal dinner, I was exhausted. I was ready to sleep until we had to come back and do it all again, but I still had a speech to write.

I was just as anxious to leave as everyone else trickling out, but unfortunately, Sofia was our ride, and she was taking forever to finish up with her wedding coordinator.

"I have an idea that might change the mood you've been in all day." Mila sank into the chair next to me.

"I haven't been in a mood." I tried to sound convincing, but I could never fool her.

"You remember I dated you for two years? I know when something is bothering you." She managed to pull me up. "Come on, let's go."

"Sofia was our ride, remember?"

"Levi's waiting for her while we take her car for a little spin." The exhaustion I felt just minutes before was the furthest on my mind as I followed her without a second thought. I was surprised Sofia had let Mila get her hands on the keys to her brand-new Ford Bronco. Then again, I let her drive my Mustang, which was my most prized possession, so I guess I wasn't the only one who could never tell her no.

We peeled out of the parking lot and drove down the dark, open road in the opposite direction of my house. "Where are we going?" I asked over the wind whistling outside.

My heart skipped a beat when she looked over with a wide smile. The thought of having nothing but the memory of it for the next years of my life made me uneasy. "You'll see."

When I looked out the window again, woods surrounding us became familiar, and I knew exactly where we were headed. It had been six years since I'd gone to my spot; I couldn't bear the memories of all the times I'd been there with Mila. "You remembered," I said.

"Of course. It's the second best view in town," she teased, the way she used to when we'd debate on whose view was better. When she brought the car to a stop, I climbed out first and rushed to her side to guide her out. "What are we doing here?" "You always said The Bluffs were the place that got you out of your head. It looked like you needed it." I didn't know whether to be glad or curse that she still could read me so well. We walked through the same tall grass we did years ago, which led to The Bluffs, and I basked in her closeness as she stayed glued to me like Velcro. "I still hate this walk. It's eerie as hell." I chuckled under my breath as we found our way through the woods lit only by the moon.

All I could do was stand in frozen awe when we finally reached the view that was my escape as a kid. The green acres still spread for miles and surrounded the beautiful lake I'd always admired. The only thing that had changed was the number of lights coming from the houses in the town over; it seemed to have doubled over the years.

Mila brought me there to cheer me up, but all it did was remind me of the first time I ever took her there, and how hooked I was the second I saw a glimpse of the girl she was scared to show everyone else at Willow High. I sat on the ledge so only my legs hung over, and I took a sharp breath when she joined me. Her warmth traveled into every crevice of my body. "Can I tell you something, Mila?"

"Shoot."

"You were right. I pulled some strings with my coach for that A on our presentation." I tucked my lips to contain the laughter on the verge of erupting.

"I knew it!" Her laughter echoed into the open space ahead of us.

"I saw my one shot and took it." I wasn't even a little sorry.

She nudged me as a soft smile pulling at her lips. "For what it's worth, I'm glad you did." Silence fell between us as we admired the view, until she spoke again. "You know you can talk to me about what's bothering you, right?"

I soaked in her perfect face. "I know." I was tempted to spill out everything I'd kept hidden and hope for the best outcome, but the night before only proved she was in love with someone else. I couldn't ignore the voice in the back of mind saying, maybe it overpowered the love she once felt for me.

"I came here after you left."

A soft gasp escaped her before she swallowed hard. "I've tried to forget that day, if I'm being honest."

"You're lucky. I can't seem to forget it." No matter how many times I replayed that day in my head and wished for a different outcome, it ended the same, like reading the same book and hoping for a different ending.

"I wanted to be mad at you, but after a few years, I understood. We were just kids who were hit with the reality of the real world too fast. Maybe it's as simple as us not being meant to be."

She didn't see the moment I flinched. "Do you really believe that?"

She folded her hands in her lap. "I mean, I kind of have to, right? I never would have fallen in love with Greyson if things didn't play out the way they did."

I kept a straight face while my heart shattered into a million pieces. "Maybe you're right."

"I loved you, though, Julian. I didn't want to say it before, but I am now." *Loved.* Past tense.

First loves were supposed to be beautiful, but no one warned me how shitty it would feel the moment it died.

twenty-four

JULIAN

6 YEARS EARLIER

As our principal, Mr. M said in his closing speech, high school graduation was the first day all our lives truly started. The unknown of the real world filled me with a sense of excitement, especially after spending my entire life in a small town, surrounded by the same faces.

When they finally called my name to cross the stage, I ignored everyone else and focused only on Mila in the second-to-last row, smiling proudly. With her help, I graduated with a higher GPA than my dad and grandpa combined, but for the first time in my life, I did something without them in mind and only thought of myself.

"Congratulations, class of 2018," Mr. M said into the microphone before my classmates and I erupted in cheers for the last time and threw our caps in the air.

Elijah found me almost immediately through the crowd. He planned to stay in California, a few hours from Willow's Cove while he attended UC Davis. His dad wasn't too happy he wouldn't play football while majoring in communications, but in true Elijah Fisher fashion, he didn't care.

"I heard New York isn't everything people make it out to be, Perez," he joked.

I laughed under my breath. "I'm gonna miss you too, Fisher," I didn't know when we'd see each other again, or where we'd be in our new lives when we did, but I was confident it wasn't the last time.

He brought me into a tight embrace. "Take care of yourself, JP. I want to hear about all the exciting shit you and Camilla have done the next time I see you."

We were suddenly joined by Damon, who wrapped his arms around us both. "You're having a group hug and forgot me?" "How could we? I heard your smart ass remarks from across the field," Elijah said, before dismissing himself to take pictures with his family, leaving me and Damon alone. He had his moments, but senior year was when he tried to be better, making him easier to be around.

"You're really going to New York?" he asked.

I nodded. "Yeah, we leave in a few days to get settled in our new apartment." We were both silent, because we knew after seeing each other everyday for eighteen years, it was about to change, but you don't say goodbye to the kid who's seen you through every phase of your life; it's always see you later.

"I'm happy for you and Camilla, really. I know I was an asshole, but I'm taking my year off to go find out who I want to be outside of high school." He was the only senior who didn't apply to any colleges, but knowing Damon, not having a plan, was the plan.

I hugged him so tight, I was nearly out of breath. "You know I'm here whenever you need me, D. We're brothers."

He hid his red, swollen eyes when we broke apart. It was the first time I ever saw him cry. "Thanks for being my best friend, even when I didn't deserve it." As he walked away, all I pictured was the kid I met in kindergarten, who wore a matching superhero shirt with me.

I felt a tap on my shoulder. "Can I hug my brother now?" I turned to see Sofia in a flowy purple dress.

"I guess so," I said as I picked her up off her feet and squeezed her tightly. We hadn't seen much of each other since I'd stormed out of my house, alternating between crashing on Elijah's couch and Mila's bed, but there wasn't a day she didn't call to check on me. I wasn't surprised she was alone, since I knew my parents couldn't give two shits about their oldest kid graduating high school.

"I'm proud of you, J," she said as I placed my graduation cap on her head. She cowered with disappointment. "I'm sorry it's just me who showed up."

"I'm not. I only wanted you here anyway." I shrugged.

"You're finally being nice to me right before you leave for New York?" She was the reason I felt a hint of dread to leave town. I'd miss her sarcasm, her witty jokes, and most of all, her sunny disposition that always reminded me everything we faced at home would pass.

"Speaking of, can you sneak me through the window later so I can pack my stuff?"

She beamed a smile up at me. "Only if you let me visit you during New York Fashion Week."

I playfully rolled my eyes. "Deal." What she didn't know was I planned to have her visit as much as she could so I could keep an eye on her. Even thousands of miles wouldn't stop me from being her big brother.

When her eyes darted behind me, I knew Mila was there. "I'll let you guys have a moment. I'll see you back at the house."

I didn't have time to prepare before Mila leaped into my arms and kissed me. "Hey, graduate," she said against my smile.

"Hey back. You look beautiful." I brushed away her wavy hair to get a look into her blue eyes.

"You sure you can't come to dinner with us?" As much as I wanted to join her family, and finally get to know her dad, we were moving states in a matter of days, and I had nothing packed.

"We'll have plenty of time together in New York, but I have to go pack. Go have fun with your parents, and I'll call you later."

My heart swelled when she ran her fingers through my hair with a warm smile. "I love you."

"I love you more." Holding her in my arms made me even more eager to pack up my old life for the new one we were starting together.

THANKFULLY, Sofia remembered to leave her window unlocked for me to sneak in after dark. I didn't know how my dad would react if he saw me, and I didn't want to find out. The house was quiet, so I was sure he was passed out drunk somewhere, but I still felt the familiar dread I always did stepping foot inside.

I found Sofia in front of the mirror applying makeup, which I thought was odd, but I assumed she was getting ready to leave with her friends.

"You want to help me pack so I can get the hell out of here?" I asked.

"Yeah, sure," she said with her face hidden behind her hair. "Why are you hiding your face?"

"I'm not. Let's go pack your things." I stood in front of her door so she wouldn't be able to leave. After years of living in that house, I knew it wasn't nothing. I felt anger radiate through every crevice of my bones when I moved the hair from her face, and saw the red mark on her cheek she was unsuccessful at covering with makeup.

"What happened?" I already knew, but I had to hear it from her.

She pushed my hand away. "Me and Dad got into an argument when I gave him shit about not going to your graduation. It's my fault for making him upset. I didn't want to tell you because I knew what you'd do."

My hands curled into fists at my sides, and I saw nothing but red as I stormed downstairs where I knew he'd be, ignoring Sofia's pleas to stop as she followed behind on my heels. It was too late to turn back—he made the mistake of doing the one thing I told him not to. I'd taken a few hits from him and never told anyone as long as he never laid a hand on Sofia. The moment he hurt her, all bets were off.

"You know what'll happen if you confront him; it's not worth it," Sofia said with panic in her voice.

"When is it gonna be enough, Sof? He's treated us like shit our entire lives and has gotten away with it because we always say he's not worth the trouble. I'm done."

Just as I suspected, he was passed out on the couch, a case of beer curled up next to him, my mom passed out with a lit cigarette in her hand. I kicked the couch so hard, they both startled awake. "Julian? What the hell are you doing here?" my dad shouted.

"The better question is, what the hell is on Sofia's face?"

He stood up and looked me directly in the eyes with a sinister smirk. It was embarrassing to admit I once looked up to him, but it just showed how little I actually knew him. "You're leaving, so it doesn't concern you. She's my business now." There was a voice in my head telling me he was punishing Sofia for my choice to go to New York.

The smell of whiskey flooded my nose the longer I stood in front of him. "I told you what would happen if you ever hurt her." All he cared about was his reputation in town, and I was sure once people found out how he treated us, his worst nightmare of being forgotten would come true.

"You won't do shit." I only had one intrusive thought enter my mind: *fuck it*. I swung my arm back and hit his face with all the strength my body had. One punch laid him flat on the ground, unconscious. My mom finally showed concern, but it was towards him lying on the floor. I always felt sorry for her; I knew she disassociated because she was stuck in a loveless marriage, but at that moment, I saw the worry she had for him instead of her daughter, and I no longer felt anything for her.

"When he wakes up, tell him never to come near my sister again," I gritted out before pulling Sofia back upstairs.

Her face was pale and held a look of horror as she stood in the middle of my room. "Holy shit. You've never hit him before."I started frantically shoving my stuff into boxes to distract myself from how angry I was. "Yeah, well, it was long overdue. Are you okay? Let me see your face."

She cried out when I gently ran my finger across the mark already starting to bruise. "I'm fine, J. I'll just crash at a friend's house until it cools off here." She deserved better. We both did, but it wasn't fair I was getting out and leaving her to fend for herself in that hellhole. I knew the only person would suffer the consequences for what I had just done was her, and I couldn't sit back and do nothing.

"No. I'm gonna finish packing, you're going to grab as much of your things as you can carry, and we're crashing at a hotel until I can figure out what to do."

I didn't want to admit it yet, but I knew there was only one way to fix everything, and it meant I'd have to make the ultimate sacrifice.

I LAID on the floor of the hotel room and gazed up at the ceiling, getting lost in the mess of my own thoughts. Every scenario I came up with landed me on the same decision, which would cost me everything—Mila.

"Sof, you up?" I whispered.

She turned on her side and looked down at me from the bed. "I'm not sleeping at all tonight. What's up?"

I mustered up the words heavy on my tongue. "I'm not going to New York." I wanted to vomit from how definitive it felt.

Her eyes narrowed. "What the hell are you talking about? You have to go, Julian. You have college, and Cami, and—"

"I need to be here, Sofia. You realize once I'm gone, Dad will have only you to take all his anger out on? I have to protect you until I can make sure he won't bother us again."

She pried herself from under the blanket. "How are you gonna do that?"

"Don't worry about it. I'll handle it." I could only focus on one problem at a time, but I had one idea I was hoping would work.

She sighed and joined me on the floor. "I can't ask you to give up your entire life for me, J." Her voice cracked, as if she was on the verge of tears.

"You're not asking. I've made up my mind—I'll use the money I had saved up for New York to get a place where we'll stay while you finish up school. After that, we'll figure it out. Together." I wrapped my arm around her as she laid her head on my shoulder, just like when we were kids.

She sniffled. "What about Cami?" I winced when images of the life waiting for us flashed. The idea of missing out on it was excruciating, but before I was Mila's boyfriend, I was Sofia's big brother, and I had an obligation to protect her, even if it meant losing the thing I held closest to my heart.

"I can't hold her back, Sof." I didn't have to say anything else for her to know what my decision meant. "I'm sorry."

I forced a smile as I wiped tears streaming down her cheek. "Get some sleep."

If I had a normal life, I would've packed my things, had a farewell party with friends, and left town like most people did after graduating high school; but as much as my family tried to pretend, our life was far from normal.

twenty-five

CAMILLA

I COULDN'T HELP but think of Greyson and how I wished he was there as I stood in front of the mirror in my bridesmaid dress. When I woke up the next morning, I'd be going back home, and throughout all the chaos in my head, the one thing I knew for sure was I wanted to be in his arms.

"So, you're leaving tomorrow, right?" Taylor came to stand behind me and spoke through the mirror.

I nodded. "Yeah. Don't worry, I was going to say goodbye first thing in the morning." I wasn't going to make the same mistake twice.

She ran her fingers through my hair. "Good, because I didn't want to fly to New York and hunt you down." Our laughter carried over the other voices in the room.

It probably was neither the place nor the time to explain myself, but after she'd let me back in her life without hesitation, I owed it to her to tell her the truth. "I'm sorry I didn't reach out after I left, Tay. I wanted to every day, but I—"

She stopped me by grasping my shoulders. "Cami, stop. It doesn't matter what you did. I'm sure you had your reasons, and I used to want to know, but who am I to judge you for them? All

I want you to do is promise me you won't forget about me again."

I wasn't worthy of her forgiveness or kindness, but that was Taylor—gracious in every aspect, even to people who didn't deserve it. "I promise." Another thing I knew for sure was, I didn't want to go another day without her again.

Everyone in the room paused when Sofia entered. She looked like the image of perfection in her white dress. Her long, brown hair fell in beach waves down her back, and her makeup only enhanced her natural beauty. The dress was even more stunning than I remembered from the day in the store, the long train cascading behind her gracefully.

Taylor gasped and looked at her with adoration while I held back tears. "You look amazing."

"We all do." Sofia looked around the room and beamed a smile, tears threatening her shimmery eyes.

I rushed over and blotted her with a tissue. "Don't cry. You'll ruin your makeup."

"Thank you," she said softly, then turned towards the girls who were putting the finishing touches on their makeup. "Could you guys give Cami and me a minute alone, please?"

Taylor smiled over at us before shutting the door.

"You really are the most beautiful bride Willow's Cove has ever seen, Sof." I adjusted the lace veil she'd let me pick out while I choked on tears.

Her freshly manicured hands gripped mine. "Thanks, Cami. I just wanted a moment alone with you since today's gonna be crazy, and I know you're leaving tomorrow." I blotted away a tear that had managed to run halfway down her cheek. "I know you must have a beautiful life in New York, but I hope you know you'll always have a place back here with us too, so don't let it be six years before we see you again."

I didn't plan on crying until the ceremony started, but she

managed to break me. "I promise I won't." It was her turn to fix my makeup.

"I'm sorry my brother is an idiot for not going after you."

My breath caught in my throat. "It's okay. Some things just aren't meant to be, but you and Levi are the exception." I had no doubt in my mind she was marrying the person she'd be with forever, especially when her face lit up just at the mention of his name.

Taylor slowly made her way back in. "Everyone is set, Sof. Ready to get married?" Her high-pitched squeal made the air in the room feel lighter. "Absolutely."

"We'll meet you at the end of the aisle," I said.

"I'll be the one wearing white." She threw us a wink and dragged her dress' train behind her to a private room while Taylor led me down the hallway where the rest of the bridal party waited. I peeked behind the curtain that separated us from the guests to see the room filled to the brim with people smiling from ear to ear. It was like the whole damn town was invited, but I wouldn't be surprised if they were, since the Willows were like royalty there.I met with Julian's firm chest that nearly knocked me over. He'd hardly spoken since we got back from The Bluffs. I couldn't put my finger on it, but I knew him long enough to know something was bothering him.

He looked down at me with his eyes wide and a subtle smile. "You look beautiful."

"Thanks." I got on my tiptoes to adjust his crooked tie. "You look nice too, Perez."

He grazed my arm with his fingertips. "I'm sorry I've been a little on edge lately, Mila. I promise, today will be different." The familiar light in his eyes was gone, and I hated to admit I missed it.

"Okay, everyone, let's take our places. Sofia and the mayor will be making their way out in a few minutes." While Sofia's wedding coordinator directed each couple to our designated places, I was stumped with a question I hadn't thought to ask before.

"Hey, why aren't your parents here? I would assume your dad would be the one walking Sofia down the aisle instead of Levi's."

His face grew tight, and his face blanched, as if he was going to vomit. "They couldn't make it back in town on time." His answer was brief and sharp, which told me not to ask for any clarification, but I wondered what kind of parents would miss their kid's wedding? I hadn't spoken to my dad in years, yet I knew he'd move mountains if I was getting married.

The music started, and I watched each couple descend down the aisle until it was our turn. "Please don't let me fall on my face, Julian," I whispered close before we walked out with our arms tangled, just like we'd practiced.

"Never."

It was hard not to notice the eyes glued to us and the whispers that followed. Almost everyone in that room knew us both in some way, so they were probably shocked to see us together after nearly a decade.

"Don't worry about the stares. They're just jealous I get to walk down the aisle with you and they don't." He could always get me to believe anything that came from his lips, no matter how absurd it sounded.

I hid my laughter behind the bouquet of lilies in my hand. "That was cheesy, but it worked, so thanks." I was relieved when we reached the end and all attention turned to Sofia. She'd always been graceful and poised, but that day, she radiated in a way she'd never had before. Marriage already suited her well. Her smile lit up the entire room, but it was only aimed at Levi, whom she hadn't looked away from since she entered. He looked at her like she held the moon and sun, and everything started and ended with her. It was how every girl wanted to be looked at.

I was able to hold back my tears until the vows started.

"Levi, I didn't think it was possible for someone to own my heart until you, but I'd let you have it in any lifetime. You're engrained in every good moment of my life, and even in the moments that weren't, you managed to make me see the light. Your kindness and your ability to see not just me, but everyone around you, is something I'll admire about you forever." Her voice became muffled as I locked eyes with Julian, who was already gazing at me with an intensity that made heat rise on my neck.

I couldn't help but compare Sofia's vows to words Julian had confessed before. I also couldn't help but think if it would have been our wedding everyone was attending, if he'd made a different decision six years before—that idea came with an overwhelming pit of guilt.

"CAN I JUST GET A WATER, PLEASE?" I sat at the bar to get some distance from the crowd, but I avoided any alcohol to avoid a repeat of the bachelorette party.

"Camilla? I knew it was you walking with Julian, but I had to be sure."

I turned around to the familiar voice. "Jaime Torres." She wrapped me in her arms before I could process her new look, but I immediately thought blonde hair suited her better than brown.

"I was hoping I'd see you." Despite her stilettos, her gold-specked dress dragged behind as she took the seat next to me. "Congratulations on selling out the bookstore last week. I had to work, but I wish I could've been there."

Her pleasantness made me grow suspicious. "Thank you."

She didn't seem to get the hint that I was avoiding any further conversation by taking a swig of water. "You're the last person I expected to see back in town. I wouldn't have blamed you if you never came back after living in New York."

"I didn't plan on it, trust me. I was only supposed to be here for the book signing, but I got roped into staying." She followed my eyes to where Julian sat at the table, then back at me with a knowing smile. "I knew you two would find each other again."

I laughed under my breath. "We're just friends."

She waved the bartender over and ordered a red wine. "It's funny, because I swear, I heard that in high school right before you started dating." She shook her head. "Take it from me, Camilla: you and Julian can never be friends."

I was on the verge of going stir crazy. "Why do people keep saying that?" She was the last person I thought I'd be talking about Julian with, but maybe I needed an outsider's perspective.

She chugged down her wine and ordered another. "I say this as someone who used to hate you two together. Once you and Julian became a thing, there was no chance for anyone else. If you paid any attention, you'd see he still looks at you the same way he did back then."

The funny thing was, I *had* noticed a glimpse of what she was talking about. I just didn't let myself acknowledge it because doing so would betray everything I had with Greyson. "Maybe if you were this pleasant in high school, we could have stayed friends." As our laughter carried over the live band, I was taken back to middle school when me, her, and Taylor had inside jokes about boys.

"I'll admit, I wasn't the nicest, but you know how brutal high school was if you didn't fit in, so I made sure I did." I suddenly realized I couldn't blame her for the way she acted back then; it was eat or be eaten. I chose to stay invisible until Julian forced me out of the shadows.

I let a genuine smile touch my lips. "I never thought I'd say this, but I'm really glad I ran into you, Jaime."

We were suddenly joined by Julian, whose hand came to rest on my back. "How about that dance, Mila?"

"Julian, you remember Jaime, right?"

His lips parted in shock. "Jaime Torres?" She raised her glass up at us. "The one and only." She subtly threw me a wink before getting up from her seat. "I should get back to my date, but you guys enjoy the rest of your night."

Julian pulled me towards the dance floor. "I never thought I'd see you laughing with Jaime Torres of all people."

I looked over and saw her greet a man at her table with a kiss on the cheek and a bright smile. "We just have a new understanding of each other."

I didn't notice we were dancing to a slow song until we started to sway. "How do I always let you rope me into slow dancing?" I craned my neck up to look at him.

"I can be pretty persuasive." His smile made my heart flutter. "There it is. I thought you forgot how to smile."

He towered over me even when I was in heels, so he had to crouch lower so our foreheads were nearly touching. "I'm sorry, Mila. It's been a weird couple of days."

I tightened my grip around his neck. "Trust me, I get it. I know coming back, especially with a boyfriend, must've been weird for you, but it means a lot you let me stay and see the house. I'm leaving knowing it's in good hands."

He winced. "Will you ever come back?"

I didn't have an answer for that, because I wasn't certain *if* I came back, I wouldn't find a reason to stay. "Can we just have fun tonight, instead of thinking about the future?" We never seemed to be good at that anyway.

"Whatever you want, Mila." The clinking of glasses made me back away from his heated stare.

"I'd like to make a toast." Levi's dad pulled the attention to him. "Sofia, you're all we could ask for our boy, and we promise to take care of you forever. Welcome to the family. To my son and new daughter."

I felt when Julian stiffed at my side, and I sympathized with how hard it must've been to see Sofia be greeted into a powerful family that would take over his job of protecting her.

"Since we're doing speeches, my big brother should have one I'd like to hear now."

I nudged him forward when Sofia raised her champagne-filled glass. "Duty calls."

He forced a smile. "Try not to laugh." I could tell he was nervous from the way his chest heaved in jagged breaths, but the sip of champagne he took before raising the glass above his head seemed to help him speak confidently.

"I think I can speak for everyone when I say, to be around Sofia, is to know what sunlight feels like. She's special, so I knew whoever she decided to spend her life with, had to be too. I'll admit, it's hard to see my baby sister all grown up. I never thought I'd trust her with anyone else, but now, I know she's in good hands." He quickly glanced over at me. "Take care of each other, learn from one another, and take it from me: once you have something good, hang onto it for dear life." He raised his glass higher. "To the newlyweds."

I stood frozen while everyone around me drank and clapped for his beautiful speech. *Take it from me: once you have something good, hang onto it for dear life.*

If only he'd listened to his own advice.

It was a little after one in the morning when the reception ended, and since Julian had a little too much to drink, I drove us home, my head spinning the entire time.

I had a flight in nine hours to leave everything behind again, but the thought was unbearable. I was so fueled with my desire to escape the first time, I forgot how much Willow's Cove had ingrained themselves into my soul—I would miss Sofia's humor and free spirit, Taylor's ability to know what I was thinking without having to say anything. I'd miss the smell of fresh coffee accompanied by the sound of bacon sizzling in the morning, picking out fresh fruit from Mr. and Mrs Asher's booth at the farmer's market.

"Alright, we're here," I said as I parked in the driveway.

He entangled our hands as we climbed out of the car. "How about one last visit to the cove?"

I had to get some sleep if I was going to be able to function the next morning, but I got the feeling he didn't want me to say no. "Can you even walk?"

He chuckled. "I'm not that drunk, Mila. Besides, the breeze will sober me up." He was right about being persuasive, because I followed him down the hill towards the ocean without a second thought.

"Actually, let's go down to your secret spot, for old times' sake."

I'd been avoiding going to my spot to spare myself the reminder of all the moments I shared with Julian. The secret cave was exactly how I'd left it, and the view of the open ocean was as beautiful as ever. I memorized how peaceful it was, how my feet felt when they sank into the warm sand, the aroma of salt in the air.

"Do you come down here a lot?" I asked as we walked along the edge of the water.

He shook his head. "I haven't been here in six years. I couldn't come back to the place that reminded me of you."

I let silence fall between us so I could listen to the sounds of the waves crashing against each other. "Promise me something, Julian."

We stopped to look at each other. "What?"

I sucked in a sharp breath. "Promise me, after I leave this time, you won't just sit in that house and let your life pass by."

The smile he'd had moments before turned into a frown. "I can't, Mila."

"Why not?" I pleaded, but deep down, I knew what his answer was. He inched closer and traced my face with his fingertips. "Because a life without you is meaningless."

His words poured over me, making me aware of the gravity I could always feel but never see that tethered me to him from thousands of miles away. The only question was, why did it decide to pull us back together when we weren't the same people as when I left Willow's Cove?

"Julian…" I'd waited years to hear those words from him, but they came too late.

"Stay here, Mila." I looked for any sign he was joking, but his face was stern. I knew there were so many unsaid words between us, but I hadn't prepared myself for those three. "I…I can't do this right now."

I tried to walk away, but his desperate voice called me back. "When can we talk about it then, Mila?"

I only pictured Greyson's face when I turned back so quickly, he nearly plowed into me. "Fine, you want to talk? Let's talk. You can't say things like that. I can handle your sly smiles, the reminiscing, but not that. You had years, Julian, so why now? Why do you want to ruin everything when you know I have a life back in New York with someone else?"

"I've seen something in your eyes this past week. You miss the person you were here, with me. You said so yourself, you weren't sure if New York was the place for you anymore."

I felt mascara run down my cheek as I shoved him back so hard, he nearly lost his footing. "Screw you, Julian."

I tried walking back up to the house, but his voice followed me. "You know I'm right, Mila. You're just too stubborn for your own good, like you've always been. If you were so happy in your new life, you wouldn't have agreed to stay in Willow's Cove."

He didn't even know me anymore, yet he felt the right to make assumptions about my life. Maybe it was for the best we were parting ways for the last time. I'd only been back for a week, and somehow, we ended up arguing, just like we always did.

Rage suddenly turned me numb, and I shouted as loud as my voice could carry. "It was supposed to be us, Julian! All of this was supposed to be *our* life, but you made it clear you didn't want it. I went out and gave my heart to the guy who made it clear he does, and I'm going home to him tomorrow, so I'm gonna ask again: why now?"

"Because I'm in love with you, Mila. Maybe it's a goddamn long shot to admit now, but I can't imagine waking up another day and not seeing the morning tangles in your hair, or watching the sun beam on your face as you read on the hill. I've loved you since I was sixteen, and I can't just shut it off. Look at me and tell me you haven't felt anything since you've been back." When I first moved to the city, I always imagined getting a knock on my door one day, him telling me he was crazy for letting me go, but he never did. There he was, saying all the right words, but it was six years too late.

"I haven't felt anything. There, you happy?" Before I could react, he pulled me in and crashed his lips against mine. It was only for a second, but that second made my head rush. "You feel anything now?" he whispered against my lips.

I shoved him back. "I hate you. You're the one who ended us, do you remember that? You don't get to say you're in love with me."

"I never wanted to hurt you, Mila." His voice broke.

"Then why did you, huh? Why?" I couldn't control my hands as they shoved his chest harder and harder until our feet hit the water. "I waited for you! You knew where I was for six years, Julian, and you never came for me. Why?" My words came out as sobs.

"I didn't know you wanted me to!" He shouted with his brown eyes rimmed with tears, his legs getting hit with waves.

Everything stood still. We'd gotten into arguments before, but never like that one. I wiped the evidence of tears from my face, and spoke sternly. "I'm going to bed. When we wake up tomorrow morning, this never happened."

Had we always brought out the worst in each other? Did my mind just leave out all the bad parts because he'd once taken up so much of my heart?

twenty-six

JULIAN

6 YEARS EARLIER

How was I going to tell the girl I was in love with that I couldn't start the life we planned together? I couldn't, so I pivoted. After lying awake that entire night, I still came up short on what to say to Mila; if she knew the truth about why I was staying, she'd stay back with me, but there was no way I was going to be the one to hold her back from her dreams. There was only one way to get her to leave.

"Don't hate me forever," I whispered to myself as I trembled up to her front door where she waited. I selfishly took a moment to soak up how her face lit up the moment she plunged into my arms. I couldn't do anything but memorize how she was right before I broke her heart.

"I wasn't expecting you until later. Come on, you can help me pack the rest of my stuff."

I wanted to stall as much as I could, but the thought of trying to act normal while my heart was heavy made me feel even more shitty. Her face fell when I stopped her from dragging me further. "I can't go up with you, Mila."

"Why not?" I couldn't say the words while looking into her beautiful blue eyes, so I looked down at my feet instead. "I'm not going to New York."

Any sign of light immediately vanished from her face, and her voice shook as she spoke. "What do you mean? Are you going to drive down another day?" Her optimism was salt in the wound; it meant she never saw my betrayal coming.

"I changed my mind. I don't want to go." The lie felt like acid on my tongue. All I wanted to do was hold her, but she flinched when I reached for her, and I felt like I was going to be sick.

"What about everything we talked about? Our plans? Our future? You don't want that either?"

She could always see right through me, so I kept a straight face as another lie lit my throat on fire. "No." I'll never forget the moment I saw her sparkle die, the gut-wrenching feeling I had knowing I was the one who'd killed it.

"Let me get this straight: just yesterday, you seemed pretty set on our future, and today, you show up telling me you're not. Give me some kind of explanation, Julian. You owe me that." I watched her struggle to speak through her sobs in agony. *Just like I rehearsed.* "It's just happening too fast, Mila. We're only eighteen and have the rest of our lives planned out. Maybe I want something different." I didn't want different. I wanted *her*, but I knew she wouldn't get everything she wanted out of her life if she'd stayed in Willow's Cove, and I wasn't sure how long I would have to stay behind. If one of us was going to get out, it had to be her.

She sucked her tears back. "Fine. If we're done, say the words. I won't be the one to end us."

I took mental images of every detail of her face in case it was the last time I saw it—ocean blue eyes that reminded me of the waves at the cove, dark brown hair that fell in salty waves, and full lips always swiped with green apple flavored gloss. She swatted my hand away when I tried to caress her naturally rosy cheek, which only made the next words feel heavier.

"We're done, Mila."

I didn't know those three words would echo in my head for years to come, like a recurring nightmare. If we had any chance at a future, I'd stomped on it and lit it on fire, but I knew that was the only way she'd leave.

She straightened her shoulders and wiped any emotion off her face. "I guess it's settled then. I'm going to New York to start my life, and I hope you figure out what it is you really want out of yours, Julian. I won't be waiting around if you decide you finally want me." *I'm always going to want you.*

While it shattered my heart to see her love for me dim, deep down, I couldn't help but swell with pride she wasn't letting me get in the way of her dreams. I would just have to love her the way I loved the waves at the cove—from afar.

twenty-seven

JULIAN

I WOKE up the next morning with a pounding headache and the memory of Mila's tear-filled face as her words echoed in my head.

I followed everyone's advice and asked her to stay, and we ended up in a screaming match. All hope she wasn't getting on her plane that morning was lost, but at least I had the memory of her lips. Kissing her was stupid, especially after she'd just screamed at me, but I couldn't let her leave without her lips pressing an imprint on mine one last time. If that made me self-ish, then so be it.

I couldn't ignore she was leaving as much as I couldn't shut off my feelings for her. It was quiet when I walked out to the kitchen, with no sign she'd made coffee or was even awake, until I noticed the door to her room cracked open. I lightly knocked as I pushed it open. "Mila? You in here?"

Her half-packed suitcases were laid on her bed. Clothes were scattered, books were shoved inside the pockets of her suitcase, and the only thing lying on her nightstand was the silver-studded C necklace I'd gotten for her at the farmer's market. I'd seen it around her neck at the wedding, which meant she'd taken it off after our heated argument, and I only had myself to blame.

Suddenly, I heard the front door close, and I hurried out to catch her rummaging through the fridge. She tensed the moment we met eyes, and I felt as if I wanted to vomit. "Good morning. Where were you?"

"Taylor's. I told her I wouldn't leave without saying good-bye." The thought of us saying goodbye made me nauseous. "I should go finish packing."

She started down the hall, but I reached out to stop her. I didn't have any more room for regret, so I ripped off the band-aid and swallowed my pride. "Mila, I know things got out of hand last night, but I want you to know, I'm sorry. I also shouldn't have kissed you." I kept the thought to myself, how I couldn't forget how soft her lips were as they wrapped around mine, or how for a split second, I felt when she wanted to give in.

She walked back and eased into the chair closest to me. "I thought hard about whether I should be mad at you this morning, but I decided I don't want us to leave on bad terms again. We both said things I'd rather just forget altogether."

Was I a coward for finally accepting the truth that I was once again letting her slip through my fingers? "What if I can't forget?" I rushed out before I could psych myself out.

"Julian, I don't want to fight—" I cut her off before she could say anything that would leave my heart in pieces again. "Then we won't. I can't let you leave without knowing the answer to the question you asked me last night."

Her blue eyes softened.

After I'd threatened my dad to leave town and never contact me or Sofia again, or else I'd tell everyone what he'd done to us, we swore it would stay our secret. It wasn't only to save us from the pity, but once she got involved with the Willows, we knew we'd be a story in the local paper if it ever got out.

"I lied, Mila. Of course I wanted to go with you to New York, but I couldn't because…" I forced the secret that had been ruining my life for years from the depths of my throat. "I needed to stay back with Sofia to protect her."

Her eyes roamed over my face with concern. "Protect her from what?"

"Our dad." My mouth was sour after speaking about him after all those years, but if there was any chance of getting her back, I had to take it.

"What do you mean?"

My leg shook as I imagined myself as a kid in that hellhole I grew up in. "He was a drunk who took his anger out on the people around him, and it was usually me, but it happened once to Sofia the night of our graduation. I had to make sure he was gone from our lives forever before I felt comfortable leaving Sofia in Willow's Cove."

Her face drained of color. "Wait, why didn't you…I could've…If I'd known that, I would've—"

I saved her from finding the words. "You would've stayed."

She nodded because that was Mila—selfless, brave, and headstrong when she set her mind to something. Who was I to keep her hidden away from the world just because I couldn't stomach the thought of being without her?

"I'm sorry you both went through that. You didn't deserve it," she spoke gently. "So, everything you said that day…" She could barely form any sentences through her jagged breaths.

"It was to get you to leave me behind. I wanted the life we talked about. I *still* want it. Why do you think I'm living in this house?"

She shot out of the chair and tried to gather herself as she paced around the living room. "You didn't think to tell me this the whole time I was here instead of springing it on me an hour before my flight?"

I seared my eyes into hers. "Would it have made a difference?" I knew the answer when she didn't respond, and I'm glad she didn't say it out loud, because I wouldn't have recovered.

She shook her head and wiped her eyes as they started to water. "For four years, I held onto hope you'd show up or call. I would've followed you anywhere, Julian, but that was then. Now, there's Greyson. Even though you didn't do it intentionally, he mended the heart you broke, and I can't just throw that away."

There was suddenly a hollow hole where my heart once was. Some things, you just can't take back, no matter how hard you try. That dreadful moment was one of mine.

"I just want you to be happy, Mila." It's all I've ever wanted, even if it meant living without her. She wiped a tear that streamed down her face, but before she could speak again, a knock on the door interrupted us. Sofia was on a plane to Paris for her honeymoon, and I was sure Elijah was passed out in his hotel room, so I hesitated to answer. All the blood in my body rushed to the surface when I saw a man in a perfectly tailored suit and dark sunglasses hovering in my doorway.

He scanned me up and down and offered me his hand. "You must be Julian. I'm Greyson."

twenty-eight

CAMILLA

IF ELENA WAS in that room, she'd say something like *shit has hit the fan,* and she'd be right. I couldn't bring myself to move as I stared at Greyson hovering in the doorway, then at Julian's face washed of all color. The air grew suffocating from the fact that neither knew each other existed until a few days before.

Greyson looked as handsome as ever in his fitted Ralph Lauren suit. You couldn't catch him dead in jeans, even on his days off from working at the office. His messy, wavy hair was held out of his face by his designer sunglasses on top of his head, and his grey eyes still shined when he saw me.

He brushed past Julian to pick me up and kiss me hard enough for me to lose my breath. "I missed you so much, Cami."

I couldn't bear to look over at Julian, especially when my head was still spinning from our conversation. "How...how are you here?" I asked in a daze.

"I wanted to surprise you. You can thank Elena for giving me directions to this place. She also canceled your flight so we can fly back together in my dad's jet."

"You didn't have to come all this way," I said.

"I just couldn't wait any longer to see you." When he moved

to tuck a strand of hair behind my ear, I saw the hurt flash in his eyes when I flinched back. "Are you okay?"

I nodded. "Yeah. I'm just surprised to see you." Maybe it was guilt making me uneasy, or the surprise he was in a small town like Willow's Cove, much less in Julian's living room.

"We'll go to that Thai restaurant you like as soon as we land." He took out his wallet and walked over to Julian. "Before I forget, thank you for letting Cami stay here. How much do I owe you?"

He meant well, but I knew Julian took offense when his jaw tightened as he looked down at the hundred dollar bills offered out to him. "No need. I was happy to have Mila here."

Greyson's brows flickered with confusion at the nickname he'd never heard before. "Thanks. You must be some friend." There was a hint of sarcasm in his voice.

"If that's what you want to call it." Julian snapped back. Despite there being a window letting fresh air in, the more I stood between them, the more my chest tightened and I couldn't breathe.

Greyson adjusted his tie and turned back to me. "Are you packed, Cami?"

I shook my head. "No. I was just going to finish before you showed up, but I don't think the clothes I bought while I was here will fit in my suitcase."

"Where's the nearest store? I'll go get another one while you finish up." I wasn't surprised he didn't hesitate for a solution; he was constantly willing to go out of his way for people.

"Just follow the road you took until you hit downtown. There's only one market here."

He chuckled under his breath. "God, I hate small towns. I'll be right back." He kissed my forehead and left me and Julian in echoing silence.

"So that's the infamous Greyson. He seems like a good guy." His tone didn't reflect the look of despair all over his face.

"He is." When neither of us said anything for what felt like forever, I took it as it was—goodbye. I sympathized with what he and Sofia went through, and I wished more than anything he would've just told me the truth, because at least whatever decision I made after would've been my own. But, I couldn't just throw away nearly three years with Greyson because I suddenly knew. I had to accept that Julian was another chapter in my life I had to close.

"When Greyson comes back, I'm leaving with him, but I'm gonna say something just once, and then walk out of here."

He nodded distantly.

"I love him, Julian, but I'm always going to love you too. Maybe I did feel something while I was here; I just didn't want to admit it because it won't change anything." Tears threatened my eyes but I held them back. "Maybe, in another life, we did it right." I knew if I looked at him again, I'd get sucked back in, so I turned away for the last time.

twenty-nine

CAMILLA

6 YEARS AGO

I REPLAYED my last conversation with Julian until my eyes were puffy and sore. His words cut a wound deep enough to last a lifetime, but I couldn't shake how the look in his eyes was unfamiliar, like he was pleading out to me. I just couldn't figure out for what.

So many unanswered questions filtered through my head: were we really moving too fast? Why would he plan a life in New York if he had any doubt about leaving Willow's Cove? Why was there a small part of me that still wanted him to change his mind? I let out the sobs buried in my chest when I turned and faced the boxes stacked in the corner, ready to be stuffed into the car Julian and I had reserved weeks prior. I wouldn't admit it out loud, but I was terrified of starting a new life in the city all on my own.

The sudden sound of my parents shouting downstairs startled me out of bed. I followed their voices to the living room but stood hidden on the staircase to eavesdrop. They fought often, but their anger echoed through the house in a much different way than usual. "You've only been back a day, and you're already going off to be with *her*?" I was too stunned to even breathe.

"I came down for Cami's graduation, and now, I'm going back to my life. That was the deal, right, Liv? We stay married so you get to live in this big house with my money while I get to do whatever the hell I want." The string that tied my relationship with my dad was already thin after I found out about his affair, but it was cut after hearing his hatred towards my mom. Memories of him teaching me to swim down at the cove, dancing on his feet in the living room, and watching him build the swing in the front yard started to fade one by one.

My chest caved at the realization that living with the burden of harboring the "secret" was for nothing. I thought I was keeping our family together by not saying anything, but not only did Mom know the entire time, she allowed it. The pedestal I'd once held her on crashed down, and she was suddenly someone who went against everything she'd ever taught me growing up.

"I'm not lying for you this time. You can call your daughter in the morning and tell her you left for another work trip." I watched him gather up his bags and slam the door behind him, and as soon as he was gone, my mom's whimpers carried up the stairs and thudded in my ears.

I was dizzy from my entire world being flipped upside down, but I gained the strength to call after her. "Mom? Are you okay?"

She tried to wipe away any trace of sadness from her face before I approached her. "Of course. Your dad had to leave, but he's gonna call you in the morning." I'd seen her plaster on a fake smile enough growing up to recognize it immediately.

I took a deep breath before dropping next to her on the floor at the end of the stairs. "I heard everything." For the first time, I looked into her eyes and saw how lost they were. I couldn't do anything except cradle her when she sank into my lap and started to sob, just like she did for me as a kid. Seeing someone you grew up admiring crumble right before your eyes was life-altering.

She spoke through her sobs. "I'm sorry, Cami. You deserve better than this." In that moment, she and I were more similar than we'd ever been. She was my mom, but also just a girl burdened by a broken heart. "It's okay," I whispered.

"No, it's not. I should've divorced him as soon as I knew about the affair." I knew it was stupid to ask before I opened my mouth, but curiosity ate at me.

"Why didn't you?"

She wiped her tears but stayed in my lap as she spoke in an almost whisper. "I've never told you this, but I had a scholarship to Berkeley waiting for me after high school. I came to Willow's Cove for the summer to visit a friend, but then I met your dad. My head exploded from how in love we were, and when he asked me to stay, I gave it all up." I always assumed she hardly spoke about her life before me because there wasn't much to tell, but it turned out, it was because it hurt to admit what she'd left behind. "To answer your question, I had to sacrifice having a life and a career of my own to raise you, which I'll never regret, but because of that, staying with your dad is how we have financial security for things like this house, and sending you to NYU to live out your dreams."

I sometimes resented the way she was always tough on me about good grades and making sure my transcript for colleges looked perfect, but I suddenly had a new understanding that she was nudging me towards a life she never got the chance to live.

"I'm sorry you had to give up your dreams." I pictured her my age, full of life and ready to take on the world, and then losing that spark as time passed.

She ran her manicured finger across my cheek with a gentle smile. "*You* are my dream, Cami. I'd make that same sacrifice a hundred times over if it meant I get you."

She wiped away the tears that rimmed my eyes. "I love you,

Mom." I'd always said I'd never want to turn out like my parents, and while that was still true, I would've been lucky if I was half the woman my mom was.

"I love you more, my sweet girl." She ran her fingers through my hair with a gentle smile. "Enough about me, where's Julian? Shouldn't you two be packing up the last of your things together?"

I didn't want to say the words because then, it would be real. "He isn't going with me."

Her face blanched. "What?"

"He said it's because we're moving too fast, but there's this pit in my stomach telling me it's something else, that he needs me. I don't know what to do." I leaned on her shoulder so she wouldn't see me cry, but as much as she tried soothing me, nothing filled the void in my chest. New York was waiting for me, but was I a bad person for leaving if I had a gut feeling Julian needed me here?

She sighed, as if she struggled to find the words. "I'll tell you what you're going to do. You're gonna go to New York and start your new life. You know I love Julian, but you can't stay in Willow's Cove, Cami. Take what life has to offer you outside of this town, unlike me. If you and Julian are meant to be, you'll find each other again, but right now, you have to go and not look back. Promise me."

I blinked away the tears before I said the two words I would live by for the next six years. "I promise."

"You have to leave without saying goodbye to anyone. Otherwise, you'll find reasons to stay." I wasn't supposed to leave for another day, and there was so much I hadn't done yet— visit the bookstore one last time, stop by Mr. and Mrs. Wilson's bakery, one more movie night with Mom, but most of all, say bye to Taylor and Sofia. They'd hate me forever for it, but I knew my mom was right. I had to leave, and it had to be then. Otherwise, I never would.

thirty

JULIAN

6 YEARS AGO

I KNEW IT WAS SELFISH. I'd spent the entire drive convincing myself to turn back around, but I couldn't let Mila leave with our last moment together being a bad memory. She had to know that, one day, when I felt worthy of her, I'd find her again.

I decided to use her front door instead of scaling her roof, but I froze when Mrs. Vega appeared on the other side of the door with puffy eyes as if she'd just finished crying. "Hi, Mrs. Vega. Can I see Cami, please?" She didn't have to say anything for me to know she was gone. My heart suddenly felt the absence.

"You just missed her. I'm really sorry, Julian." The look on her face when I saw her last flashed through my mind. That couldn't be the last time I ever saw her. I refused to believe it.

I kept my voice from breaking in front of her. "Could you just give her a message for me the next time you talk to her? I doubt she'd pick up any of my calls."

She smiled tightly. "Come inside. You look like you've had a rough couple of days." Was it that obvious there weren't enough words to describe what was scrambling in my mind?

I sat on the couch and stared at the framed picture of Mila on the table beside me. I knew it was from kindergarten because I remembered what she was wearing the first time I saw her.

Mrs. Vega sat across from me on the chair with her hands in her lap. "Is everything okay, Julian?"

I nodded. "I'm fine." She had the same look Mila did when she knew I was lying. I never noticed how much they resembled each other until her blue eyes bore into mine.

"Really? One minute, you're going to New York with Cami, then you're not. Before she left, she said she had this feeling it was because something else was going on, and you needed her. Was she right?"

My head snapped. "She said that?" I should have known. She was always too smart for her own good.

"As a mom, I sort of have these instincts that tell me when someone is spiraling. You don't have to tell me what you're going through, Julian, but I have to ask why you felt like you couldn't tell Cami."

I ran my hands through my hair as I tried to find the right words without giving too much away. No one could find out about my dad—not for his sake, but for mine and Sofia's. "I couldn't be the one to hold her back from her dreams."

Her entire face lit up as she held a hand over her chest. "I can't tell you how much that means. I've always wanted what's best for her, and now I know you do too."

"Of course I do. I love her, Mrs. Vega," I choked out.

"I know, and it's because you love her that I'm asking you to do something for her sake."

I agreed with no hesitation. "Anything."

"I made her promise not to come back to Willow's Cove, but I know you're the only person who could get her to break it, so I need you to promise me you won't contact her for a while."

My entire body tensed. "How long is a while?"

"At least until she finishes college. She has a chance most

people in this town don't get, Julian. Neither of us can jeopardize that." I was spiraling after being without her for a day; the thought of living without her for four years made me nauseous, but if staying away until it was the right time for both of us meant she'd have a chance to make something of herself, then I'd make the sacrifice a hundred times over. "Okay. I promise."

She smiled. "Now promise me in the meantime, you'll take care of yourself. That way you'll be the best version you could be when she comes back to you, because she will. That's *my* promise." It was funny how my own parents couldn't give a damn about me, but she did.

"I'll hold you to that. Thank you, Mrs. Vega. I guess I'll be seeing you around." I got up out of the chair and offered her a smile before walking to the door.

"One more thing." She called out. "Make sure she knows where to find you." I looked back at her one last time, only thinking of Mila's face.

I had every intention of getting in my car and driving away, but when I looked up at her window, I knew I had to go in for my own sake.

I used the tree branches I'd climbed plenty of times to scale her roof, and of course, her window was unlocked. Maybe it was my mind playing tricks on me, but I had a thought she'd left it that way because she knew I'd come. I sat down on her bed and looked around at the walls that had been stripped of all the posters, the desk empty of CDs, and her bookshelf nearly empty, because there was no way she'd leave the state without her favorite books.

I sat on her bed, realizing I'd never sneak in just to see her face again or scare her while she was reading. Four years apart was going to feel like hell, but for her, I was willing to wait a lifetime.

As I crawled back out of her window, my eyes caught the framed picture of us lying flat on her desk. I'd seen it hundreds of times, but that time, there was a note with Mila's cursive handwriting tucked in one of the corners.

I held it together until I traced my finger over the three words.

forever and always – Mila

thirty-one

JULIAN

THE AIR DIDN'T FEEL the same after Mila left Willow's Cove. The ocean wasn't quite as blue anymore, and everything around me felt lifeless as I sulked in my own regret. I'd been collecting dust as I waited for her to come back, and then, she was gone again.

As I picked at the food on my plate, I pictured her across from me, smiling as she drowned her strawberry pancakes in syrup. After I lost her the first time, I lived off the hope we'd make our way back to each other someday, but that time felt definitive. Final.

I did everything right—got her to leave Willow's Cove to go to college, kept the promise to her mom, waited for her for six years, and in the end, I still ended up without her. I wondered if it was it all worth it?

The sound of a car pulling up made me grunt out of frustration since I'd purposely been avoiding having any visitors. Seconds later, Elijah let himself in through the front door with his hands up, and behind him was a familiar face.

"Damon?" It had been years, and suddenly he was someone with a mustache and tattoos.

"Miss me, JP?" I didn't waste any time to bring him in a tight embrace. When he didn't show for the wedding, I thought I'd never see him again. "Sorry I missed the wedding. I couldn't get off work, but your sister has been blowing up my phone saying you needed me. Don't shoot the messenger."

I should've known Sofia knew about Mila being gone despite being in another country. News traveled fast in Willow's Cove, especially gossip.

I turned to Elijah. "I thought you left town, Fisher?" He was only in town for the weekend, so I figured he couldn't have gotten out fast enough. He sat across from me and let a subtle smirk show.

"I'm sticking around for a little bit. I figured this town could use a little fun."

I'd known him long enough to know there was another reason. "Does this have anything to do with how you couldn't leave Taylor's side at the wedding?" He'd never smiled so much around someone, so it was something worth noticing. I faintly remembered him having a crush on her in high school, but Elijah had a lot of crushes, so I never thought anything of it.

"We're not here to talk about me."

"Will someone fill me in on why the hell I had to get on a plane to come see you? I can't leave until I have something to report back to Sofia. I forgot how scary she is." Damon chimed in.

I couldn't help but laugh at how she found time to threaten him while on her honeymoon.

"You can tell her I'm fine." Had no one ever heard of self-loathing in peace? It had only been two days since I'd been burdened with a Mila-sized hole in my chest, and I just needed a little time to myself.

"After all this time, you're still a shitty liar, JP." Elijah said.

"What is this, a tag team?" I joked.

I didn't want to admit my failure to get Mila to stay out loud.

It was bad enough I had the memory of it, but I knew they wouldn't leave until I did.

"What do you want me to say? Camilla left. I did what everyone told me to do, and she still left back to New York with another guy, and I'm still here." The wound I'd been trying to patch up for days suddenly reopened.

"Camilla? As in Camilla Vega? Damn, nothing changes around here." Damon threw his head back before walking over to my fridge for a beer.

"Shit. That's rough." Elijah folded his arms across his chest. "I'm not really good at this kind of thing, but maybe everyone saw it wrong. Her coming back wasn't so you would get a second chance, but instead, to finally get closure." How could I accept that? How was I supposed to live the rest of my life without Camilla Vega?

I shook my head and sank against the countertop. "I should've fought harder for her."

"If she already had her mind made up, not even you could've changed it." Damon said. The two of them lecturing me about Mila really made it feel like old times.

"I mean, I should've fought harder six years ago." I thought I was doing the right thing by keeping that goddamn promise, but it only landed us back in the same place we always did—apart.

They looked to each other, then rested their hands on my shoulder. "I know it's hard to see, but maybe she did you a favor. You went so long thinking about the what-ifs, and now, you can finally move on." Damon said softly.

Coming to terms with that was a bridge I didn't want to cross yet, and honestly, I wasn't sure I ever would.

2 weeks later

thirty-two

CAMILLA

MY LEG TAPPED against the marble floors as I waited in the room stacked to the brim with books. After spending two weeks drafting the first couple of chapters of my book and submitting it to Lucy, we were asked by my publisher for an in-person meeting. I wasn't sure if it was good or bad news, so I braced myself for either.

"Stop fidgeting, Cami. You're making me nervous," Elena said. The anxious feeling in my stomach reminded me of how I felt the day of my book signing in Willow's Cove.

It had been two weeks since I'd left, and every day since, New York hadn't felt as lively as it once did. I could no longer drown out the sounds of traffic outside my window, the crowded sidewalks made me feel boxed in, and I found myself looking for anything that reminded me of everything—and everyone—I'd left behind for a second time.

"Camilla, they're ready for you." A woman at the front desk smiled and guided us over to where another woman I'd only seen once, sat at her desk. Elena always tagged along for important meetings because when I tended to freak out. She always managed to keep her cool. "It's nice to see you again,

Camilla. Thank you for coming on short notice." She smiled politely.

"No problem. It's good to see you, Jane." I hid my shaking hands under the table.

"I received your pitch and read some of the chapters your agent sent over, and with your first book continuing to chart, I think this book will have no problem selling as well. I do have one question."

My eyes quickly darted to Elena. "Ask away."

"What inspired this manuscript to be so different than the last?" I knew the answer right away, and I spoke while running my fingers over the *C* necklace I hadn't taken off since I'd landed back in New York.

"My first book reminded people what it felt like with their first love: the innocence, playfulness, and maybe even a little confusion sometimes, but I think that's why they gravitated towards it. My second book will be about what it feels like to lose it."

I was convinced she was going to back out when the room grew silent, but then a soft smile tugged at her red lips. "I don't read many books that come across my desk because I'm surrounded by them all day, but I did read yours, Cami. It took me back to when I was a teenager and was so head over heels in love, I couldn't think straight. I have high hopes for the finished manuscript for the next one, but I just have one request."

I nodded. "Anything."

"Since we're marketing it as a romance, the ending should have them end up together."

I had no plans for an ending yet, but it was no shocker they wanted a happily ever after since romances were supposed to sell the dream, despite it rarely happening in real life. "Okay. Deal."

She stood and reached her hand out to me. "Then we have ourselves a book to sell next year. We'll be in touch about your deadlines, and I'll send your contract over to Lucy."

"Thank you. It means so much."

Before Elena and I walked out of her office, she called after us. "By the way, does it have a name?"

After sitting at my kitchen table for hours scribbling down names, there wasn't one that felt right. "Not yet, but I'll get right to it."

When I walked out of the building, I let out a breath. *Holy shit. I did it.*

"Well, you handled it pretty well without me. Since I just sat there and looked pretty, coffee is on me today." Elena's red bottom heels tapped against the pavement as we walked to the nearby coffee shop where we were regulars because they had the best matcha latte in the city.

"I can't believe she liked the pitch." I thought my first book deal was just a stroke of luck, but hearing directly from Jane that she was anticipating my next book lit me up inside.

"Why wouldn't she? You're a great writer, Cami. I'm not just saying that because you pay me."

"Remind me to give you a raise for being a kiss ass." I smiled.

"Don't worry, I will." When she whipped her hair around to open the door to the café, I found us a table by the window while she ordered our drinks. I usually loved people-watching, especially when I first moved to the city. Everyone moved like they had somewhere to be, and that once excited me as someone who grew up where nothing happened. But since I'd gotten back, I'd been chasing the spark I felt when I first moved to New York. It was nowhere to be found.

"I have a question," Elena said as she took the seat across from me and handed me my matcha latte. "Shoot."

"What really happened with that Julian guy? Because your pitch sounded eerily close to home." Right until she brought him up, I'd almost gone the whole day without thinking of him or the devastated look on his face when I left.

"Nothing. I stayed in his guest room for a week; now, I'm back home." I took a sip of my perfectly sweetened matcha to avoid her burning glare.

"Whatever you say."

My eyes narrowed. "What is that supposed to mean?"

She folded her hands in her lap before a knowing smirk tugged at her lips. "I was in a room with you two for five minutes and could see he was in love with you. Anyone with eyes could have."

I contemplated if I should let Elena into the past I'd hidden from Greyson or let it stay buried, but maybe, she could've made sense of my tangled thoughts. "You know how my publisher said she fell so head over heels for someone, she couldn't think straight? That's how I felt about Julian in high school. While I was in Willow's Cove, I guess lines started to blur, and I remembered why I fell for him so hard." Her eyes held no judgment as I continued. "When he asked me to stay in Willow's Cove, of course I said no, but there isn't a second I don't think about him. That makes me a shitty person, doesn't it? What about Greyson?" If he had any suspicions my mind was elsewhere since coming back home, he didn't tell me about them, but every night, when we'd eat takeout at our kitchen table, I couldn't help but think of Julian and his home-cooked meals.

"Considering I've never been in love with one person, much less two, I'm probably the wrong person to give advice. Have you talked to your mom about it?"

After giving my dad an ultimatum and finally divorcing him, she moved into a one bedroom apartment in lower Manhattan not too far from me and Greyson. I hadn't stopped by to see her since I'd been back. The last thing I wanted was for her to find out I was reeling over the same guy I was at eighteen. "Not yet."

Her eyebrows furrowed as she sipped from her cup, seemingly in deep thought. "Then I guess I'm your only voice of reason. It doesn't make you a shitty person, Cami. It's just like you said: lines got blurred, so of course you're going to be confused. First loves have a way of reeling you back in, but you decided to come back with Greyson, so that should tell you all you need to know about where your heart lies."

I barely touched my latte as I sat in anguish. "Don't you want to judge me even a little for juggling two people at once?"

She chuckled before throwing me a wink. "Since when is that my thing?"

She was right about knowing where my heart lies. I'd come back with Greyson, but I couldn't ignore how that same invisible string I'd felt for six years was pulling me back to Willow's Cove.

thirty-three

JULIAN

I SAT at the top of the grass hill and watched the waves turn over each other. After two weeks of Mila gone, I finally realized maybe everything did pass like the tides, even my time with Mila. It was clear she wanted to keep her life back in New York, and that life didn't include me.

I didn't turn to see whose footsteps approached me until I saw Sofia from the corner of my eye. I prepared myself for the smart remark I knew she had, but instead, she watched the high tides in silence with me, and it was nice. "Should I even bother with a lecture?"

I'd already given myself plenty. "Nope. Let's talk about something else, like...how was the honeymoon?" Levi had splurged on a trip to Paris and used a friend's connections for Sofia to talk with fashion designers she'd grown up admiring. The photos he'd sent of her in infamous drawing rooms spoke a thousand words.

"Amazing, but I didn't come to talk about me. Are you okay?" It turned into a recurring question anytime someone was around me—Elijah, Taylor, people in town, my sister. I was far

231

from okay. My heart was shattered into fragments, and I felt incapable of putting it back together.

"Who told you?" I didn't tell her about Mila because I didn't want to ruin her trip, but of course, she had her ways of finding out.

"News travels fast in this town, especially when it's bad." It explained the weird looks I got from people when I went into town for groceries.

"Well, I'm fine, Sof." She saw right through my forced smile. "You're really bad at lying, but for what it's worth, I'm sorry about Cami."

No one could possibly be as sorry as I was. The worst part was, I only had myself to blame. "Yeah, me too."

She aimed a smile behind her at the house. "It looks great, by the way." It was practically finished when Mila left, but to pass the time while she was gone, I stayed up all night making final touches, like planting a garden to line the pebble walkway and adding shutters to the windows. "I'm glad you think so, because I might sell it."

Her jaw dropped. "What? Julian, you can't."

I shrugged. "Sof, all I've ever thought of since I was sixteen is Camilla. I even bought this house to feel closer to her, but now, I have to sit in it alone. I have to go figure out who I am without her." I'd thought long and hard on whether to sell or burn the house to ash, but Mila's words about not sitting and watching my life pass by stuck with me. I'd spent the last six years doing nothing but hoping she came back, and I never figured out what I really wanted out of my life.

"Can you just stop and think for a second? Your life savings went into the renovations, J. What will you do?"

I couldn't look her in the eyes as I said the next words. "I'm thinking of going back to the Air Force. It'll help pass the time while I figure things out." It's easy to lose track of time when you're serving, so I figured, why not enlist for another term?

"You're going to leave again? I just got you back. There are other ways to get over Cami than disappearing again, Julian." I knew that, but other ways took time. Besides, she had Levi to protect her, so she no longer needed me.

"Everything I touch turns to shit, Sofia. My relationship with Dad, your relationship with him, Mila. I need some time to clean up the mess."

"What if Cami comes back one day?" Her tone held an underlying hint of hope, but I didn't have any of that left.

"She's not." I finally entered the acceptance stage. Some people might have said I'd lost it, and maybe I had.

thirty-four

CAMILLA

OF COURSE, Greyson chose our favorite restaurant to celebrate our three year anniversary. Instead of sitting in our usual spot, he'd paid for private dining, which didn't raise any eyebrows, since he always did extravagant things on a whim. There was no need to look over the menu; I always ordered the same dish. Greyson decided to be spontaneous and ordered the most expensive wine on the menu.

"That bottle is a thousand dollars," I whispered across the table when the waiter left us alone.

"Only the best for tonight." His smirk disarmed me the same way it had for over a thousand days. Even though my mind was somewhere else after I came back from Willow's Cove, every time I looked at him, my future became more and more clear. I wasn't sure how I got so lucky.

When the waiter came back with the bottle, Greyson adjusted his tie that matched his black suit, and ran his fingers through his slicked-back hair.

"To us, and you, for securing another book deal. I'm so proud of you, Cami."

I smiled. "Who would have thought we'd be celebrating an anniversary after being paired up during freshman orientation?"

He was the most unlikely person I thought I'd fall for—we came from two different worlds, and I pegged him as someone who could break my heart into even smaller fragments, but ironically, he was the one to patch it back together. I wouldn't have made it in the city as long as I did without him, college would've been a disaster, and I wouldn't have known that I was capable of loving again. The moment he entered my life, he lit it up.

"I did. I was just waiting for you to give me a chance." I thought for sure he would have given up after the first dozen times I turned him down, but thankfully, he had an inability to fail and persisted for another four years. "I love you." All I could do was admire him fondly as I said the words.

He reached across the table and entwined our fingers. "I love you more." I always knew the words came from the depths of his heart just by the way his smile brightened as they slipped from his lips.

When the waiter returned to the table, not only did he have our plates of food that looked delicious, but he placed an extravagant bouquet of red roses in the middle of the table. When I looked up at Greyson, his breathing turned heavy as he knelt down to the floor on one knee.

"Greyson…" I could barely get his name out before he opened a velvet box and revealed a beautiful marquise diamond that made me lose my breath. We'd stayed up so many nights talking about getting married when the time was right, but when the moment came, I froze.

His hand trembled as he grasped mine for dear life. "Camilla Vega, from the moment we met, you made me see the world in a different light, and I want to see it that way with you forever. Will you marry me?" My eyes darted from him to the diamond, then back to him again.

After coming back from Willow's Cove, I was riddled with confusion about whether my life in New York was still the life I wanted, but the answer was in front of me the entire time. Wherever Greyson was, that was where I was supposed to be too."Yes," I choked out as tears ran down my face. His grey eyes lit up as he slipped the ring on my left finger and swooped me out of the chair. His big arms wrapped around me as he smiled. "It's you and me forever now," he whispered before wrapping his lips with mine.

When I said yes, I meant it with every bit of my heart, which was why I was confused on why the second I said it, I pictured the way Julian looked under the sun next to the cove.

thirty-five

JULIAN

I was a man possessed by unwavering thoughts. It'd been almost a month since I'd seen Mila, and every day, the house echoed in her absence. Every room, corner, and crevice held the memory of her smile or voice.

The sun had barely greeted the day when my sister graced me with an unwanted visit. I knew whatever news she had was urgent because not only was she not an early riser, but we hadn't spoken much since I told her I was considering re-enlisting.

"I didn't even know you woke up this early," I said from under the hood of Bill's truck he'd dropped off earlier that week. Fixing cars had been a nice distraction, since I couldn't fix the mess in my head.

Instead of throwing back a smart remark, she stood quiet, which was the first red flag something was wrong. Rather than her usual perkiness, her face was void of color. "Who died?" I asked sarcastically.

She spoke so soft, I could barely hear her. "I saw this when I woke up this morning." She flipped over her phone and showed me a photo of Mila with a diamond ring on her left hand, the guy who was standing in my living room a month prior next to her, a

237

smile on her face. If I hadn't been grasping the truck's hood, my legs would have buckled and sent me straight to the floor. She was getting married—to someone else. The last month had been hell, and seeing her completely fine and moved on shattered what was left of me.

Everything started to spin, but I kept myself upright in front of Sofia. "Why are you showing me this?" Whether it was to rub salt in the wound or to remind me it could've been me next to her in the picture if I hadn't fucked up, it was working.

"What really happened with Cami before she left, J? It's just me." I'd had enough of people trying to force my hand. They all told me to pour my heart out, and when I did, it was for nothing. They all wanted an explanation, but what good would it do? She was gone.

The tool in my hand slipped out as I threw it against the side of the house in an explosion of frustration. "That's just it. She left!" I collapsed into my hands when I saw the flash of fear in her eyes that resembled when my dad would shout at us. Who the hell was I?

"Fuck, I'm sorry, Sof. I'm just…"

I was brought back down when she squeezed my hand. "I know."

"I thought I could fix everything when she came back. I even told her about Dad," I said.

Her mouth dropped open, and her voice rose in surprise. "Holy shit. I haven't even told Levi." When we said we didn't want anyone to know, we meant it. Everyone had skeletons in their closet, and ours happened to be our childhood.

"She doesn't know about the promise you made to her mom, does she?" I shook my head. She hardly knew anything of the lengths I went through in our time apart.

"Do you want my advice?" I knew she was going to give it whether I wanted it or not. "Go to New York and tell her. Maybe she'll see you're who she's supposed to be with."

I had to make sure I heard her right. "What did you say?"

"You heard me." The fact she'd just gotten married but was completely okay with me potentially ruining someone else's engagement was very on brand for how she saw opportunities and took them, no matter the stakes.

"She's engaged, Sofia. I can't just show up at her door and pour my heart out again. I can't afford a plane ticket to New York, even if I wanted to go." Not only was it absolutely crazy, but after being shut down twice, I wasn't sure I'd survive a third rejection. "Besides, you don't say yes when someone asks you to marry them unless you're sure. It's over." My voice broke.

"Deep down, does it feel over?" I went silent.

She looked down at her purse and pulled something out. "If it were me, I'd want to know everything, and I think she deserves to. You gave up your future with her for me, so the least I can do is buy your flight to get her back." She put a credit card in my hand and gathered her things to walk away. "You have the same two options, J. Go to New York and leave everything out on the table, or live without her knowing that maybe, things would have turned out differently if you had."

I hated how she left me alone with my own thoughts, as if she didn't throw a bomb on me. The last thing I wanted to do was drop in on her new life and mess it up again, but what if Sofia was right? Would her knowing the entire truth change everything? It felt like I was grasping at straws, but I knew I'd regret it for the rest of my life if I didn't try.

thirty-six

CAMILLA

I OPENED my eyes to a bouquet of roses on the pillow next to me, with a note in Greyson's handwriting.

Got called into a last minute meeting. I'll pick us up some dinner. I love you - your fiancé

I stared at the two-carat diamond on my left hand with longing. It happened so fast, yet so slowly, all at once. One day, he was just my best friend who would walk me to my dorm room every night, and then my stuff was being moved into his penthouse. Once Greyson wanted something, he went to the ends of the earth to have it, and it was nice being wanted.

I followed the same morning routine: make breakfast, let the housekeepers in to straighten up while I headed to the corner cafe to pick up a matcha latte, then check emails before getting some writing done. It came as second nature to follow the same pattern, but that day was different.

I had just finished replying to my agent's email when a knock on my door startled me. I didn't bother to look through the peephole, since I figured it was Elena, but I stood frozen in my doorway when Julian stood there with lost eyes and a bag in his hand.

I couldn't figure out if he was real or if I was imagining him. "Mila." His deep voice settled in my chest after a month without hearing it.

"Julian. What are you doing in New York? At my house?" I started with the most obvious questions.

"Can I come inside, please?" My eyes darted to the dark bags under his, which told me he'd probably been restless since I left. I let him brush past and shut the door behind me.

"How did you know where to find me? And how did you get on this floor without the code?" I asked as he roamed the penthouse with a stoic expression. "Your assistant is a tough one to crack, but I got an address out of her eventually. As for the code, I said I was food delivery." I was definitely going to have a conversation with Elena, and the front desk.

I had to sit down to stop my head from spinning in circles while he stood by the window overlooking lower Manhattan perfectly. "It's one hell of a view from up here. I never pegged you for a penthouse kind of girl," he murmured with a hint of mockery. I picked at my nail beds. "It was Greyson's before we started dating. I'm sure you didn't come over two thousand miles to see the view, Julian."

"No." He sat across from me in the chair Greyson always did and met my gaze. "I came here to tell you what has been on my conscious for too long, and all I ask is you let me finish. If you still want nothing to do with me after, you'll never hear from me again, I promise." He'd come all the way from California to New York, so whatever it was had to be important. I brought my knees up to my chest and listened intently. "Okay."

He swallowed hard and spoke with a wary tone. "I knew about Greyson long before you told me about him." My face twisted. How could he have possibly known? "The military was the fastest way I could make the years fly by, but as soon as I was discharged, I came straight to New York. I remembered the first apartment we picked out together, and I must've searched that whole goddamn building, hoping you were still there. Right as I was about to give up, it was like a sign from the universe or something—I saw you coming out of your publisher's office. I was only inches away from you when Greyson came up and kissed you, and you kissed him back. That was a little over a year ago, and the last time I saw you until you showed up in Willow's Cove."

I couldn't move. I felt like I couldn't breathe, and the room suddenly seemed to cave in. I spent four long years looking over my shoulder, wondering if he was there, and one day, he was. "You came back." I shuddered when I realized I hadn't said it in my head. "Why did you wait so long?"

His brown eyes glossed over. "I promised your mom I would. Technically, I only had to wait four to go after you, but I had to wait for Sofia to graduate until I left for the military, so it turned into five."

Every time he spoke, I was left with more confusion, and my life started to make less sense. "My mom?" I whimpered.

"I went back to your house after you left. I wanted to see you one last time, but instead, your mom invited me in to talk. We both agreed the best thing for you was to stay where you were, so I promised her I wouldn't try to get you back until after you finished college."

In all of the conversations I'd had with my mom, the one she had with Julian never came up. How could she keep that from me? Would things be different if she had? My entire life felt like it was planned out by everyone else around me. All the tears I shed, the restless nights I'd stood up replaying my last moments with Julian were for nothing.

"Why didn't you tell me?" I asked.

"Probably for the same reason you didn't tell me your book was about us."

My breath caught in my throat, and I masked the inner turmoil that grew inside me. "What are you talking about? My book is fictional, Julian."

He chuckled under his breath before reaching into the bag he'd brought with him and pulling out a copy of my book. "Page 134. As I watched him sleep next to me, I knew it was the moment forever began. I whispered *forever and always* while brushing my fingers through his wavy locks."

His brown eyes looked past mine and into my soul. "Forever and always, Mila. This was *us*. I tabbed every page that resembled a moment we shared." He flipped through the book to show almost every page was tabbed. "I went inside every bookstore I passed for a year and bought every copy they had in stock because I know you wrote our love story for a reason. It wasn't over for you either. I went back to Willow's Cove so you'd know where to find me when you realized it."

There was so much to process, I became overwhelmed with emotions I couldn't afford to acknowledge. "What do you want me to say, Julian?" We looked at each other with the same stars in our eyes as before.

"Say this changes things. Now you know everything I was a coward for not saying before. I'm telling you now, hoping it's enough."

Tears slid down my cheeks as I thought of the life we could've had. We'd live in the house by the cove, where we'd make breakfast every morning before going for a walk down at the beach. Farmer's market trips every weekend, where we'd get so much fruit, we wouldn't know what to do with it. Get married, show our kids our secret spots—a simple, yet meaningful life.

Then, there was the life I already had with Greyson. All around me were the memories of our laughter when we moved my stuff into his penthouse and couldn't fit through the doorway. We took walks in Central Park every Sunday, and I'd lost count of how many times we'd burnt food in our kitchen when we failed at cooking. I recalled all the nights I laid on his chest and counted his heartbeats.

I spoke through tears. "Julian, I said yes when Greyson asked me to marry him, I can't just—"

"I don't have as much to give as him, I know that, Mila. I can't give you a life with a penthouse and a private jet, but you'll have my heart. I'm not saying we'll be perfect. We'll bicker like we did as teenagers, and there will be days when it's really hard, but there isn't anyone else I want to go through all of that with. It's me and you, Mila." He grabbed my hand and held it over his heart that was beating rapidly against his chest. "Whatever you choose, my heart is yours whether you want it or not."

I couldn't hold back my sobs any longer as my eyes darted from him to the ring on my finger. I thought of being greeted by Greyson when he'd come home from work, then being greeted by Julian when he came from the beach with sand still in his hair.

When I cupped his cheek with my hand, he leaned into it, his eyes shut as if he was memorizing my touch. "I'm always going to love you, Julian." I knew no matter what happened, when he walked out my front door, there would always be a part of my heart reserved for him.

"Isn't that enough?" he sobbed.

"It used to be, but we're not kids anymore. Greyson needs me, and—"

"Please stop." He slipped away from my hand, taking his warmth with him. I stood painfully still as he bent down and left a kiss on my forehead. "I really wish we could've done it right in this lifetime, Mila."

Me too.

I couldn't watch him leave. It wasn't until he closed the door behind him that I saw the copy of my book left where he'd been sitting, and I let myself collapse into a puddle of tears.

thirty-seven

JULIAN

I WAS elbow deep in garden soil when a truck pulled up my driveway. The past weeks since leaving New York, I dedicated all my time growing vegetables in my front yard. The alternative was letting myself go stir-crazy as I recalled my rejection. I call bullshit to whoever said it was easier to move on when you have closure.

"Officer Lopez?" I asked as the familiar face started to come into view. He was out of uniform, which meant it was a formal visit.

"Julian Perez. Your file came across my desk today, and I thought there was no way in hell it was you. I had to come check for myself."

I shook his hand and smiled. "It's right, sir. My physical said I'm still in great shape, and I'm more than qualified to be a crew chief for another term."

His grey mustache tipped up. "You might be in great shape on paper, but how's your head? Because you're stupid if you think I'm approving this."

I blanched. "What?"

He'd helped with my long registration process the first time, so we dropped formality when we talked, unless he was in uniform.

He looked out at the widespread view and sighed. "I've always saw potential in you kid, so this conversation is off the record. You have all the skills the Air Force can give you, so why drag yourself back for another four years?"

"I guess, I'm having trouble finding my purpose. Maybe going back to the military will help me find it." The words didn't sit right on my tongue when I said them out loud.

He gripped my shoulder. "I'm talking to you like you were one of my own now; I can't stop you from reenlisting, in fact, I'm supposed to encourage you, which is exactly why you should listen to me. You're smart, but you seem troubled by something. You have a beautiful home, your sister just got married, you seem to be building something good for yourself. I promise, you won't find what you're missing by running away for another four years. Once I sign those papers, there's no going back."

Images of everything I'd leave behind flashed through my mind—I wouldn't see Sofia's smile every morning, or hear how married life was treating her. Elijah wouldn't pop in randomly to steal my beer, I wouldn't get to pretend to hate Levi. Damon was staying in town longer than expected, so I'd miss out on hearing how his new life was treating him.

"She'll come back to you, I promise." Mrs. Vega's voice suddenly echoed in my ears, hitting me over the head with a realization.

What the hell was I thinking? I'd been so busy trying to escape my problems, I forgot what I would leave behind. Besides, I made a promise to stay right where Mila could find me if she ever came back, and I had to keep it.

"On second thought, sir. I think I'm gonna stay right where I am. I'm sorry for wasting your time."

He held back a smile as he saluted me. "Not a waste at all."

I watched as he drove away, and immediately rushed to dial the number I'd contemplated deleting dozens of times. I wasn't sure if I was disappointed or relieved there was no answer. "It's Cami. Sorry I didn't pick up, but leave me a message, and I'll try to remember to call you back."

I smiled when her voice played over the message. "Mila. I know I said you wouldn't hear from me again, but there's one more thing I didn't say back at your apartment. If all I have now are memories of you sitting under the sun at the cove, reading your beat up copy of *Persuasion* by Jane Austen, I'll consider myself lucky. I'm going to love you for the rest of my life, and no matter how many years pass, or who we become, if you're ever back in Willow's Cove, I'll be right where you left me."

thirty-eight

CAMILLA

I HADN'T BEEN by to see my mom in weeks, not since Julian showed up at my doorstep and made me question how long I had been surrounded by secrets.

I fetched the spare key from under the mat and let myself into her quiet apartment she'd been living in since finally getting the guts to leave my dad five years before. I took partial credit, after begging her to finally start living her own life, since she no longer had to worry about me.

The last time I saw my dad was sophomore year of college when I told him I'd known about the affair the entire time, and as long as he had another family, he wouldn't be mine. You can guess who he chose.

"Mom?" I yelled out in the empty space.

"I'm in here, Cami." When I walked down the long hallway to her room, I found her snug in her sweater and tucked under the blankets. "There's my girl. I've been wondering where you've been." I took her cold hand when she reached out to me and sat beside her bed.

"How are you?" Some days, she was perfectly fine, but others, when her lupus flared up, she could hardly get out of bed because of the pain. I'd hired a nurse to check on her every day, and her boyfriend of three years constantly kept me updated. Still, nothing compared to seeing her bright blue eyes in person.

"It's a good day today, but I want to hear what's new with you, other than that giant rock on your finger." I rushed to her place as soon as Greyson and I left the restaurant the night we got engaged. She'd never smiled harder.

The realization of why I originally went to her house suddenly hit me. "Julian showed up at my place and told me the promise you had him keep."

Her face fell before she used all the strength she had left to pull herself up. "I've been meaning to have this talk with you, but never found the right time. Yes, I made him promise to wait, but only because I wanted you to have the chance I never had, Cami. I won't apologize for making sure your dreams came true."

I stayed eerily silent. My entire life had always been a web of lies—my dad and his affair, Mom knowing about it the whole time, Julian's reason for staying away. They all led me there.

"You didn't think to tell me?" We talked nearly every day; surely, it should have come up at some point.

Her fragile touch grazed my face. "I was, Cami. After you graduated college, I was going to tell you everything so you could find each other again, but then—"

"Greyson." My voice wavered when I said his name.

She nodded. "You finally looked happy again, and I didn't want to take that away from you. For that, I'm sorry." I held onto her shaking hands and let her sweet perfume comfort me. I felt like a puppet, my strings being pulled by the people around me, who kept secrets to do what they thought was best for me.

"Julian also asked me to go back to Willow's Cove with him." I shook away the memory of his tear-filled face.

"Is that what you want?" Her words made the room grow cold.

"I thought I was so sure of everything I wanted out of life, and then one day, I woke up and didn't know who I was anymore. When I was in Willow's Cove, I started to remember, but I can't just drop everything just because the first guy I loved popped back up. Right?"

Since I was eighteen, I stood firm on keeping the promise I made to her of not going back to Willow's Cove, but when I had no obligation to stay away anymore, did I still want to? "I know better than to try and persuade you again, but just ask yourself something, Cami. In five, even ten years from now, who will give you the life you want? Don't think of anyone else, just you, because you're the one who has to live with the decision you make." The question made the hairs on my body stand, and while I took her advice to heart, I couldn't let myself face it at the time.

"I should get back home. Greyson and I are looking at wedding venues today." I would've missed when her face went grim had I not been staring at her.

"I love you, Cami," she said. I kissed the top of her head and tucked her back under the blankets. "I love you too. I'll come by later to check on you."

My head swirled with thoughts as the brisk air hit me in the face. I went to get answers, and that's what I got, but I left more confused than when I walked through the door. Whoever said moving on was easier when you had closure was full of crap.

As I put in the code in the elevator to take me up to the penthouse, I dug through my bag and realized my phone was missing, but I was sure I left it on the table that morning. "Grey? Are you ready to leave? Our appointment is in fifteen minutes," I shouted as I walked through the door, but I was met with silence. I walked until I found him sat at our kitchen table with a look of devastation while holding my phone in a tight grip, as if he was on the verge of smashing it. "You forgot your phone."

I kept my voice calm as I rushed over to him. "Why do you have that look? What's wrong?"

He could barely look at me when he finally spoke. "Julian wasn't just a friend, was he, Cami? Before you lie to me again, please don't."

Time stopped. I was a deer caught in headlights. "He was my first boyfriend."

"That makes this make more sense." He laid my phone on the table and let a message that sounded like Julian's voice play on speaker. "Mila, I know I said you wouldn't hear from me again, but there's one more thing I didn't say back at your apartment. If all I have now are memories of you sitting under the sun at the cove reading your beat up copy of Persuasion by Jane Austen, then I'll consider myself lucky. I'm going to love you for the rest of my life, and no matter how many years pass, or who we become, if you're ever back in Willow's Cove, I'll be right where you left me." I looked up at Greyson, then back to the phone with my heart battering against my chest.

"Why didn't you tell me he was here?" His jaw was clenched, so I chose my words carefully. "I didn't want you to think anything happened. He just stopped by unannounced."

His laughter was anything but light. "He flew over a thousand miles to tell you he was still in love with you. I don't think that's just stopping by, Camilla." He hadn't called me by my name since we first met.

"I'm so sorry. I should have told you. It didn't mean anything." I was relieved when he let me grab his hand, squeezing it tightly as tears threatened his eyes.

"You know the worst part? I think you didn't tell me because a part of you is still contemplating which one of us you want. Am I right?"

I shook my head and grasped his hand for dear life. "I'm still here, Greyson. When he asked me to stay in Willow's Cove with him, I said no because I love you." I choked on the tears sliding down my cheeks.

"Do you love him?" he asked. I expected him to be angry, but he waited for me to speak with a touch of sadness in his eyes. It made the next words feel all the heavier. "Ye-yes." I swallowed the lump that formed in my throat as our eyes met from across our kitchen table—the same table where we'd shared countless meals and conversations.

After reading endless books and watching every rom-com under the sun, I always wondered how people fell in love with two people, but that summer, I found out just how easy it was. The choice was laid out in front of me—Julian, who was part of my past I thought I'd left behind, and Greyson, a part of a future I thought I was sure of.

"Who do you love more?" he asked.

I froze. Goddamn Willow's Cove. Everything was fine until I went back and got my life turned upside down. "You," I said.

"I wish I could believe you, Cami, but I keep thinking if you loved me more, there wouldn't be a reason for you to choose in the first place."

"Julian and I just have history, and I guess when I went back to Willow's Cove, I got confused, but you know I love you, Grey."

He smiled faintly, but I could tell it was forced. "You know, I read the end of your book. How the guy chased her down and told her everything she'd wanted to hear, and they lived happily ever after. It was never about us, was it?"

He took my silence as an answer. "Can you please just tell me if you're gonna walk away? Because if I have to see that, I'll never be the same again." We were both crying, our faces red.

"As long as you want me, I'm not going anywhere." I was clinging to the last threads of us for dear life.

"Do you still want to marry me?" he asked.

I nodded without hesitation. Our life together was all I'd

known for three years, and I didn't want to let it go. He wiped away the tears in his eyes before leaving kisses all over my hands and arms. "I still want you, Cami. Say the word, and we'll forget this happened, but we can't build a life if even a small part of you wants one with him. I won't share your heart with anyone else."

Of course, he was willing to forgive me. That's the kind of person he always was. Greyson Carter—the guy who wore his heart on his sleeve but was always too scared to let people see it.

In five, even ten years from now, who will give you the life you want? Mom's voice repeated in my head.

I'd always planned my life so far ahead, but suddenly, I couldn't picture what the near future looked like. I *chose* the life I had with Greyson, so why did it feel like I gave up a part of myself when I let Julian leave?

Greyson deserved all my heart, but could I give it to him?

Either choice I made, someone gets hurt. My entire life, people made decisions on my behalf, and suddenly, I was faced with the question: what did *I* think was best for me?

thirty-nine

JULIAN

It hardly rained in Willow's Cove, but the way it was coming down seemed to be enough to last the entire year. I'd always preferred the sun, but nothing beat hearing the sounds of droplets hitting the ground.

When the timer on my microwave went off, I twisted in disgust at the frozen dinner I thought would look appealing. Instead, it looked more like dog food. I couldn't bring myself to make a homemade meal when I all I thought of was making enough for two. You'd think after being shot down by the same girl three times in the span of a month, I wouldn't still hold onto hope that one day, she'd show up at my doorstep.

I looked down at my new roommate when it clawed at my leg. "You want this food instead?"

Instead of moping around and letting the days pass alone, I'd gone down to the animal shelter and adopted a three-year-old golden retriever, Cooper, who had been sitting behind a cage for most of his life. The girl at the shelter said he'd been returned twice for having "too much energy", so I figured he'd be able to burn it off down at the beach every day. With my days filled with making sure he was taken care of, there was less time to miss

Mila. Still, she was my last thought before I closed my eyes and the first when I opened them.

The sound of a car pulling up caught both of our attention, but I couldn't think of anyone who'd be crazy enough to drive in that rain. When I looked out my window, it was too dark to see the car parked in the driveway, so I waited until there was a loud knock at my door.

Cooper knew to stand by me when someone was at the door, so he was glued to my side as I swung it open to find Sofia's wet hair dangling over her face.

"Sofia, what the hell are you doing?" I pulled her in past the threshold and wrapped her in a towel I kept by the door.

"I was on my way here when the rain started. I brought you a warm meal because I know you were probably eating that frozen crap." I gawked at the pan of lasagna she held out in front of me, and while it looked delicious, I wasn't stupid. "Thanks, Sof, but you don't have to make me food as an excuse to check on me."

I put it on the counter to save for later. She'd made up every excuse in the book to come by and make sure I was okay, but it was supposed to be the other way around. People were afraid of me being alone, but everyday that passed seemed to get easier.

"How could I be your annoying little sister if I don't come annoy you?" She made me smile on the hard days, I'd give her that. "Where's that husband of yours?"

"At home. He wanted to come, but they have him signing a stack of papers in his office. I guess when his dad is through with being mayor, Levi is next in line to run." I saw the flash of something sad in her eyes, so it was my turn to make her smile. "So, my sister is going to be the mayor's wife? That has to come with special privileges, right? I plan to cash those in." I was still getting used to her being a married woman, but the moment she said her vows, she had a certain glow to her she didn't have before.

Her laughter echoed through the kitchen before it died off.

"It'll definitely be weird, but I knew what I was getting into when I married Levi, who's great, by the way. He told me to tell you that so you don't threaten him again, and to invite you over for dinner soon." She lived on the other edge of town in the gated community of mansions I typically avoided.

"I'll bring lasagna," I joked.

Her bright smile reminded me of when she was a little girl and she'd try to make me laugh after I was on the receiving end of my dad's wrath. It was a nice reminder that no matter how much older we got, no matter the paths we took, we'd always be there to cheer each other up when we needed it.

"I should get back before Levi gets worried, but I'll think of another excuse to come by and check on you tomorrow." As much as her drop ins got under my skin sometimes, she was the only family I had left, so I knew I would be okay as long as she was around.

She hugged me before she left, and for the first time, I allowed it. "Drive slow, okay?" I called said as I watched her back out of the driveway.

Only minutes went by before another knock on my door startled me. I wondered what Sofia could have possible forgotten as I swung the door open with Cooper stuck to my side.

"What'd you forget this—" I expected to see my sister, but instead, Mila stood in the doorway dripping wet, tears welling in her eyes, suitcases at her sides.

"Mila? What are you doing here?" I asked.

I couldn't even move to let her past the threshold, because I was trying to convince myself I wasn't dreaming. I had to be if she'd come back. "Did you mean what you said in your voicemail?"

I resisted the urge to reach out and touch her. If I did, I wouldn't let go, and I needed to know she was mine before I did that. "Every word."

She handed me a green journal, *Cami* written on the front. "It has every entry I've written since I was sixteen. They're all about you."

I skimmed over pages and pages with my name scribbled on every one, along with so many *I love you's,* I lost count.

"I gave the ring back to Greyson."

I froze. "You what?"

"It's you, Julian. I don't want the penthouse, private jet, or any of those things you said you can't give me; I want the life we talked about. I want *you.* I'm sorry it took so long for me to figure it out. I was just scared you wouldn't catch me if I fell for you again, but you jump, I jump, right? I hope you'll still have me, because I'm completely in love with you." The words came from the depths of her throat as she pleaded.

There was no hesitation. I'd been given a second chance, and there was no way in hell I was wasting it. I spoke over the rain splattering on the pavement. "I'm warning you, Mila. If you walk over this threshold, I'm never letting you go again."

A smile appeared on her lips. "Then I have a new rule: don't." She dropped her bags and leaped into my arms before pressing her lips to mine and sealing our forever.

epilogue

JULIAN

1 YEAR LATER

THANKS TO ELENA, I was about to pull something I only had one shot at not messing up. My hands shook as I made my way to Mila, who sat in front of her computer, Cooper glued to her side. I'd repurposed the empty room into what it was always intended to be—the office and library of her dreams. I'd built a bookshelf into the walls and attached a ladder so she could move between them with ease, put her desk directly in front of the window so she could write accompanied by her favorite view.

I stood back and watched her for just a moment. Almost a year ago, she showed up at my doorstep, dripping wet from the rain, and since then, I considered myself the luckiest man alive.

My heart swelled when she turned around and greeted me with her ocean blue eyes and bright smile. "Good morning."

"Good morning." I showered kisses all over her face.

"Shouldn't you be getting to work?" I should've, but I knew the boys would be okay running drills with their new assistant coaches. After going down to the school to speak with the team like Mr. M requested, he offered me a full-time position as the varsity head coach. I had my doubts, but after pondering it over with Mila, we agreed it was a good way to bring the sport I once loved back into my life, untainted by my dad. I did have one catch; my assistant coaches had to be people who loved the sport just as much as I did. I thought of only two people—Elijah and Damon.

"Do I smell coffee?" I smirked at how predictable she was beforeI revealed the breakfast spread I'd made for her: pancakes with strawberries from Mr. and Mrs. Asher, eggs, bacon, and a fresh cup of hot coffee. Usually, we ate together at our table, but that morning was different.

"What's the occasion?" Her lazy smile made my heart leap. "I have a surprise for you." Her shoulders straightened as she perked up with interest. "What is it?"

I pulled a book from under my shirt and offered it to her. After watching her write in every spot in the house for months, I felt it was only right she had the very first copy of her second book.

She pried it from my hands with a gasp. "You didn't."

"You can thank Elena." I didn't know how, but she pulled a miracle and got her hands on an early copy just so I could surprise her. Since Mila moved back to Willow's Cove and Elena still lived in the city, they hardly saw each other, but there wasn't a day they didn't talk on the phone.

She ran her fingers over the cover we'd approved together a few months before. "Open it."

My heart pounded in my chest as she read the four words I'd written on the very first page.

Will You Marry Me?

I had Sofia and Taylor to thank for the idea. Only they would have the creativity to think of asking her to spend the rest of her life with me using the book about our love story.

She met my eyes with her mouth gaping. "Are you serious?" When I said I'd never let her go, I meant it. It was her or nobody. We went from being two kids who knew nothing about love, teenagers who desperately tried to figure it out, strangers who still held a piece of one another, to two people growing more in love each day. I never wanted to know a life without her again.

"It's you and me forever, Mila."

With tears in her eyes, she grabbed a pen sitting on her desk and scribbled next to my handwriting before handing the book back to me. One word in her cursive stared back at me.

Yes

I cupped her face and devoured her lips until I could no longer breathe. "I love you," I whispered as our foreheads touched.

"Forever," she said.

Lying next to us was the book we'd written together about our love story, with the only title that felt right—*Right Where You Left Me*. I never gave up hope she would come back to me, and now, we had forever to make up for lost time.

acknowledgments

If you told 21-year-old me she'd be writing acknowledgments for her THIRD book, she'd scream. If I'm being honest, this book was the hardest I'll probably ever write for a multitude of reasons, but also the most special. It's because of the love and support from the people mentioned in this acknowledgment that it's in your hands.

Dad, thank you for your pep talks and for sitting with me at the table while I ripped my hair out over a scene. Your push for me to always follow my dream is the reason I'm still here. I love you. <3

Grandma, thank you for always telling me I'm not crazy for wanting to be a famous author. Anytime I start to doubt myself, I hear your voice. <3

Kayla, thanks for picking up all my FaceTime calls so I can spew about my fictional characters' love lives. You're my OG beta reader. <3

MC Larios, the kind of author friend everyone deserves to have. Thank you for being my voice of reason when I feel lost, and for sitting on FaceTime with me for hours while I edit. <3

Grace Elena, my formatter, thank you for making yet another one of my books look beautiful. Your talent always amazes me <3

Layla Brown, my cover designer, thank you for making my cover even better than I imagined in my head. I can't imagine creating something with anyone else. <3

Alexa, my editor, your ability to tolerate how many times I

use "that" in a draft deserves an award. I can't imagine working with anyone else on getting my book published ready. <3

My ARC team, beta readers, and anyone who's been involved with making this book what it is, thank you from the bottom of my heart. I love every single one of you. <3

The readers, where do I begin? As always, thank you for changing my life. It's not an understatement when I say because of you, I get to wake up and do what I love everyday, I never take it for granted. <3

Here's to more books to be written!

coming soon

Willow's Cove Series
titles TBA

also by lana vargas

Summer in Phoenix

The Darkness that Follows Us

about the author

Lana Vargas is a Mexican-American Romance Author who resides in California. With her debut novel Summer in Phoenix landing her in the top 40 on Amazon, followed by her Sophomore novel The Darkness that Follows Us landing in the top 20, and winning Best Romance Novel in the Literary Romance category from Wolf Media Festival, she is proof that anyone can make their dreams a reality. She plans to continue to show women that we all deserve great love stories one book at a time.

Printed in Great Britain
by Amazon